THE BLOOD IS LOVE

THE DARK EYES DUET #2

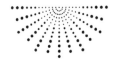

KARINA HALLE

Cover Design: Hang Le Designs

Edited by: Laura Helseth

Proofed by: Chanpreet Singh

DEDICATION

For my Finnish mother for giving me her *sisu* (but please, don't ever read this book)

"You stare, there's smoke in your eyes, I get close, my blood is the price." – Parsonz Curse, Royal Thunder

"There is no place I can go, there is no place I can hide. It feels like it keeps coming from the inside." – The Big Come Down, NIN

"Touch your lips to mine, that we may make a kiss that can pierce through death and survive." – The Blood is Love, Queens of the Stone Age

PLAYLIST

Just like I did for Black Sunshine, there's an important playlist to go with The Blood is Love. You can find it here on Spotify and I've also listed some of it below:

"The Blood is Love" - Queens of the Stone Age
    "Fangs" - Purple Hearse
    "Blue" - Royal Thunder
    "Do You Love Me?" - Nick Cave & The Bad Seeds
    "American Witch" - Rob Zombie
    "Furious Angels" - Rob Dougan
    "Hostage" - Billie Eilish
    "Telepathy" - Crosses
    "Parsonz Curse" - Royal Thunder
    "Phantom Bride" - Deftones
    "Bitches Brew" - Crosses
    "I Would For You" - NIN
    "Big Dark Love" - Murder by Death
    "Speed Me Towards Death" - Rob Dougan
    "Captain Midnight" - Tomahawk
    "Somebody's Sins" - Tricky

"Digital Bath" - Deftones
"Left Me for Dead" - Rob Dougan
"Ruiner" - NIN
"Live With Me" - Massive Attack
"Stripsearch" - Faith No More
"Head Like a Hole" - NIN
"Someone's in the Wolf" - Queens of the Stone Age
"Engine Number Nine" - Deftones
"Dead Skin Mask" - Slayer
"Clubbed to Death" - Rob Dougan
"Satellite"- NIN
"Spell" - Nick Cave & The Bad Seeds
"You've Seen the Butcher" - Deftones
"I Let Love In" - Nick Cave & The Bad Seeds
"Hell is Around the Corner" - Tricky
"I'm Not Driving Anymore" - Rob Dougan
"We're Not Alone" - Peeping Tom
"Death of it All" - Rob Zombie
"Constant Fear" - Bohren and Der Club of Gore
"Pit Stop (Take Me Home)" - Lovage
"Girl I Love You" - Massive Attack
"In This This Twilight" - NIN
"Inertia Creeps" - Massive Attack
"Option" - Crosses
"Sin" - NIN
"Surprise! You're Dead!" - Faith No More
"The Big Come Down" - NIN
"Skeletal Remains" - Bohren and Der Club of Gore
"King for a Day" - Faith No More
"Death Bell" - Crosses

PROLOGUE

FINNMARK, 1350

ON THE THIRD DAY, IT STARTED TO RAIN BLOOD. AT LEAST, that's what it looked like to Ivar Skarde as he surveyed the sky from inside the cave. A brilliant red sunrise lit up the clouds to the east, saturating the horizon, just as rain began to fall. Each shimmering droplet reflected the sunrise in such an otherworldly way that it could have been beautiful if Skarde had been in the mood to see things as such.

But he wasn't. The plague was spreading north throughout Norway, and it was only a matter of time before it would reach him too, in the desolate, cold and blurry border between his home country and the Kingdom of Sweden. Though the Sámi people he had been living with didn't rely on the grains in which the disease spread (of course, at the time they had no idea it was caused by rats which would often feed on the grains), Skarde didn't feel safe. Death taunted him at every corner. He wouldn't rest until he could somehow be free from the threat of death forever, whether it came from the plague or something else.

Skarde used to be a warrior for King Magnus VII. A formidable one. Death was present at every battle as the king

1

levied his crusade against Novgorod, and it was one that Skarde would always conquer, without fear, even as many of his comrades succumbed to it in violent ways. But that all changed when he almost lost his life, an errant sword during the battle of Orekhov. As Skarde lay there bleeding outside the fortress, snow falling on him like tears, he lost consciousness. Became one with the dark. And there he saw things so horrible, that when he woke up in the infirmary, he had a new appreciation for death, one born out of fear. Fear that when he died, he would be sucked into the black hole, the endless void, of pain and suffering for all eternity.

It took ages for him to heal back in Norway, and when he finally did, the black plague was spreading throughout Oslo. Skarde took the opportunity to leave, to head north, up and up and up, hoping to leave all the death behind him, the death he felt was coming for him, like it had lost its chance and wanted a rematch.

Eventually, Skarde heard things on his travels up north. That many of the Sámi people hadn't converted to Christianity, that some of them were shamans, that the mystical legends of the frozen north were true.

That there were things you could do to cheat death —forever.

So Skarde went to them. The Sámi people were not a monolith and their religious practices, even language, differed between regions and tribes, and many were distrustful of a former soldier for the king, especially since monarchies had tried to wipe out their ways. But eventually he found one tribe that took him in. This tribe lived in the low mountains, keeping a small herd of reindeer for food, clothing and transportation. They also practiced animism, their own form of witchcraft, and harbored a supposed connection to the underworld.

Seppo was the leader of the group. Though Skarde didn't

speak their language, Seppo seemed to understand what Skarde wanted. But Seppo wouldn't give it to Skarde so easily, not something so heavy, that came with such a price. Skarde ended up living in a cave by himself, set apart from the tribe, for a year before Seppo deemed Skarde ready. In that time, Skarde had picked up on the Northern Sámi dialect that the tribe spoke, allowing him to converse with Seppo, who told him the following: A *noaidi*, a mediator between the human world and the *saivo*, the underworld, would come for him one day and take him on a journey. This would happen after three things happened on three days:

The first day there would be a small earthquake, a sign that the underworld was waking up.

The second day lightning would strike the ground, as Tiermes, the God of Thunder and protector of humans, would try and warn Skarde, or anyone foolish enough to go against the laws of the world, that they were making a mistake.

The third day, the sky would rain blood, signifying the sorrow and pain that was to come.

This was the third day, rain against a red sky. Yesterday there was a lightning storm that struck a pine tree in the distance, blasting all the branches off of it until all that was left was a charred pole. The day before that, the earth shook for a minute. At first Skarde was convinced it was just a reindeer herd stampeding nearby, but after the lighting and the blood rain, he knew that his time had come.

He stared at the rain falling for a moment, that blazing red sunrise permeating the crisp white snow, making it look blood stained, then he turned around to get his fur hat and coat, preparing for the journey.

When he turned back around, there was a man standing in the entrance to the cave.

Skarde had a fright.

The man was dressed in a long heavy black coat, different from the Sámi's traditional wear, and instead of a face he had a deer skull with short, three-pronged antlers.

Skarde stared at the man, wondering how the skull was fastened to his head. He peered at the deep dark and empty eye sockets, trying to see a glimpse of the man underneath, but there was none to be found.

The man raised a hand, fitted with a furry glove, and pointed to the horizon.

We go, the man said, but to Skarde the voice didn't sound like it was coming from the mask. It sounded like it was coming from inside his own head.

Skarde nodded, feeling nervous now, and as the man turned from the cave, Skarde followed him.

They walked past the gathering of huts where this Sámi tribe lived, and as the reindeer skinned door of the largest one opened, Seppo stepped out. Seppo's face was grave. Skarde had thought that Seppo would at least be happy that Skarde's time finally came. If not for that, then at least Skarde, who was feeling like he was a nuisance to the tribe, was leaving for good.

But Seppo didn't look happy. And as others came out of their huts and stared at the deer skull man and Skarde, they watched with a mix of revulsion and fear. One of them even spit on the ground and Skarde wondered if it was for him or for the noaidi.

Skarde raised his head high, remembering that this was what he wanted, and that he was a warrior, and that he wasn't afraid (even though he was) and he followed the man. They walked for hours. Past rivers and treeless plains, over hills where snow still lived at the top, down through mossy pine forests. The walk was silent. There were no birds, they saw no animals, and the noaidi didn't say a single word to Skarde.

Eventually they came to a stop in front of a large rock that sat adjacent to a steep hillside. The rock was huge, at least twenty feet high, and a smooth dark gray. It didn't seem to fit in with the surroundings at all.

The man moved to the back of the rock, to the dark space between the rock and the hillside, and motioned for Skarde to follow.

Skarde didn't want to go. He knew there was something very wrong about the rock, that it didn't belong there, that the dark space that the noaidi was disappearing into was a space he'd never come out of. There was death in that darkness, the very death that Skarde was trying to escape.

Death, and evil.

Skarde swallowed hard and stood his ground. Perhaps if he turned around he could find his way back to Seppo. Maybe they would take him in again. Maybe he could stay with them until the plague was gone and then he could go back down to Oslo and start life over, find a wife, have a child, do the things he never got a chance to do. Skarde was old, in his early sixties, but he was handsome and strong and he had money put away and he knew he could still carve out a happy life for himself.

Death will always find you, a voice said.

It seemed to come from the dark space, where the noaidi had gone, but the voice didn't belong to the skull man.

The voice belonged to Hell itself.

I will find you, the voice went on, raspy and inhuman and disembodied. Dripping with malice. *Ivar Skarde. You cannot cheat death again. I will come for you and you will be back inside that void, to suffer for eternity. No escape.*

Suddenly, a cold, icy wind smelling of sulfur came out of the dark space behind the rock, blowing back Skarde's long black hair, chilling him to the marrow of his bones.

You only have two choices, the voice continued. *To run away knowing there is truly no escape. Or to come forward and join me. Become one with the darkness you try so hard to avoid. You cannot escape death, but you can become death.*

Become death? Skarde thought to himself.

A coward would run away, the voice said. *A warrior would step forward and choose to become something greater than he is, greater than he'll ever be. Greater and more powerful than any creature in this world. You can become death, and in becoming death, you will live forever. Your blood will be eternal. You will have nothing to fear. All will fear you.*

The wind blew again, and this time it seemed to tug at Skarde like invisible hands, pulling him to the dark space.

All will fear me, Skarde thought. *Eternal blood. Eternal life.*

He fought against the wind for a moment, waited to hear more from the voice, but the voice had ceased.

He made his choice.

He stepped forward and the sulfur wind pulled him to the space behind the rock and Skarde stepped through.

The space was dark and dank and there were a million screams filling his head and the wind kept pulling Skarde along, but soon there was light reaching his eyes and Skarde had the impression that he wasn't going into a cave, but just going around the rock and out the other side.

And he stepped through the crack and into the light, expecting to be on the other side of the rock.

He was. But nothing looked the same.

There was snow on the ground where there wasn't snow before.

There were trees, pine and birch.

There was a stream.

Beyond the stream, where there couldn't physically be an ocean, was an ocean. Churning waves. Above that, dark clouds that sent out forks of lightning that struck the surface.

And this world was a red world.

The leaves on the trees were red.

The stream was red.

The ocean was red.

The lightning was red.

It was a beautiful bleeding world.

The noaidi stood in front of him as before, ever stoic, ever silent, and raised a hand to point to the distance. Skarde noticed the hand didn't have the mittens anymore. The hand was human, and it was only bone. A living skeleton. And then Skarde knew there was no face under that mask, that it wasn't a mask at all.

But he was no longer afraid.

And he followed the skeleton finger as it pointed to a castle in the distance made of crumbling stone, a sprawling, decaying place.

Skarde started walking to the castle, but the noaidi stayed behind by the rock. Perhaps guarding it, perhaps because this was something that Skarde had to do on his own.

Skarde walked along the crimson river. At times he was certain it was actual blood flowing, like he was following an artery of some giant beast. Other times, it looked like red-tinted water. Sometimes he saw hands poking through the surface, and if he looked too closely, he saw faces too.

He followed the river as it led him toward the ocean shore and the castle, and as he approached, he saw two people on horseback set off from the crumbling entrance, coming toward him. There was something about them that was off-putting, like the horses didn't move the way they should, or didn't seem quite right, even at a distance.

But as the horses got closer, Skarde saw what was so strange about them.

They were made of bone and metal and stone.

A crimson mane and tail of twigs and leaves.

Fire that leaked from their nostrils.

And above them sat cloaked men with no faces, only dark space beneath the hoods.

They were his escorts, waiting patiently for Skarde to approach them before the faceless men turned their horses around, one on either side of Skarde, leading him to the castle.

Skarde kept glancing at the horses as they walked beside him at an uneven pace, at their hooves of iron, their skeleton legs of copper intertwined with muscle and veins. Smoke leaked from the horses' eye sockets and mouths, nostrils that belched flames. With each hit of their iron hooves on the ice-crusted snow, sparks shot out.

Eventually they reached the castle and, up close, Skarde could see it was just ruins. Inside everything was red and black and soulless.

The horses and their riders stayed out front, guarding the entrance, and Skarde stepped inside, the stone flooring beneath his feet uneven, snow and red leaves blown inside the cavernous, cold room, making it look like it was splattered with blood.

Come forward, the voice said again. It came from the darkness at the back of the castle, where the room disappeared into a void. *Come forward and claim your throne.*

Skarde hesitated, then stepped forward, stopping where the light started to fade into black. It seemed as thick as tar and he had the notion that if he stepped forward, inky hands would drag him in.

"A throne?" Skarde asked into the void. "*My* throne?"

The voice said nothing.

"Where am I?" Skarde went on.

You are in the Red World, the voice said. *This will be your world, once you claim your throne. There are many worlds, many layers, of which you will discover, places you can go that no humans will be able to go. Some of these places you will be able to create yourself. This is one of them.*

The way the voice said *humans* gave Skarde a pause.

"Are you not human?" he asked.

The voice let out a mirthless laugh. *I am not. And soon, neither will you be. You will become something else. One with the darkness, one with the madness, one with the power of eternal life, a power you can grant to others, to make them just like you. The power and control of blood.*

Skarde stood where he was, feeling fear once again.

Do not be afraid, the voice said. *Fear is something for humans, not for what you will become. Fear is what they will feel when they look at you, knowing the darkness that has replaced your heart and runs in your veins. Now, come closer and look me in the eye and I will give you what you've come here for.*

Skarde took in a deep breath, wanting to turn around and leave. But at the same time, he realized it wouldn't be so easy. He was in this world now, not the one he knew, and he was at the mercy of this place, of that voice. He had no choice.

This was what he wanted. This was what he asked for.

He took a step into the darkness and as he imagined would happen, the darkness reached out for him. He let it take him into the black until it brought him to a stop.

His eyes adjusted.

He was in some big dark space, with walls that turned into smooth, leaking rock, like a cave, like he was underground, that stretched up and up into a red lightning sky.

In the flashes of crimson, he saw a giant creature sitting on top of an equally large throne. A glimpse of horns and eyes and battered wings and decay. A sight so terrible that Skarde had to quickly look away, as if every human instinct he had knew that no one living should ever see such a thing, could ever comprehend it. To stare at it was to die.

He looked down at the base of the chair instead.

At the cloven hooves of the beast.

At the voluptuous naked woman at the creature's feet.

She was lying there on her side, staring at Skarde with so much love and adoration that he was immediately hard, and his blood was running hot.

"Who is she?" Skarde asked, keeping his eyes on the woman, with her dark eyes and dark hair and red lips and full breasts. Skarde was so hard now that it was physically painful, and he was being driven by this other strange urge, not just to fuck but to feed. To drink her blood.

It made no sense to him but it didn't matter, because he was being driven mad by the sight of her, the smell of her.

She is the key, the creature said. *And she is for you. Take her and take your place.*

Skarde approached the woman, keeping his eyes on her, not on the awful creature. The woman smiled, eyes heavy lidded, running her hands over her breasts, down her soft stomach, to the wetness between her legs.

Do what you want, the voice urged him on. *Take her, defile her, bleed her. Take everything she has and make it yours.*

Skarde didn't want to hurt the woman, but he was no angel. He had killed several women in his lifetime, war makes people do things they don't want to do, but need to.

So he stood above the woman, his nose filling with the stench of death and sulfur, and he stripped off his clothes. Naked, his cock larger and harder than ever, throbbed painfully in his hand.

The woman spread her legs for him, spread her folds with her fingers, beckoned him.

He knelt down, salivating, and with one hard, brutal thrust, drove his aching cock deep inside her.

The woman screamed.

Not from pleasure, but from pain.

Skarde stared at her in surprise but it was too late.

He wouldn't be stopped.

Yes, the voice went on. *Fuck her, drink her, eat her. Until there's nothing left.*

Skarde's vision went red with lust.

He fucked her hard against the stone floor, her head banging against it, her screams echoing in the room, and those screams only ended up spurring him on more, making his blood dance and sizzle, like there was a fire inside him that would not be put out. The more pain he caused, the harder he got.

The blood, the voice said from above him. *The blood is life. The blood is release. Drink from her.*

Skarde continued to drive his cock inside her at a punishing pace, his orgasm close but never close enough. The thought of drinking her blood felt like it could bring the relief he wanted.

And the vein in her neck was dark and rigid against her pale skin.

Inviting.

He leaned in and bit her neck. His canine teeth weren't very sharp, dulled by the years, and it took a lot to break the skin. He had to snap his jaws shut, like a rabid dog, and move his head back and forth until the skin began to tear and the blood started to flow into his mouth. He swallowed it down in big gulps, all salt and copper and sulfur.

Yes, drink me.

But it wasn't the woman talking. She wasn't even screaming anymore. She was cold, lifeless, dead.

It was the voice talking.

The creature.

Skarde stopped, the blood spilling from his lips and he looked above him at the creature, going against every instinct.

The creature was smiling. If it could be called a smile. If

that really was a mouth and not a hole to some Hellish eternity.

Skarde looked back down at the woman.

She was gone.

There was no woman at all.

Instead it was a tail.

Leathery and dark and hard. Rough pebbled skin that had a small tear in it where blood flowed freely.

The creature had tricked Skarde.

There was no woman at all.

There was only this beast.

He had bit through its skin.

He had drunk its blood.

Now it is complete, the voice said. *You will take your place here, you will have your eternal life. You will live with the darkness that you are and you will cheat death because you are death. Because death is all you'll bring this world and the next and the next. You need to never fear death again.*

Skarde didn't even have the time to feel disgusted because his body immediately started to change. It felt like his bones were breaking, his organs shifting, like his heart stopping pumping and the air left his lungs. His teeth fell out, rattling across the stone floor, and fresh, sharp canines painfully pushed through his gums.

"What am I!?" Skarde screamed in horror, voice echoing in the room as his body transformed and contorted and became something inhuman.

The creature chuckled.

You are my son now, Skarde. And you will become Hell on earth.

1

LENORE

PRESENT DAY

"Excuse me, miss. Are you okay?"

Sure. I've just forgotten how to breathe, that's all.

I lift my head and look over my shoulder to see a man in a heavy coat and unkept beard, a face marked by an unkind life. He's staring at me in concern, which I'm not taking too lightly. For this stranger to be concerned about me means that I must look really rough.

I give him a quick smile, even though I'm shaking on the outside, screaming on the inside. "I'm okay. Thank you."

Lies. All lies.

He watches me for a moment, still staying in the shadows of the alley. I don't know how I ended up so close to the Tenderloin district, I guess I wasn't paying attention to where I was walking. The moment I left the house, I was in a dream state, not caring where I was going, as long as I got to the water. For some reason I thought seeing San Francisco Bay would put my heart at ease and clear my mind and remind me that I'm still the Lenore Warwick I've known my whole life. That I'm still me, no matter what I am now, no matter what I've done.

But my walk has brought me closer to areas in the city most people know to avoid, especially at night, and now I'm in the grips of a full-blown panic attack, frozen on the spot, leaning against a dirty building and trying to breathe. It doesn't matter that I could technically go without air for an inhuman amount of time, thanks to my vampire blood. It doesn't matter that I'm sure there's some kind of spell that would ward off such attacks, thanks to my witch blood.

Nope, all that matters is that right now it feels like I'm going to die. All rational thought has left my head, all I feel is fear, that choking, pressing horror that I'll never take a deep breath again, that my heart is going to punch right through my skin, that I'm going to collapse to the needle-strewn ground. I don't care that some homeless guy is watching me have a freak-out right here on the street.

Okay, I care a little bit. It's enough to distract my brain, to make me focus on him instead. Not that I'm scared of him, per se, but I am a twenty-one-year-old girl in the wrong neighborhood, conversing with a transient, and I'm clearly not at my best.

I try to straighten up and push myself off the wall, feeling immense vertigo as I do so. I want to bring out my phone, jam my thumb on the digital button on the panic attack app I have and have it talk me through this, remind me that it's all in my head, but I don't feel like flashing an iPhone around.

"You sure you're okay?" the man says, shuffling forward.

I nod quickly, pressing my lips together. I feel like I've troubled him and I need to make it okay. I reach into my crossbody purse and quickly rifle along the bottom, collecting the loose coins and some bills. I'm not sure how much I have but I take a step toward the man and hold out my hand.

"Here, maybe you could use this," I say.

The man looks surprised and holds out his palms and I drop the money in it, mostly quarters and a five-dollar bill.

Before he can thank me, I turn on my heel and walk swiftly down the street, letting the adrenaline carry me along.

You see, you're breathing, I remind myself, going over what the panic attack app mantras normally tell me. *Trust your body to do the breathing for you. Your body is keeping you alive. Also, you're really hard to kill.*

Okay, so it doesn't say that last one. But it's because I'm so hard to kill that I'm having these panic attacks in the first place.

I make it to Market Street and block out the lights and sounds and crowds until I find myself beside the ferry building, leaning over the railing and watching the dark waves lap the wharf, the night sky stretching above. Even though it's chilly out and the water is choppy, there's something soothing about it, like the water is taking my bad energy and mixing it up, leveling me out a little.

The adrenaline starts to leave my body, like a balloon slowly deflating. Soon, I'll be hit with so much exhaustion that I'll need to take an Uber home. Except the idea of being alone in a car with a stranger also feels panic-inducing.

A month ago I was abducted by a vampire. Believe it or not, that was the second time I've been abducted by a vampire this year. His name was Yanik and he attacked me in broad daylight, as my father was driving me through Hayes Valley. We were only a few blocks from my parent's house, stuck in traffic when it happened, and I can't stop seeing his face. Can't stop seeing the way that Yanik walked over to the car, and my father, my good-natured father, asked him what all the traffic was for, and then Yanik lowered his head so I could see him and...

His eyes...his black, fathomless eyes, eyes that held only evil behind them.

It's all I keep seeing in my head, then my father being attacked, then Yanik coming for me and I'm trying to escape and I can't and I lose all consciousness. The world slips and spins and goes black, goes to that place of pure evil.

Later, I would kill Yanik by setting him on fire with a power that I still don't understand (and haven't been able to conjure up since), but it's that early moment when I was afraid that my father was dead, when I felt so hopeless and powerless and lost, that's one reason I keep having panic attacks over.

I was doing fine, too. I spent two weeks with Solon at Shelter Cove, his remote and very private beachside estate north of the city, bringing myself back to life, letting the slow life and the ocean waves and Solon's arms heal me. Then we came back here and I officially moved into Solon's room and...

The panic attacks started. At first I was having nightmares, the kind where you wake up soaked in sweat, and then they started to morph into day terrors, like I was experiencing it all again, while awake.

Suffice to say, things haven't been all rosy for me. Not only am I trying to deal with what happened to me, but I'm also trying to deal with all the other shit that's happened in the last few months. Trauma upon trauma. First, being taken by Solon and Ezra and held prisoner in their basement, then discovering I was a vampire, then going through *The Becoming*. That was all a piece of cake compared to my tussle with vampire slayer Atlas Poe, who then killed my best friend Elle. Then I found out that I'm the daughter of a famous evil warlock called Jeremias. Then there was my ex, Matt, whom I attacked in a fit of bloodlust and Solon had to kill him. Finally, Yanik kidnapped me on the behest of

Skarde, the dark King of the Vampires, Solon's father and sworn enemy, and I made him and the cloaked servants of the Dark Order go up in flames, murdering them all.

So, yeah I've been processing a lot of shit, on top of the fact that my entire life has been a lie and everything I knew about my future has been forever altered. You don't just discover you're both a vampire and a witch and expect everything to go back to normal.

It's just...I want things to go back to normal. Badly. I love Solon, I really do, and I like Wolf and Amethyst and Yvonne (still not sold on Ezra). I love the feeling of found family in that house, as spooky as it can be at times. But I miss my parents, the parents that I knew them as, not actual witches, not people who murdered my birth parents. I miss living below them, I miss coming up to use their coffee, miss listening to my dad yammer on about his beard. I miss spending my weeknights studying about the art of ancient Mesopotamia, spending my weekends with Elle at The Cloister and getting shit-faced. I want to wake up with a hangover and head to Salt and Straw around the corner to get some strawberry and balsamic ice cream. I miss my damn tattoos. I miss being a normal human fucking being.

And in a blink of the eye it's all just...gone. I haven't had any time to really process it and now, now that I'm back in the house, and my parents are okay, and I'm settling into this new life with Solon, a life as half of many things but never a whole thing, I feel like I'm scrambling to catch up.

Hence, the panic attacks. Tonight I was having dinner with Amethyst (because my human side controls my appetite), while the vamps were in the Dark Eyes club drinking with some bloodsucking buddies. Suddenly I felt like the dining room was closing in on me and I was drowning. I told Amethyst I was going for a walk, that I needed fresh air and time to be alone and she dutifully let me leave the house. All I knew was that maybe if I got to the water, if I got to the bay, I'd be able to breathe again.

But even though I just wanted to be alone, I know I'm not alone.

I know it because suddenly the cold is at my back. Like icy wings brushing over my hair, my shoulders, my spine. The sign of a vampire, but in my case I know exactly who it is because the hair is standing up on my arms, and it isn't from fear.

Solon.

My vampire.

"I should be offended you keep running away," his voice rings out, as cool as the ocean air wisping past.

I sigh, staring out across at the lights on the Bay Bridge. "And I should be offended you're still stalking me, everywhere I go." I slowly turn around and eye Solon. "You know we're in a relationship, right? You don't need to keep tabs on me."

He doesn't smile. I didn't expect him to. But there is a faint twinkle in his blue eyes as he appraises me. I appraise him right back. As usual, I'm struck dumb by how otherworldly beautiful he is. I know that's what every girl in love thinks when they look at their lover, especially when the relationship is shiny and sparkling new, and it's also what someone thinks when they're staring at a vampire, particularly one that looks like him.

From his gray wool overcoat, and expensive dark suit underneath (his standard uniform when he's entertaining at Dark Eyes), he looks insanely put together, a picture of class and strength, with that carnal hint of elegance in the way he carries himself, like he'd be able to pounce on your jugular before you could open your mouth to scream. His brows are black and arched over his eyes, creating shadows, making the blue of his irises seem sharper, his gaze unforgiving. His hair is black, long-ish, always falling perfectly around his face, showcasing a broad forehead, sublime nose, strong jaw and chin, and full lips that have the ability to make your eyes roll back in your head when he's putting them to good use.

At the moment though, he's keeping his distance. In a way it's hard to believe that this man is in love with me. I don't mean that in the *oh woe is me, how could this ridiculously hot, smart, deadly centuries-old vampire be in love with little ol' me, I'm just your average college student from the Bay Area*, kind of way. I mean in it in that while he's told me he's in love with me, he's not the type to say it all that often. Not that I was expecting to have him shower me with declarations of love over the last few weeks, because that's really not his style, but even so...there's a wall that's up that wasn't there before.

Or maybe it was always there and it's something he actually has to push down, with effort. Maybe being in love doesn't come naturally to him, maybe it's something he has to keep working at.

He raises his hand and delicately taps his fingers against his temple, his eyes searing me. "You're thinking too much," he says in a low voice, in that mild accent that flits between British and American.

"Why is your accent British?" I ask him, changing my thoughts before he has a chance to read them. He can do that sometimes, and the last thing I want him to know is that I'm analyzing whether he loves me or not. Our relationship is new and I'm sure the last thing he wants is me coming on too strong. God, what a normal thing to worry about.

He tilts his head slightly, like a bird. A bird of prey. "My accent?"

"Yeah. I thought it would be Scandinavian or something."

"I spent a lot of time in England," he says after a moment. "I told you as much."

"How much time is a lot of time? You mean, like how

Madonna moved to London and six months later had an accent or...?"

"Two hundred years," he says simply. "Enough to pick it up." He pauses, gaze flitting over my features. "Why did you run from me?"

"I didn't run from *you*," I tell him, folding my arms against the night air and leaning back against the railing. "You were downstairs. I just had to get out of the house."

"You should have told me."

"I'm not going to tell you every time I go somewhere," I tell him, though part of that is because I'm stubborn. "You don't trust me?"

"It's not a matter of trust, my dear."

"Just plain old being possessive then?" I ask, my tone more angry than it should be. I just wanted some air, damnit. A chance to be alone. You're never alone in that house, there's always someone there, and even when there isn't, either the paintings on the walls are watching you or you're surrounded by ghosts. Sure, I can't see them, but I know they're there. It's the crack house for the supernatural.

He gives me a steady look. "A little of that, yes. But surely you can't expect me not to be worried about you."

"You shouldn't be worried," I say, though it sounds like a lie. For levity I add, "And don't call me Shirley."

His forehead furrows. "I beg your pardon? Who is Shirley?"

"Oh, so you're totally immersed in Sesame Street, but you've never seen Airplane?"

He continues to stare at me and I'm this close to explaining how his favorite vampire, apparently, is Count Von Count from Sesame Street when he shrugs. "Just because you have all the time in the world, doesn't mean you've seen every film known to man. Regardless," he says, taking a step toward me in a rather menacing way that makes butterflies coast up my spine with icy wings, "just because you escaped from Yanik, doesn't mean you'll be so fortunate the next time."

I fold my arms, trying to buffer myself against the chill that his words bring. "Gee, way to instill confidence in me, Solon."

"Is it my job to bring you confidence?" he asks curiously, searching my face.

I open my mouth and then close it, trying to find the words. "It's not your job, no, but...you give me confidence anyway. And when it comes to being a vampire, well, it kind of is your job to show me the ropes right? You did kidnap me, after all."

"You're going to bring up this me kidnapping you thing for the rest of eternity, aren't you?" His lips twist in soft amusement.

"Absolutely," I tell him. "We're not even yet. I don't recall you saying sorry."

"I *have* said I was sorry," he says wryly. "And that apology means something, just so you know. One thing you'll learn over the years is how to guard your apology. People these days, especially young people, especially women, especially *you*, apologize for far too much. You need to conserve them, only for when you really mean it and it's actually warranted."

There's a thing that Solon does which is a little like mansplaining, but it comes less from him being a man and more from his life experience of hundreds of years. I call it vampsplaining. Wolf, his partner in crime back at the vampire frat house, does it a lot too.

"Ever thought about writing a self-help book?" I ask, biting back a smile. "Something like, Vampires Don't Apologize?"

His eyes dance. "Like the Guidebook for the Recently Deceased?"

"So you've seen Beetlejuice, but not Airplane?" I laugh, looking away. I shake my head, all the feelings from earlier flooding back. "I don't want you to worry about me," I say solemnly. "But maybe you should. It's just...I don't know what's happening to me."

"You're still in *The Becoming*," he says, with a gentleness that nearly unravels me. "That's what's happening to you. You're still dealing with, how some might say, growing pains." He takes another step until he's right in front of me, moving with preternatural fluidity, and places his hand at my cheek. My eyes flutter closed. "You're grieving, my dear. For the loss of the life you had. For the loss of your friends. This is entirely normal."

I manage to shake my head, keeping my eyes closed, my heart feeling waterlogged. "None of this is normal, Solon. None of it."

"Grief is normal," he says quietly. "For humans, vampires, animals. Grief is a constant in all our lives. You don't get to escape that. And the longer you live, the more grief you'll see. Believe me, moonshine, this is only the beginning for you."

I swallow hard and open my eyes, tears clinging to my lashes. "There you go, trying to make me feel better."

Solon isn't big on sarcasm, even though he's fluent in it himself. "I only tell you the truth because the truth is all I know."

"Says the guy with a secret room full of skulls."

"Not so secret anymore, is it? I'm an open book with you, Lenore."

I laugh softly and his hand drops from my face. "Is that so? Then tell me what's going on between us. Why the distance? We've been back from Shelter Cove for a couple of weeks and yet...yet it feels like everything is already changing."

"It *is* changing," he says adamantly. "You're changing.

We're changing. What we are to each other is changing with every second of the day. That bond we have, it's only growing stronger."

"Then why does it feel like you're staying away?"

"You're in my bed every night, aren't you?"

"Sex isn't the answer for everything."

He raises a brow. "Says the woman fucking me every day."

The vulgarity catches me off-guard. I love it when his façade slips a little and a hint of that beast comes out.

"Look," I tell him, feeling more emotions bubbling to the surface. I'm just a walking time bomb now. "I just…I don't want to come on too strong. But I do need some reassurance, especially when my world feels upside down half the time."

"Reassurance about what?"

I stare at him dumbly for a moment. My god, he can be so dense sometimes. Guess living for centuries doesn't make you any wiser when it comes to women.

I gather up the courage, hating that he's making me say this. "I don't know. Us. The fact that I'm in love with you and even though you told me the same, I just don't know it anymore. I'm…I'm afraid you've changed your mind."

He blinks at me, slowly.

I sigh, looking down at my boots, feeling my cheeks flush.

"Changed my mind?" he repeats.

"It doesn't matter," I tell him quickly. "Just forget it."

"I do love you," he says in a heated rush, his voice cracking, eyes turning wild as they take me in. Those precious words cause fireworks to explode down my spine. "But this is new for me too. Loving someone, loving you. I'm not made for it, you must believe me on that. My heart isn't built for it. I don't think any vampire hearts are, especially those born from such a dark place."

He reaches out, his fingers press up against my chin, lifting it so I meet his eyes. "You are mine for the ages,

Lenore, and that will never change. Please forgive me if I don't seem to show it, if I don't say it as much as I should. Just know that I feel it. I *feel* it. This black heart belongs only to you, my dear."

He takes my hand and presses it against his chest. "It's doing the best it can."

Well fuck. From the weight in his words, to the way he's staring at me so deeply it's like he's taking laps in my soul, I kind of feel like a jerk now to even doubt him.

"Sorry," I say. "I—"

"Shhhh," he interrupts, brushing his mouth against mine. "What did I say about apologizing?"

Then he kisses me, his lips and tongue telling me more than his words ever could. Immediately my body relaxes against his, all the panic and tension and fear I've been carrying inside me dissipating. Lust makes the perfect kindling, coaxing the flame until my veins run hot and the world is forgotten and I'm lost in the slow, sensual slide of his tongue, the hard way he grips my hair.

I have his blood inside me, he has my blood inside him. I never feel quite whole until our bodies are joined in some way. I said that sex isn't the answer for everything, and I still stand by that, but there's no denying the magnetic way that we connect. Sometimes it feels like too much for this world.

I don't know how long we stand there on the wharf, kissing each other. I feel like a teenager again, like I could just kiss this man for hours on end, succumbing to the soft, languid tease of his mouth.

Then I feel a wet splash in my hair and break away to look up, just in time to have a fat raindrop land on my forehead. We had two days of hot weather earlier in the week, but I guess it was just a false summer start, as usual.

"Come on," Solon says, grasping my hand as he peers up

at the dark clouds. "We should head back. I left my guests waiting."

I stare at him. "You ditched them to come after me?"

"Of course. You are what's most important to me. Not them." While those words sink in, he turns and waves his hand in the air, creating flames. I quickly look around to see if anyone is watching—it's impossible to know. Surely some vampire-looking dude creating flames out of mid-air will catch the eye of even the most jaded San Franciscan. "No one can see," he adds, noting my wary expression. "The door doesn't appear to the average person."

"I'm sure us disappearing into thin air might though."

"I'll only let people see what they need to see," he says, vague enough to make me guess that it's some borrowed magic.

"That aside," I tell him, "I don't want to go through there."

"Why not?"

"Because the last couple of times I've tried to go into the Black Sunshine, I felt like someone was watching me. Following me. In there. Creeped me out too much, I had to leave."

"Well yes, that was probably me," he says. Then he gives me a fleeting smile. "We'll do it the boring way then. An Uber."

I scoff. "Boring? You forget you had Ezra kidnap me in an Uber?"

"Bringing that up again?" he asks, but he grabs my hand, giving it a squeeze as we walk through the rain.

2

LENORE

I WAKE UP AT DAWN, COVERED IN SWEAT, STICKING TO THE black silk sheets. Though I don't sweat as much since I turned vampire, it still seems to happen when I'm having a nightmare, and the effect is totally jarring.

As is the fact that I'm totally alone. I slowly sit up, the hairs all over my body standing on end, goosebumps prickling every inch of skin, my hand sliding over the empty space on the bed next to me where Solon should be. I know he gets up early sometimes, especially when he can't sleep, or if his dog Odin whines at the bedroom door to go out, but usually I hear him get up. And anyway, it's not that he's gone that has my heart thundering in my chest, but that I still feel a presence in the room, even though I know he's not here.

The light is dim as always, the black-out curtains drawn against the gray morning, the ebony wallpaper sucking away all light like a collapsing star. A vampire's bedroom through and through. My eyes only need a moment to adjust, the room gradually brightening as my night vision comes into effect.

There's someone standing in the corner of the room.

I gasp, my breath catching in my throat, terror seizing my limbs.

At least…I think it's someone. It's a long, tall shadow that seems solid enough, and my imagination is running wild, thinking of the Dark Order and their cloaks. But when I manage to move my eyes, just a bit, it looks less solid. Like it's dissolving into the air and is becoming nothing more than the wallpaper.

It's gone.

"Holy fuck," I breathe out, my voice shaking. I don't know what that was but that had to be something, right? Even if it disappeared? Though I couldn't see anything of substance, I felt it look at me, eying me, like it wanted to devour me whole. It seemed all black but at the same time there was a white space, like a skull, but too elongated to be human. There was a strong sense of…I don't know, evil, or hatred or something disturbing, and even now the feelings are settling on me like ash.

Closing my eyes for a second, I take in a deep breath.

Then I open them. Look around the room. Exhale.

It seems as before. All scary, fucked-up vibes gone.

What the hell?

I throw back the covers, and slowly get out of bed. Is that why I was sweating in the first place? Because I thought someone, or something, was in the room? Or was it a bad dream? Am I still dreaming?

I go over to the curtains and pull them open, wincing at the harsh light, hoping it will make sure I'm awake. When I finally pry open my overly sensitive eyes, I notice something moving on the windowpane.

A moth.

A death's-head hawkmoth, to be more specific. You know, the one with the shape of a skull on its back, made famous by *The Silence of the Lambs*?

KARINA HALLE

It doesn't creep me out though, even though it's totally odd to have a moth inside the house. This isn't the kind of place where you leave the windows open, much to Yvonne's frustration when she's trying to air it out.

"How did you get in here?" I ask the moth softly. Against my better instincts, I put my hand out toward the moth and it flutters up in the air, landing on my finger. I bring it up to my face and peer at it. I've never been a fan of moths, especially when some kid at camp told me they like to crawl into your ear while you're sleeping, but I don't fear them anymore. And this one apparently doesn't fear me.

I remember what Solon told me ages ago (at least, it feels like ages ago), that the creatures of the night would seek me out. Well, I guess I'd rather have it be moths than bats.

"You want to go outside?" I ask, and the moth raises its antennae toward me, as if it's actually listening. Whoa. I'm one step closer to being a gothic Disney Princess. Maybe a flock of moths could help me get dressed in the morning.

I open the window with some effort, the old metal latch having not been opened for some time, pressing the panes wide, the smell of exhaust and the ocean wafting in, wiping away all the terror of earlier.

The moth hesitates and then flies away, up into the misty morning sky.

* * *

"ODIN, LEAVE HER ALONE," Amethyst says, as the black pit bull shoves his nose at my hand. It might seem like he wants me to give him some much-deserved scritches, but every time I do so, he just snuffs and snorts and moves his head away. What he really wants are treats. Lots of treats. And I don't have any at the moment.

"I'll give you something later," I tell him, and I swear the dog glares at me. He's extremely well-trained for a dog—most of the time—and so hyper intelligent that sometimes I think he might actually understand English. He at least seems to talk to Solon in his head. I called him out on it once but Solon looked at me like I was ridiculous for even thinking such a thing.

Still, I wouldn't be surprised. Solon isn't your average vampire, plus he's got a boatload of magic that he's bartered for, more than I have in my humble witchy beginnings. So I wouldn't put anything past him, including figuring out how to have a conversation with his dog.

Odin snuffs again and then gives up, leaving the room with that head hung low, disappointed walk that only a dog can do.

I'm sitting on the end of Amethyst's bed while she does my makeup for tonight's party at Dark Eyes. I'd say it's become a fun, girly tradition between us, but it's only happened twice before and neither of those events were "fun." The first time was because I was about to be auctioned off to the highest bidder (though Solon insists he would have never gone through with it, I'm not sure I believe him), and the second time I was attacked by someone working for Yanik, which resulted in my beloved ripping out the vampire's heart and setting it on fire.

And, actually, this time will be the first time I've been to Dark Eyes since I got back from Shelter Cove, so I'm more nervous than anything else.

"Are you okay?" Amethyst asks, her fluffy blush brush paused at my cheek. "You seem miles away."

I try to give her my most reassuring smile, but from the way her violet eyes keep locked on mine, I don't think she buys it. "I'm just...anxious. I guess."

"I heard what you said to Solon earlier. That you thought you saw someone in your room this morning."

And here I was thinking the vampires had the best hearing. For a human, Amethyst sure has them beat.

"It was nothing," I tell her. "Seeing things."

As soon as I got up this morning, I found Solon with Wolf down in Dark Eyes, talking about something that seemed rather important. As I had guessed, Solon had gotten up early that morning to take Odin out. Of course, I told him exactly what had happened, but he didn't seem all that concerned, least no more than normal.

"Seeing things?" Amethyst says. "Well, I suppose it could be a ghost. Even I've seen them around here. Why do you think I have the brightest bedroom in the house?"

I look around, trying not to squint. She has all the curtains open, letting the evening light reflect off the cream-colored walls. Despite her rather goth style—I mean, she willingly lives in an old Victorian house of vampires—her room is a cheerful place (aside from the fact that she collects those American Dolls and she keeps them all in a closet—not in their boxes like a normal collector would, but stacked in there all loose, legs and arms akimbo. I opened it one time looking for a shirt she borrowed and I got the fright of my life, like I stumbled onto the world of *Annabelle* or something).

Anyway, when it came to what I saw that morning, Solon didn't mention ghosts, but he did say it could be Shadow Souls. Those are the trapped souls of those lost in the Black Sunshine. I've seen them there, but he says it's not uncommon for them to cross over into this world. Apparently they're attracted to depression, which I guess might fit the bill when it comes to me. Along those lines, he also said that it might just be my imagination, since I'm having such a hard time processing everything that's happening. The shadow could represent a guilty conscience.

I sigh as she dusts some blush on the tip of my nose. I

hope I don't look like a clown now. "But I'm mainly anxious about tonight," I admit.

"Oh. Why?"

I shrug lightly as she puffs her brush into a large compact of bronzer. With my skin alabaster pale now, I will take all the bronzer I can get. "I don't know. I guess because this is the first party I'll have been to since everything happened. Everyone knows who I am now. Everyone probably knows I was kidnapped too."

"And they would know you destroyed Yanik."

"Exactly," I tell her. "An evil, powerful vampire who was working for Skarde. They'll fear me, and if they don't fear me, they'll hate me. Or both."

Amethyst gives me a small smile. "Is it such a bad thing to be feared?"

"*Yes*," I tell her adamantly. "I'm supposed to be one of them now, right? I don't want them all to hate me. I have to be with this crowd, well...forever. That's like living your worst years of high school for eternity, never fitting in with the cool kids."

She rolls her eyes. "Look," she says. "The vampires that hang out at Dark Eyes don't even like Solon most of the time. They tolerate him, and they only tolerate him because they fear him and because he gives them what they need. A place to feed safely. They know there are consequences for doing so outside of these walls. There may be no vampire police, but there are slayers who are more than willing to take them out, plus there's the fact that even vampires can be implicated for murder, and the fact that a lot of vampires don't like to kill people. They aren't different from humans in that way. Just because I eat beef, doesn't mean I'm going to walk around slaughtering cows. Same thing goes for them. So they need Solon. And because they need him, they'll need you too."

That doesn't make me feel any better. It's not like I grew up with this innate need to make people like me. I always knew I was different, and people treated me accordingly. But now, I feel so unsure of myself, unsure of my role in this new life, and who I am and what I can do and what it all means, that the idea of both being a vampire and having other vampires treat me as different, well, it kind of sucks.

"I just want to fit in," I tell Amethyst, adjusting myself on her lavender bedspread. "I know that sounds lame."

"It doesn't sound lame," she says, giving me a small smile before tilting her head sympathetically. "But you're not going to fit in, Lenore. Hate to be a Debbie Downer on you, but you're half-witch and half-vampire and that's never going to change. You won't fit in on the witches side any more than you'll fit in on the vampires, so you might as well not try and just be yourself instead."

I give her a withering look. "Did you go to Solon's School of Confidence Building or what?"

She laughs. "I'm sorry. But if it makes you feel better, you fit in this house and you fit in with me and that might just have to be enough."

I ponder over that as she finishes up the rest of my makeup. She's right, of course. That I won't fit in so I shouldn't even bother trying. Vampires and witches have always been sworn enemies, so the fact that I'm part witch will always be something that the vampires see when they look at me. Not only that, but that I'm the daughter of Jeremias, a skilled sorcerer in the black arts, powerful enough that vampires seem to cower in fear at the mention of his name. And even though I feel like my powers amount to nothing, I did kill one of their own. I guess they do have every right to fear me.

But maybe that shouldn't matter. Maybe all that really matters is that Amethyst doesn't fear me. Neither does Solon or Wolf or Yvonne or Ezra. Maybe everything I ever need will be inside this house. Maybe it's more than enough.

When she's done pulling my hair up into an artfully messy updo, I'm ready to go. I'm already wearing my dress for the evening, an Alexander McQueen black leather calf-length number, with a bustier top and belt across the waist, that clings to my every curve. It's certifiably bad-ass, and when I slip on my black stiletto heels, I feel a lot more confident than I did earlier. It helps that the heels make me super tall, and ever since I turned vamp, the preternatural grace that comes along with the bloodline has made walking in heels effortless now. Not that you still won't find me stomping around in my combat boots, but it's nice to wear a pair of "fuck me" heels too.

"Okay," she says to me. "You're all set."

I get to my feet and glance at myself in her full-length mirror. Despite the fact that I haven't worked out in like two months, my muscles are compact and sleek. If I look fucking strong, it's because I am.

Amethyst playfully rests her chin on my shoulder and stares at me in the mirror, her black hair a contrast to my highlighted locks. "I have to admit, I'm kind of jealous," she says wistfully.

"Why? You're going to be there tonight."

"Working," she points out. "Always working. And anyway, no one looks at me like I'm some all-powerful creature. No one even looks at me at all."

I give her a wry look in the reflection. "You're a human in a room full of vampires, I'm sure everyone is very aware of you all the time."

"Are you aware that I'm human right now?" she asks. "Are you smelling my blood? Am I making you hungry?"

"Well, no."

"Because you're used to me. So are all the vampires."

I laugh at how disappointed she sounds. "You mean you *want* to be on the menu tonight?"

She doesn't say anything to that, and that's when I realize she's not really talking about the other vampires. She wants to be on one vampire's radar in particular—Wolf. I'm starting to think Amethyst is holding out hope that Wolf is going to randomly bite her one day.

"Here," Amethyst says, handing me my jewelry box where the Burma ruby earrings that Solon gave me are nestled. I wince as the earring posts punch new holes in my ears (because of the way I heal, they close up the moment I take earrings out). Then, when Amethyst gives me the final seal of approval, I leave the room and go down the hall to the stairs, passing by the roses that Yvonne puts on every level.

As usual, the red roses are dead, so I point my fingers at them and think *bloom* and then I watch with glee as the flowers start to rise, coming alive and dripping with blood. They aren't exactly the same as they were before (pretty sure you can't pick up blood-drenched roses from the Whole Foods floral department) but it makes me feel good that not everything has to die around vampires. Even though I swear one of the vamps in this house is purposefully killing them to annoy me. Every time I make them bloom again, I'm reminded of that *Pink! Blue!* color-changing dress scene from *Sleeping Beauty*.

I climb all the way up to the tower, just as Solon is stepping out of our bedroom, dressed in a tux. He looks hella sexy, as usual. No one can pull off a tux quite like he can, in the way that you immediately want to pull it off of him.

His eyes trail over my shoulders, my chest, over my hips, their intensity kicking up a notch, his pupils dilating until his eyes nearly look black. "You look beautiful," he says in a low voice, smooth like cream, that makes a shiver run down my spine. "Those shoes," he adds, his heated gaze lingering on them.

Of course I'm grinning because it was just the reaction I wanted. "Glad you like them."

He squints at me. "You should have come up earlier," he says, sliding his hand down over his crotch in an overly suggestive manner, bottom lip sucked in through his teeth, a hint of fangs like he's both horny *and* hungry. "My cock is going to be preoccupied with the thought of you all night."

Jeez.

"Is that such a bad thing?" I tease, though the same heat that's making his gaze molten is now flaring up through me.

He comes forward, engulfing me in his natural scent of roses, tobacco, and cedar, my blood pumping hot through my veins, buzzing in response. His hand reaches out and grips me at the back of my neck, holding me possessively. "Thinking of you is never a bad thing," he murmurs, his eyes locked on my mouth, my lips already tingling at the thought of him kissing me. "But when I can't get what I want, I tend to become irritable."

I give him a lazy grin. "You? Irritable?"

He lets out a low rumble in response before kissing me, hot, wet, and deep, his grip on my neck growing tighter and tighter. If he keeps fucking my mouth with his tongue like this, I think we're going to be very late for the party.

I press my hand against his chest, managing to push him back an inch, enough so that our lips break apart. "I can't afford you mussing me up. I have to make an impression on your guests."

"Fuck them," he growls, brushing his mouth over mine, breathing heavily. "The only impression that counts is the one you leave on me." And with that he takes my hand and presses my palm against the hot, hard length of his cock.

God, I love having him in the palm of my hand like this—literally, and figuratively.

I grip him until he lets out a low hiss, his eyes pinching shut, and my god I would do anything for him.

And I will. But if we don't go to the party, I'm going to lose the nerve to go at all.

"Later," I whisper to him, taking my hand away.

He grumbles at me, eyes flashing. "You deserve to be tied up and tortured with my tongue, with not even a hint of release."

"Promise?"

I kiss him quickly and then turn around, patting my hands over my hair. We walk down the halls and stairs. Every bleeding flower droops and withers and dies when he walks past them, then blooms again when I silently ask it to. The faces in the paintings watch us as we go, perhaps amused by this little game.

"You know," I say to Solon as we reach the main level, heading for the final set of stairs that will take us below to Dark Eyes, "I was thinking about what you said earlier, when I told you about the shadow in the room this morning, the feeling of something being there. Something bad. And how you said that it could be a manifestation of my feelings." He eyes me to go on. "Well, do you guys have a therapist or something?"

He stops on the landing and blinks at me. "You guys?"

"Yeah. Vampires. You vampires. Do you have a vampire therapist? Because if you don't, I think that's a thing that's sorely needed. Not just for those who are just turning into one, but, I mean, you've been alive for centuries and you've personally spent a lot of that time an actual beast, I think maybe vampires would benefit from talking about their problems."

He frowns. "Who said I have problems?"

I laugh and smack him on the arm. "Oh, really? Mr. I Keep a Skull For Every Human I've Killed to Remind Me Of My Humanity."

He gives me a steady look, clearly not amused. "Lenore, a therapist is for human beings. For human problems. Humans only have so many years to get their shit together. They need therapy. Medication. Whatever works for them in the short amount of time they have to make their lives bearable. Vampires, on the other hand…" He shrugs with one shoulder. "We have all the time in the world to sort ourselves out. You'll sort yourself out soon enough. I promise."

"Yeah, but how soon is *soon* in vampire time?" I mutter under my breath.

He just gives me a quick smile, leans in and kisses me on the forehead, causing butterflies to brush against my ribcage, then links his arm around mine and leads me down the rest of the way.

"Nervous?" he asks me, as we pause outside the gilded doors with their embossed roses. Once we open the doors, we step through the protection spell that's cloaking the entire house. We become vulnerable to a degree.

"How could you tell?"

"You wear every single emotion you feel, Moonshine," he says affectionately. "At any rate, you have nothing to be nervous about. To be honest with you, I was surprised you wanted to come tonight."

"I figured it was time," I tell him. "I can't hide in the house and pretend this part of your world, of my world, doesn't exist. I want to be among the vampires, even if they don't want me there, even if they fear me. I need to feel like…I need to get used to this. To what I am."

"And what you are is mine," he says.

Then he pushes open the doors and we step into the club. It's like stepping into a living, breathing set from some forties film noir, all mirrors and glass, polished mahogany and teak, leather, rugs, tapestries and fine art.

My nose is assaulted with a million scents, my brain working quickly to place them all. The scent of cigar from the lounge, even though the door is always closed and the room is airtight. The tang of booze from the bar where Ezra is currently mixing a drink for someone, on bartending duty tonight. The old leather of the chairs, the wood of the floors, the faint hint of freesia, which tells me Amethyst was in here earlier. Occasionally a hint of vanilla perfume wafts past me, and my eyes instinctively scan the crowd wondering who it can be. As a rule, vampires don't wear perfume because it's too much for our sense of smell, but sometimes a vampire says fuck it and wears it anyway.

Then again, the perfume might belong to a human. Even though I know there aren't any in the club at this exact moment, that doesn't mean that they aren't behind the steel doors of the Dark Room, where the feeding happens. Because that's the other thing I'm picking up, the very faint hint of blood. Human blood. The steel doors do a great job of keeping the smell out of the lounge (otherwise all the vamps would go wild with bloodlust), but sometimes it escapes.

That said, I don't think anyone has noticed because all eyes are on us. On me, to be more specific. There are about thirty vampires in the club, which doesn't sound like a lot, but that's thirty sets of hateful, curious, lethal eyes and it makes my human blood run cold.

Chin up, Solon's voice sinks into my head. *You're the queen of the night.*

His grip around my arm tightens and I raise my chin, faking the confidence that I don't feel.

We walk into the club, vampires in their suits and tuxes and cocktail dresses part way for us, like they'd catch a disease if we stood too close. Normally even those that aren't fond of Solon would be approaching him, paying their respects, but this time everyone seems to be staying away. Can't say that makes a girl feel good, knowing it's all because of me.

"I feel like a party crasher," I whisper as Solon leads me toward the bar. It says a lot when Ezra is the only friendly face.

"This is your party, my dear," he tells me. "You have to think of it that way. Your house, your party. And I'm your vampire. Just tell me what to do."

I give him a wry look. "You'd let me boss you around?"

That gives him a pause. "Maybe just for a moment. Wouldn't want you to get used to it."

That sounds more like it. Solon likes to be in control at all costs, even if it hurts him in some way. We stop by the bar and Solon gives Ezra a nod, which means he's going to pour us both some expensive scotch.

"So how come I smell blood?" I ask Solon as Ezra takes out a bottle. "Like, human blood." Normally when there's a big party, the vampires don't feed. They don't like to get their best clothes messed up, and apparently it's messy fucking business. Dark Eyes operates as a feeding zone three other nights of the week, so usually the vampires go to those, and these parties are just an excuse to socialize with their kind away from the paranoid eye of humans.

He looks impressed. "Your sense of smell is really sharpening," he says to me. Then he shrugs lightly. "I noticed Wolf by the door to the Dark Room. Perhaps some humans showed up, wanted to donate blood and there were some takers."

I think that over as Ezra slides us both our drinks. I grasp the glass and raise it to Solon. Even with the vampires still watching us every now and then, it does feel like we're in our own little world sometimes.

"Cheers, then," I say to Solon, and he clinks his glass against mine, his eyes turning warm as he takes me in.

"Cheers. To your first real night back," he says. "To new beginnings."

We drink the scotch, the dark liquid burning beautifully, making my chest glow with fire, all while our gaze stays locked on each other.

"Absolon," a deep voice says from behind us.

We both turn away from the bar to see a thin, dark-skinned man with bright hazel eyes, dressed in a burgundy tux, his hair long and black. I don't recognize him, but he seems amiable enough.

"Onni," Solon says in surprise, and the two men quickly embrace, Onni at least a foot shorter than Solon but still commanding in his own lithe way. "I didn't know you were in town."

"Just for a couple of days," Onni says, his accent sing song. Maybe Finnish. Onni then looks to me. "This must be the infamous Lenore," he says, but he punctuates my name with a bright smile, just a hint of fangs at the corners. "It's a pleasure to finally meet you."

He holds out his hand and I put mine in his and he places a quick, cold kiss on the back. I'm rather taken aback by how friendly he's being, considering.

"Onni is an old friend of mine," Solon explains, and I'm sure he's selling the old part short. "Normally he's in Estonia. And normally he would call first."

"You know I like my surprises," he says with a laugh. "Listen, there's a lot of people I have to see, but let's do dinner in a couple of days. I'll be starving once the jetlag wears off. Such a bitch that we have to suffer through jetlag along with the rest of the world, isn't it?"

Solon slaps him on the back affectionately. "I'll have the Dark Room waiting for you then," Solon tells him.

"I look forward to it," Onni says, his pupils briefly turning red, before he nods his goodbye and strides across the club to talk to a couple seated by a teak backgammon table.

That red look of hunger in Onni's eyes flares up something inside me. Not quite hunger itself, but the feeling of being in the dark about something, of being left behind on the fringes.

I lean in close to Solon. "I want to go into the Dark Room," I whisper to him. He turns his head toward mine, his nostrils flaring delicately, eyes sharp. "I want to watch the feeding."

3

LENORE

Solon stares at me for a moment, then blinks. "You want to watch the feeding? Tonight?"

I nod slowly. "I've never seen it before. I want to see it. I want to see what happens."

He presses his lips together, studying me. "You might not like what you see."

"You think I'm too delicate to see what vampires do? Solon, I've seen it. And I've seen what I can do. With you, and with...others." The awful flash of my teeth sinking into Matt's neck goes through my head, and I quickly bat it away before it can bring on a guilt-induced panic attack.

I can see the wheels turning in his head, trying to figure out what I can handle. Then he says, "Alright." He finishes the rest of his drink and places it back down on the bar, eyes coasting over me. "It can get, uh, rather messy in there, even for those not feeding."

I gulp back my scotch and grin. "And I'm wearing a leather dress. It'll wipe right off."

"Can't say the same for my tux," he says woefully. "It's Tom Ford, you know."

42

I roll my eyes at how vain he can be. "I know. I've seen your closet. And you have a million of them."

He takes my hand and leads me through the club. By now, most of the vampires are back to chatting and drinking fine wines and cocktails in their own little groups, but every now and then they'll watch us as we go past. If the easy way Onni approached us changed any of their minds about me, it's not apparent.

The Dark Room is located at the back of the club, near the stage, which is currently vacant. Wolf is standing outside the door, on guard. With Nordic cheekbones, and his height and shoulders, he has a most commanding presence, especially in his white tux.

"And what brings you over to my neck of the woods?" Wolf asks us, his golden-green eyes dancing.

"Someone in there?" Solon asks, gesturing to the door.

"Wouldn't be standing here if there wasn't," Wolf says, eying us warily. Between Wolf, Ezra, and Amethyst, their jobs at Dark Eyes are all pretty interchangeable. Someone mans the back door, someone bartends, and someone is in charge of the Dark Room. From what I understand, Wolf's current role is to handle the human volunteers and to make sure it all goes safely. Apparently, despite the restraints, vampires do lose their cool every now and then and flat out kill someone. Just the risk that humans take when they step inside here.

"Think they'd mind if Lenore watched?" Solon asks.

Wolf's brows go to the ceiling and he stares at me. "You want to watch?"

"Can't be a very good vampire if I don't know exactly what goes on in there," I tell him, feeling a little defensive. What on earth could be so bad? They already explained to me, many times, what happens in there. Doesn't sound much different than how I feed off of Solon, just probably a lot more clinical. Like donating blood at a blood bank or something like that.

Wolf looks back to Solon, as if to say, *are you sure?* Solon just nods.

"Okay, then," Wolf says, putting his hand on the door. "I don't think they'll even notice you're there."

Good, I think. *Wouldn't want the vampire to get stage fright or something and have me spoil their whole meal.*

Wolf opens the door and Solon and I step into the dim room. The smells of blood and sex slap me in the face, a straight shot to the brain, already setting my senses on overdrive.

"Knock if you want out," Wolf says, before he shuts the door on us.

Oh my god.

The blood.

There is blood absolutely everywhere, splashed on the steel floors, splattered on the walls. But that's not what has my jaw dropped to the floor, my cheeks flaming hot.

Right in front of us is a very buff, very naked male vampire with his arms chained to the wall, the chains long enough for him to grip the waist of the petite brunette human he's currently railing from behind. She's also naked, eyes pinched shut, mouth open in moaning ecstasy. Her back is slashed all over with deep cuts and bleeding and every now and then the vampire will lean forward and lick the blood off her back. For a moment he meets my eyes but it's like he's looking through me, his expression lost to the bloodlust.

They aren't alone in their bloody writhing. At the back of the room is a black chaise lounge, and on it is a plus-sized woman with a great rack lying on her back, also totally naked, with two vampires feeding from her. She has a vampire's cock in her mouth and while he fucks her lips, he drinks freely from her bleeding wrist held up to his mouth.

At the other end, a female vampire in a green glittering dress is chained to the wall, her blonde head buried between the woman's soft legs. Her fingers are digging into the woman's hips so sharply that she's drawing blood, little pooling droplets that run down to the chair, but she's feasting on the woman like she's the main course. From the way she raises her head from time to time, her mouth dripping red, face smeared with blood, I know she literally is eating her out. Or at least sucking her dry.

Heat presses between my legs and I know I'm wet, my pussy throbbing painfully, like a switch has been turned on inside me.

And I know Solon can smell it, because he's breathing in deeply and pulling me back against him just enough so I can feel his hard-on press against the curve of my ass.

"I told you this wasn't for the faint of heart," he murmurs in my ear, the rough quality of his voice making my thighs squeeze together even tighter.

"You didn't tell me it would be an orgy in here," I manage to say, unable to tear my eyes away from all the blood and feasting and fucking, even though I know I should. For my sake more than anything. The adrenaline and lust are so overpowering that I'm afraid I might start attacking Solon right here and join in their little fuck fest.

"I know what you're thinking," he says through a groan, nipping my earlobe as he presses his cock into me harder. "But I keep my feedings private. Always have."

"So you know I'm thinking about how badly I want to fuck you right now?" I ask huskily.

"If you're thinking the same as me, then yes," he says through a growl. Then he pulls away enough to raise his hand in the air, creating a doorway of flames.

Normally I would protest to going inside the Black Sunshine, but honestly, from the way my hormones are ripping my brain apart and leaving me without rational thought, I don't think we'd even make it upstairs to the bedroom before attacking each other.

We step through the flames and the world goes black and white and silent. The feeding frenzy has turned to writhing ghostly shapes. You can still tell they're fucking, but the moans have ceased.

And I'm still more turned on than I've ever been in my life.

I don't have to tell Solon that though.

He's already grabbing me roughly by the jaw, covering my mouth in a hard, violent kiss until I'm moving back, back, back across the steel floor and my head thumps against the wall.

We both fed the other day, but I'm suddenly so ravenous that I'm clawing at him, desperate to drink his blood, to get off, to fuck, to do everything and anything, and from the way he's handling me, hands rough, cock hard, I know he feels the same.

His hands go to the bodice of my dress, ready to rip it off me, but I manage to say, "Wait. Don't ruin it." Cleaning blood off a leather dress is one thing, having it ripped to shreds is another. I wouldn't mind wearing it again.

He grumbles in protest, his fingers moving so quickly that it feels like a rush of air at my back and then the dress is zipped off, falling to my feet, leaving me completely nude, and he's suddenly naked too, the tuxedo in a pile.

There's something so jarring about seeing Solon here like this. Not just in the black and white world of Black Sunshine, turning our bodies different shades of gray, but him standing here in this sterile room, totally nude. With the way he's standing, breathing hard, muscles primed, cock hard and erect, his hair a mess, he looks absolutely feral, like he's about to pounce on me and tear me apart.

He looks like a beast, I can't help but think. Even though there is a real beast that lives inside of him, one I only glimpsed briefly as it fucked me royally, part of me wants to bring that beast out of him again. He's warned me about it, that I can't tame that monster inside of him...but who says I even want to?

I reach back to take off my heels, utterly uninhibited about being so naked and on display, when he lets out a low guttural noise from his chest. "Don't. Keep the shoes on."

My brows go up. Okay then. I make a mental note to wear heels more often.

He takes a predatory step toward me. Then another. My eyes keep bouncing from his rigid cock, bobbing with the languid movement, to his gaze that burns so hot and deep that I feel I'm about to enter a new territory with him.

Fuck, I'm practically dripping between my legs at the thought.

"Go over to the chains," he says, voice low and rough.

I look over my shoulder. I can see the ghostly glowing shape of the chained male vampire still fucking the woman, though with the way time moves in here, it's all happening in slow motion.

"The empty chains," Solon clarifies.

Now my other brow lifts. "You want me to chain you up?"

He gives me a wicked grin. "Not a chance."

So much for me bossing him around.

I swallow hard and stare at the chains on the wall, the sleek metal links leading to soft cuffs. I went from purely vanilla sex before I met Solon to...well, I don't know how the hell I'd classify our sex life. But putting me in chains in a vampire feeding room—in the Black Sunshine, no less—is a whole other level. That would bring my sexual experience from vanilla to Ben & Jerry's Everything But The...

Still, there's no denying that the hunger was already

building inside me. I'll do whatever he asks of me, as long as we both get off. I've already made peace with this monstrously horny side of Lenore.

"What do you want me to do?" I ask.

He moves so quickly that it's just a blur. Suddenly I'm being pushed back against the wall, the cuffs locked over my wrists and Solon is grabbing my hair, making a fist in it before pushing me down until I'm on my knees, the chains straining. Now I know what the black leather mats are for.

"Suck it," he grinds out.

My eyes go wide.

And I obey.

Because I can't reach his cock with my hands, all I can do is open my mouth while he tightens his grip in my hair, pulling my head forward while he makes a fist with his other hand, guiding himself into my mouth. His dick slips past my lips, deeper and deeper, until I'm nearly choking. Thank god my gag reflex has subsided since becoming a vampire.

I close my eyes for a bit and let him fuck my face, his cock sliding in deeper and harder with each and every thrust. I stare up at him every now and then, especially as he gets rougher, and more vocal, letting out lustful grunts. I love seeing his head thrown back, his neck exposed. I watch the blood pulsing in this throat, smell how hot it is beneath the surface of his skin. I want to drink from him, suck him off in both ways.

I have no control, though. I've never given a blow job where I haven't been able to use my hands, so I'm at his total mercy, and his cock is relentless as it plunges in and out of my wet mouth.

That is, until I feel my fangs begin to lengthen, the sharp tips of them razing the rigid veins along his shaft.

Teasing.

Wanting.

Solon lets out a low hiss, his nails digging into my scalp, and he glances down at me with feverish eyes, out of his mind with lust.

May I? I ask sweetly inside his head.

His pupils turn bright red, the only color in this room.

Yes, my dear, he answers.

Feed on me.

I smile around his cock and then gently press my fangs down until they lightly pierce the skin, drawing his sweet blood.

He gasps loudly, this low rumbling sound that seems to come from the depths of his chest, but whether he's enjoying it or not is the least of my concerns right now. The moment his blood hits my tongue, all I can think about is feeding, getting my fill. The hunger is out of control and I am selfish and insatiable, my fangs sinking in deeper, the blood pouring into my mouth.

I suck and I swallow and I feast on his cock like a woman starved and his nails are digging into my head so sharply, I feel wetness in my hair, blood starting to run down the sides of my face. The pain is enough to make me slow down and step back. This is a rather dangerous time for me to get carried away.

I hungrily gulp down his blood, his life force, and attempt to control myself, pulling my fangs back enough so that I can continue to suck him off in every which way that counts.

"Fuck!" he rasps out, pushing his dick so far inside my mouth that his balls press against my chin and he's tensing and I know he's close. The blood from his nails runs over my lips as he starts fucking me harder and then the room fills with his bellow as he comes.

It's the hottest fucking sound and totally unhinged, just the way I love Solon. He's in such control most of the time, that when he comes, I finally see beneath the cold and calculated alpha exterior, see the wild, primal, disheveled vampire underneath.

I swallow him down, every part of him, his cum hitting the back of my throat as his pumping slows, and he unhooks his fingers from my scalp. Slowly he pulls out, and I stare up at him, feeling like I've come myself, my hunger satisfied.

He drops to his knees beside me and then grabs my face, the blood smearing across my skin, kissing me hard, his tongue violent.

He pulls away, lids heavy as his eyes search mine. "I didn't hurt you?" he asks, running his fingers through my hair.

I shake my head. "The better question is, did I hurt you?"

The corner of his beautiful mouth ticks up. "You did. And I wanted you to." Then he licks the blood off his lips. "Perhaps you'll let me do the same to you."

I gulp, the throbbing back between my legs, the pressure automatically building at the thought. "Okay," I say breathlessly.

His nostrils flare, pupils burning with crimson. "Get to your feet."

Thanks to my vampire grace, I'm able to get to my feet easily, even in heels with my hands in chains.

He moves forward on his knees, his face at my crotch, staring up at me with fire that singes my skin. He reaches up with his large rough hands and palms my breasts, pinching and squeezing my nipples until I gasp, then lets his hands slowly trail down over my stomach, down between my thighs.

"Spread your legs wider," he murmurs, his eyes still locked on mine.

I oblige, taking as wide a stance as possible in these high heels.

Solon reaches around my hips, placing his hand at the

small of my back to steady me and keep me in place, then dips his mouth between my legs.

Still staring up at me.

Never breaking eye contact.

I'm shivering with the bone-deep intimacy of it all, how deeply he seems to stare into my soul, how I would never be so vulnerable and trusting with anyone else, just as his lips brush over clit, his hand reaching up and spreading me open for him.

Fuck.

My eyes pinch closed, my mouth falling open, his tongue dipping low and licking up a wet, wide path, the sound so loud in the stillness of this other world. I wobble on my heels for a moment, trying to stay on my feet, the chains rattling, and then he's gripping me harder, his tongue digging deep inside me.

I cry out loudly, back arching, the dam ready to burst, but he pulls his face away just in time. I feel him blow hot air on my clit, which makes me throb with a deep, delicious ache, and I stare down at him to see him smiling wickedly.

"Tease," I tell him, my voice breaking with lust and tightly wound desperation.

He doesn't say anything to that. He doesn't need to. He knows exactly what he's doing. I come so damn easily with him that it's not uncommon for me to come multiple times when he goes down on me, but he loves to draw it out as much as possible. Prince of Darkness; King of Edging.

Then he buries his head in deeper, tongue thrust up inside of me and I'm almost screaming from how badly I want to come, wanting so badly for him to touch my clit again.

And then he does.

With his fangs.

The sharp prick catches me off-guard for a moment and I

suck in my breath, holding it in my chest while he gently drags his fangs over my clit.

Back and forth. Back and forth.

So sharp. So hungry.

And I'm waiting, waiting for the bite.

He clamps down, fangs piercing my skin.

"Fuck!" I cry out, my voice strangling in my throat. The pain of his bite is sharp and deep and delicate and it obliterates my mind. It stings and throbs as the blood pulses through me, then soothes in the most satisfying way, like each burst of agony is its own orgasm, its own hit of relief. With each precise bite, each strong suck of my blood through his lips, I'm brought to new heights until I'm coming hard, writhing on his face, riding his mouth like a woman possessed.

And Solon has given into the bloodlust, just as I had earlier. If he can't regain control, well, I guess there are worse ways to die than during an endless orgasm.

Eventually, somehow, Solon manages to regain control. I don't know how long I've been standing here for, with Solon feasting on me, sucking my clit, drinking my blood, making me come over and over and over again, but I think all the muscles in my body have been filleted and my knees are about to buckle.

"Solon," I say through a ragged gasp, "I can't."

And then I'm falling forward and he's catching me in his arms, just as the chains go taut, pulling at my wrists. He holds me up, smoothing the hair off my face, staring at me with wild eyes, my blood all over his mouth.

"Are you okay?" he asks, breathing hard, his concern fighting through the hunger.

I manage to nod. "You literally made me come until I couldn't stand. So yeah, I'm okay."

He smirks, self-satisfied. Then he leans in and kisses me

on the forehead and gets to his feet, pulling me back up. I lean against his warm hard chest, hear his heartbeat slowing, and he uncuffs me from the chains until I'm free again. I shake out my arms to get feeling back into them.

"Now you know what goes on in here," he says to me, running the back of his fingers over my cheek. "You're a lot less delicate than I thought."

"You should know that about me by now," I tell him, even though, yeah, this was a shock to my system. A shock to the girl I used to be. But I'm not that girl anymore. I'm Solon's and I belong to him, body and soul and blood.

He clears his throat. "Shall we clean ourselves up and return to the party? I have to say, I suddenly feel like I could stay out all night."

"Me too." The energy and adrenaline have me feeling so fucking alive.

We get cleaned up, get dressed, and step back into the real world.

4
ABSOLON

"Mr. Stavig," Yvonne calls out as I walk down the hall. I pause and she catches up to me, Odin trailing behind her as if he's her dog now. "That guest you are having over for dinner tonight. Is he human or vampire?"

"Vampire," I reply.

"So you won't need me to make you anything?" she asks, and I catch the disappointment wafting from her. I know it must be terribly boring to be a cook for a host of vampires when we rarely ever sit down to eat food.

"I'm afraid not," I tell her, hoping to placate her with a quick smile. "But if I do need anything, I'll be sure to let you know."

That seems to make her happy for now. She gives me a pleasant nod and scampers off toward the kitchen, Odin hot on her heels. I know I shouldn't be insulted that he's choosing to spend all of his time with my housekeeper, because I know she's feeding him scraps, even though she says she's not. She doesn't know I can smell it when people are lying.

I can also smell it on Odin's breath. Keeping him on a raw food diet is proving to be next to impossible in this house.

I ignore his lack of loyalty and head down the stairs toward Dark Eyes, knowing my guest, Onni, could be showing up at any minute. Punctuality isn't a strong suit among vampires, but jetlag could mess up his schedule.

I walk through the doors, feeling the power of the protective wards brush through me, and spot Wolf closing the door to the Dark Room.

"You manage to find someone on the list?" I ask, nodding at the door.

"There's always someone," he says.

Even though we have designated nights for feeding, we operate off a list of trusted human volunteers. I'll never quite understand why humans want to be fed on when they get nothing out of it, but I don't judge their fetish either. And if it weren't for them, the vampires wouldn't be able to live in San Francisco. A safe place to feed means that vampires can coexist with humans without suspicion. If every vampire had to go out and kill to stay alive, a lot of dead bodies would start piling up, and fingers would start pointing. That's happened in most cities across the world, but not in this one, thanks to me.

"Glad that his dinner is sorted then. Where's Ezra?" I ask, adjusting my cufflinks. "Can't entertain guests without a bartender."

"He had to go out," Wolf says. "You could always try your hand at it. I have a hard time believing you weren't a bartender at some point in your life."

He gives me his namesake grin and then heads toward the bar to make me a drink.

"You're correct," I tell him, following him over to the bar. "I did it briefly in Copenhagen. But only because I was trying to get close to a witch that frequented the bar. My drinks were bloody awful."

"I have a hard time believing that too," Wolf says, and from the damn twinkle in his eye I can tell he's not done with me. He grabs a bottle of Lapraigh from the wall of bottles behind the bar and then grabs a glass. He pops off the cork. "See, it's easy to do. First you take off the cork, then you pour yourself a glass."

I stare at him, refusing to be amused. "Very funny," I say stiffly.

He winces as he pours the scotch and pushes the glass toward me. "Wow, you're grumpy when Lenore's not around, you know that? I forget what you were like for hundreds of years."

"And you're a fucking wanker when Amethyst isn't around," I snipe right back, taking the scotch. Two can play this game. Lenore and Amethyst are both out tonight having a girl's night bar crawl or something dreadful like that. I won't deny that I'm not at my best when I don't have Lenore around me, but he'll deny it until the cows come home that Amethyst affects him in a similar way.

"Amethyst?" he says casually. Too casually. "I didn't even notice she was gone. Having a girls night, are they?"

I just blink at him. He knows they are. And I'm not going to push it either. Whatever Wolf feels for Amethyst is none of my business. Heaven knows that Lenore is constantly bringing them up around me, like they're subjects of some reality dating show and not people living in this house. She's convinced they're soulmates, and whenever I mention the fact that human and vampire relationships never end well, she ignores it. Turns out my half-witch is an incurable romantic.

"Yes, a girl's night," I say after a moment. "It's good for Lenore to get out of the house."

Wolf nods, pouring himself a drink. "You're worried about her."

I slowly turn the glass of scotch around in my hands, making the coaster with the Dark Eyes logo spin. "I don't think she's adapting very well."

"You're forgetting that she's only a half-vampire and spent her whole life being raised as a human."

"I'm not forgetting that," I snap at him. "I was there. I saw her being raised."

He raises a brow. "Then perhaps you're forgetting that it's a trying time for any vampire when they're in *The Becoming*." My gaze hardens but he goes on. "And yes, I know you aren't like most of us. Believe me. But you've told me you don't remember what it was like when Skarde turned you. You've forgotten."

"Or I've blocked it out," I say in a low voice.

"Either way, you don't remember. But I do. It was fucking rough, even though I knew my whole life what was going to happen when I turned thirty-five. I saw the same thing happen to my sister when she turned twenty-one, then my brother and, it still didn't prepare me. Now Lenore's gone through that, without any warning, and neither of us know exactly how it is for her because we don't have witch blood. I think she's adapting as well as she can, old boy."

I sigh. "I know. She is. But I'm still worried. Her body is adjusting but her mind…her heart. I'm not sure she's cut out for this lifestyle. She's too…soft."

"She is," he says, after he has a drink. "But that's why you're in love with her. Because all you've known are centuries of life being hard and sharp."

And relentless. The years have been relentless.

"I love her in ways I don't understand," I say quietly, looking off at nothing in particular.

I feel Wolf's eyes on me in surprise, silence falling

between us. Though vampires are fairly emotional and expressive by nature, I've never been one to talk much, especially about something as personal as my relationship with Lenore. Perhaps her softness is rounding my edges.

I'm not sure I like it. I need to stay hard, in more ways than one.

"Well," Wolf says after a moment, clearing his throat, "if it makes you feel any better, I don't think love is something even humans understand, let alone us. It might be for the best to let it remain a mystery." I finish my drink and he leans across the bar, pouring me another one. "And I wouldn't worry about Lenore either. She'll come into her own eventually. It just might take time."

"I know. But then why does it feel like time is something we're running out of?" I ask, unable to ignore the dark feeling that's been nagging at me ever since the incident with Yanik. "I'm so painfully aware of the seconds, minutes, hours, days when I'm with her, like time is now limited, no longer infinite."

"Maybe it's because we don't know how immortal she is," he points out. "We both know that we can live forever—if we choose to, and only if we're careful. We don't know how it is with a half-witch, half-vampire. How much can her body handle? There are three ways to kill us, how many to kill her? And even without that, how long will she naturally live for? A hundred years? A couple hundred?"

Lenore has asked these questions herself, to which none of us have any answers. Human-vampire hybrids can live a long time, like my brother Kaleid, for example, who was the first born vampire to my father. Over time, his human side disappeared. But he's also an exception. Most direct hybrids don't live forever and they're easier to kill. My brother excels because of my father's blood. Blood that was created by the Devil himself, the same blood that runs in me.

"Maybe that's it," I muse. "Or maybe it's that we're waiting for the other shoe to drop. With my father. You know he won't take what she did lightly."

Wolf breaks into a grin. "Oh, to have been a fly in that room when he found out how little Lenore bested his Dark Order. In flames." Then his brows furrow. "But you know he can't leave his homeland."

"Can't? Or won't? Two different things, Wolf. And regardless, whoever—or whatever—he sends here next will be far, far worse than Yanik."

He shrugs. "I'll be ready for them. So will you."

"But will Lenore?"

"I wouldn't underestimate her, Solon. That was your father's mistake."

He might be right, but that doesn't stop me from worrying. God damnit, I'm not cut out for this sentimental shit.

Suddenly my nose fills with the smell of aniseed and Wolf gives me a sharp nod. Onni is here.

He strides across the club to the backdoor and opens it. After their first visit, vampires get a key card that will give them access through the parking lot at the back of the house, but they still have to knock to come inside. They must be invited in.

"Onni," Wolf says, opening the door for our guest. "Come on in."

Onni comes inside, dressed in a deep pink suit. With his dark skin tone, light eyes, and long black hair, body as thin and slight as a reed, Onni embraces the fact that he's different, preferring to have people think he's an eccentric as opposed to a vampire. It works for him, but because he's so memorable, he has to change up his look every thirty years or so. The last version of him had a purple afro, which he enjoyed immensely, living in Helsinki in the 1960's, though I think he preferred the blue powdered wig he had in France in the late 1700s, modelled after his dear friend Marie Antoinette.

"Nice party the other night," Onni says, taking the seat beside me at the bar. "I was so enraptured with that vampire from Alaska that I forgot to say goodnight."

Wolf holds out the scotch. "Will this do?"

"I'll have a good red, if you don't mind me being a pain in the ass. Anything from Bordeaux? Old?"

"How old?" I ask. There's a wine cellar in the basement, but I'd rather not go searching for the rare vintages.

"Anything older than what I can get at the liquor store," he says.

"I have a Cabernet Sauvignon from the 90's, Napa," I tell him as Wolf reaches down and pulls it out. "You're in California now, Onni. You can get your Bordeaux in Europe."

Wolf pours us all a glass, since it's a terrible waste to open the bottle just for one person. "So," I say, savoring the sip. I can practically taste the weather on the day the grapes were picked. Sunshine after a morning of fog. Supple and cool. "What brings you here, Onni? You don't usually come without some kind of news from the homeland."

He grins at me, teeth blindingly white. "Absolon, really. A friend can't come say hello?"

"You don't risk jetlag to say hello. An email would suffice."

His smile is smaller now. He has a long, careful sip of his wine and then runs his tongue over his teeth. "This is quite good. I'd forgotten how much I like a Californian red," he says. Then he gives me a fixed look. "There's been some, uh, tribulations. Skarde is continuing to build his army. Whether that's the Dark Order or something else, I'm not sure. At least, Kaleid isn't sure."

I straighten up, nearly snapping my teeth together at the

mention of my brother's name. "Kaleid? You've been in contact with him?"

Onni nods. "He's back in Helsinki, for good. Ruling the roost. Seems he now has the same goal as you do, as we all do."

I frown. "And what is that?"

"To kill your father."

I almost laugh. "This is what you came all this way to tell me? Utter bullshit?"

Onni flinches at my expression, which I assume must be murderous. I'm certainly feeling murderous right now. "It's not bullshit. He's broken away."

"When did this happen?" Wolf asks, also in disbelief. Kaleid, my father's golden child, has been at Skarde's side since his life began. The two are thick as thieves.

"A couple of years ago," Onni says.

I shake my head, a bitter taste in my mouth overtaking the wine. "Impossible. I would have heard by now."

"I had to make sure," Onni says. "I've been in Helsinki, living in the Red World with him. He has plans to take him out. I swear to you."

"I thought you were in Tallinn," I grumble.

He shakes his head. "Kaleid welcomed me back."

Helsinki, Finland, was my brother's home base for a long time. My father lives further up north, where the Finnish and Norwegian border intersects above the arctic circle. Kaleid has spent centuries splitting his time between the two places.

"And your father has moved on," Onni continues, perhaps picking up on my thoughts, as some of us are known to do. "He's no longer in the village, gone north now. He's retreated further into the Red World, so deep that even Kaleid can't reach him through it. He knows. Skarde knows what Kaleid will do, so he's doing everything he can to prevent that.

There he can build his armies without interference from anyone but..." He trails off.

None of us know for sure who exactly Skarde made a deal with for eternal life when he became the first vampire. I assume the Devil, or some dark, all-knowing malevolent force. It's been rumored that this dark force has been helping Skarde all this time, or that Skarde has been nothing more than a puppet for centuries upon centuries. I wouldn't know —since my memories of my father are tinged with madness and hatred—if he's ever had full agency or not. I suppose it's never really mattered. My father is the de facto king that nearly all vampires defer to, regardless of who is really behind him.

"My father wouldn't retreat," I say slowly. "He wants to remain in control, in reach of his subjects. To go so deep into the other worlds, where not even Kaleid can get to him...he's risking the loss of power. How does he know vampires won't start deferring to Kaleid instead?"

Onni shrugs. "Kaleid has wondered that same thing. So it has to be for a reason. A big reason. It's why I'm here. To convince you to come to Helsinki, so you can team up with your brother and put an end to it."

I stare at Onni like he's lost his bloody mind, because he can't seriously believe the words he's sprouting. "You can't be serious. Team up? Do you know how ridiculous that sounds?"

"I know, but I am serious. Look at me, Absolon, you know that I am."

It's hard for vampires to lie to each other. Hard, but not impossible. "You're a good man Onni, but you're as dumb as a fucking post. You really think I'm going to go to Finland on your word that Kaleid wants to work with me?"

Onni looks rebuffed. "You don't trust me?"

"No," I tell him sharply. "I don't trust anyone. It's why

I'm still alive." I pause, studying him for a moment. I can tell he's telling the truth, which is the weird thing, but all it means is that he believes it. "You do realize this is a trap, right? Did Kaleid actually ask for me, or was this your idea?"

Onni looks me dead in the eye. "He asked for you. He told me to bring you to Helsinki if I could."

My eyes narrow, hackles raising. "Bring me?" I repeat coldly. "By any means necessary?"

He gives me a wry smile. "You know that would be impossible with you. All I can do is plead his case and ask politely."

I hesitate. "Did he mention Lenore?" I ask.

"Your little witch?" Onni asks. If I hadn't picked up on the affection in his voice, I probably would have torn him in two for using such a condescending phrase. "No."

Hmmm. Kaleid would know that Lenore destroyed Yanik, but if he isn't asking for her, then at least she's not a target. If this was a trap. Which it is.

"Well, I think you know where I stand on this," I tell Onni, before finishing the wine and getting to my feet. "I don't think you're lying, but you can hardly blame me for not trusting my brother. If he truly wanted—needed—my help, he would prove it by coming here, in my domain. For me to go to Helsinki would be walking into a noose and, forgive me, but my life has just started to get interesting again. Wouldn't want to end it so soon."

I eye Wolf, not forgetting to be a good host. "Do you think Onni's dinner is ready yet?"

Onni sits up straight, eyes wide with excitement, pupils turning red with hunger. "Ooh, I had almost forgotten. I can't remember the last time I had American blood. Please tell me it's a male. A young one."

"Beggars can't be choosers on a short notice," Wolf says to

him. "We have a female in her early thirties. Sorry to disappoint you."

Onni waves him away and gets out of his seat. "No disappointment here. I'm sure she'll taste just fine. Besides," he gestures to the room, "it's all part of the experience here. It's just so…neat and tidy not having any bodies to dispose of. Sure, you lose the thrill of the kill, but I suppose consent is popular these days. You know, Absolon, but Kaleid has started to copy you."

I raise my brow. "Copy me?"

"A little." He squeezes his finger and thumb together in show. "He now has a den outside of the Red World. He has some humans he likes to keep around. They live with him. He feeds from them. Oh, and they want to be there, don't worry. No different than your little volunteers here. Before, he was insatiable, perhaps to gather strength to fight your father, so much so that the Helsinki police started raising the alarm of a serial killer in the city. For a while he started importing Russians from St. Petersburg, but that got a little dicey. Guess your, er, respectable approach to feeding is rubbing off on him."

"I'll believe it when I see it," I tell him, putting my hand on his shoulder and leading him to the donor in the Dark Room.

And I won't be seeing it, that much I know is true.

5

LENORE

"Wow. You're hella drunk," Amethyst says as she puts my arm around her shoulder. "Like, actually drunk."

"You're drunk too," I remind her. I can walk, so I don't need her support, but I am delighted in the fact that I can't walk in a straight line. Fucking eh, I did it. I drank enough to feel human again.

"I'm buzzed," Amethyst tells me. "Happily, pleasantly buzzed. But also sober enough to get us a cab and go home."

I suppose she's right, though I'm having fun walking in the mist. We started our bar crawl down in the Castro and ended up here in Upper Haight. I didn't want to go to the Cloister because it reminded me of bad times, so we stayed at a few places on Haight Street, doing shot after shot after shot.

Okay, so maybe I was the only one doing shot after shot. I was determined to get drunk off my fucking ass, and because of my vampire blood, it takes a lot of alcohol to get me to that level. But, score one for me, all that tequila worked.

And honestly, it was much needed. When Amethyst said we should go for a girl's night, something we've been talking about having for a while, I jumped at the chance. I just wanted to let off some steam, feel normal for once, do the things I used to do.

For the most part, it worked. We talked about life, the normal life, the thing that exists outside of the house. We talked about our exes, friends (though I tried not to say much on those two subjects, considering how fresh those wounds are), we talked about our families. I was open with her about my relationship with Solon (I mean she's literally the only person who could understand what it's like to be with a vampire), but no matter what I said, I couldn't get her to open up about Wolf.

I know I'm nosy as fuck, but I can't help it.

"Hey," I say to her as we stand on the curb and she pulls out her phone, looking for a ride. I'm feeling emboldened in that too-much-tequila kind of way.

"Mmmm?" she says, thumbs firing on the screen.

"Does it, um, bother you at all that I was intimate with Wolf?"

Her eyes widen briefly as she stares at her phone. She swallows and then gives me a furtive glance. "Does it bother *you* that you were?" she asks.

I shrug. "Not really. I don't think about it. I mean, I only remember some of it anyway. But, you know, it happened, and I know how you feel about him and I don't want you to hate me or think it's weird or—"

She holds up her hand to shut me up. "First of all, Wolf is a friend, nothing more." Uh huh, sure. "Second of all, I don't hate you or think it's weird. It's part of *The Becoming* right? Solon wanted to stay in control, but you were in pain, so to speak, so he had Wolf, you know, help you. I get it."

I nod, feeling a bit better. "Okay. Good. Great. Just wondering."

"It's totally cool. I mean, it's not like you had sex with him," she goes on, back to look at her phone.

"Ummmm," I say, feeling my cheeks flame.

She glances at me and frowns. "Is that what you think happened? That you slept with Wolf?"

Uh, I really don't want to go into details here. "Well." I clear my throat. Oh, so awkward. "Yes. We slept together. I was tied to the bed and he was, you know, going down on me and…"

Her black microbladed brows tick up. "Yes?"

"And yeah…" *Fill in the blanks here, Amethyst.*

"So what makes you think you had sex?" she asks, her lips twisting into an amused smile.

"The fact that we did?"

"And you remember this?"

"Well. No."

"Have you discussed it with Wolf?"

"Uh, also negative. Though he did say we had good rhythm together."

"And that's what you're basing this on?"

I frown. "Do you know something I don't know?"

She laughs. "Oh, you poor thing. You really thought he had his dick inside you." She catches herself, cheeks going pink against her pale face. "Sorry. That was uncalled for."

I shake my head, not understanding. "Solon told me. After I woke up in the bathtub when he was trying to fucking drown me, he said Wolf fucked me for two days! Said the whole house smelled like sex!"

"Well, it did. It smelled like…um, you. I guess. I don't know. This is getting weird now." She looks back at her phone, hastily tucking a strand of hair behind her ear.

"But why would Solon lie about that?"

"I don't think he lied," Amethyst says. "Face fucking is still fucking, isn't it? All I'm saying is that if it makes any difference to you, you didn't actually have penetrative sex with Wolf."

It doesn't make a difference, not really. Maybe a little. Okay, maybe a lot. I don't remember much of that time, if anything, which was incredibly unnerving, to know your body was going through things that your mind wasn't. And I adore Wolf, I really do, and I trust him too, but there's a difference between someone you trust getting you off for days on end because you were desperately horny and in need, and someone you trust getting off *in* you, even though they didn't need to. The latter could fall into the taking advantage of you part.

"I mean, you've been Solon's property from day one," Amethyst adds. "He likes to have his control, but not enough to let Wolf brand you with his dick before he got a chance. Then again, I don't know what the hell goes on in your vampire lover's head, so I might be wrong about that. Vampires are a weird bunch when it comes to sex anyway, like it's seriously not a big deal to them. Guess that's what happens when you live for that long—you see a lot, you do a lot. Hey look, I got a car just two minutes away."

I ponder that while we wait. Solon is definitely possessive, but he's open-minded when it comes to sex, and I think as a vampire you have to be. Guess there's something erotically charged about bloodsucking and feeding off each other. Vampires are probably pretty adept at separating physical acts from emotional ones.

But I'm not like that. And Solon knows that too.

A Prius pulls up shortly and the two of us get in the back seat, but while Amethyst is chatting to the driver about the SF Giants (who knew she was a baseball fan?), the alcohol is coursing through my veins, mixing all my emotions up, the tequila feeding anger. All this time and Solon never said anything? He knew I had the wrong impression about what happened, and he still went with it.

It's not long before our ride drops us off at the house and we're walking in through the front door.

"I'm going to get a drink at the bar," Amethyst says, heading down the stairs to Dark Eyes.

"Oh me too," I say quickly as I follow her, knowing that Solon is probably down there with Wolf, just the two people I wanted to see.

And there they are. Solon, Wolf and that Finnish guy from the other night, in the cigar lounge, smoking and drinking, in a conversation about something.

Amethyst gives me a look like *please don't*, but I ignore her and march straight over to the cigar lounge door and fling it open.

"You!" I exclaim, striding toward the three vampires, nearly tripping over the Turkish rug. I stop behind Solon and he slowly turns his head to look at me, breathing in deeply and wincing slightly. I probably smell like booze. He can probably tell I'm drunk. Doesn't matter. I'm not that drunk.

"You," I say again, pointing at him now, "you liar!" He blinks at me, the cigar smoke wafting from his mouth. "You made me think this whole time that Wolf was fucking me when he was really eating me out for days on end!" I look at Wolf who is sitting there wide-eyed. "Isn't that true? Why didn't you tell me what really happened? You know I thought we were screwing."

Solon clears his throat. "Lenore, you remember Onni?" he asks, gesturing to him.

I glance at Onni who is staring at me with his mouth agape. "Yeah, hi again." I look back to Solon, hand on my hip. "So what was the point of all that? Some weird double standard where it's okay to have your friend get me off, but he can't get off inside me?"

Solon and Wolf exchange a look, like *whoa nelly*. Onni looks like he's going to start eating popcorn for the show. Perhaps I shouldn't be spewing this in front of company, but I honestly don't care at the moment.

"Lenore," Solon says delicately as he brings his gaze back to meet mine, "perhaps this is a conversation for another time."

"No," I tell him adamantly. "I don't care what this guy thinks." I gesture to Onni who looks mildly insulted. "All you vampires are so casual about sex, aren't you? It's just the same as feeding, isn't it? Fucking, sucking, it's all the same. But guess what? It's not that way to humans, and if it is to some, it's not the same to me. Okay? I totally thought that Wolf was railing me for those days I don't remember during *The Becoming*, and it turns out he wasn't! Why did you let me think that?"

"Would it have made a difference?" Wolf asks, and Solon gives him a sharp look, maybe to shut him up.

"To me, yeah!" I tell him. "I thought I was okay with it since I didn't remember and it's part of the process, but now that I know the truth, it does make a difference! And it makes a difference to Amethyst too."

Wolf's brows go up. "Why would Amethyst care?"

And oh my god. I've said too much.

"No reason," I say quickly. "I gotta go."

I turn on my heel and leave the cigar lounge, walking past Amethyst, who is behind the bar shaking a shaker full of ice.

"What is going on in there?" she asks, frowning, but she doesn't seem pissed off, which means she didn't hear what I'd said.

"Nothing. I'm drunk. Going to bed," I tell her and keep going, through the doors and up the stairs into the house.

I get all the way to the top floor when I hear Solon coming up quickly on the stairs behind me, so fast that one moment he's at the bottom level of the house and the next he's standing behind me.

"What's gotten into you?" he asks me, reaching out and pulling me to a stop just outside the door to our bedroom.

"I'm drunk," I tell him with a scowl, trying to rip my arm from his grasp. His grip is too strong.

"I can see that. How much did you drink?"

"Enough to feel normal again."

"And is your normal getting pissy at me for no reason?"

My mouth drops. "No reason?"

He shakes his head slowly. "I'm not a mind reader."

"Yes you are!" I exclaim, throwing my arms out. "You are a mind reader."

"Lenore," he says with tried patience, "I don't understand what's bothering you about what happened. You're mad because, what, because you thought...?"

I finally get my arm out of his grasp and poke my finger into his chest. "You tied me down to the bed. You had Wolf go down on me."

He blinks at me in disbelief. "You were begging for it."

"I was begging for *you*, not him."

He raises his chin. "You were in agony, Lenore. We gave you a way out."

"I couldn't take the way out *because* I was in agony. And yes, I'm grateful, for lack of a better word, that he was there to do what you refused to. I would have gone mad otherwise, I know that. I would have hurt myself, I'm sure. But...you told me that we had sex for days."

"You did," he says stiffly.

I close my eyes, frustration rolling through me. "You could have been clearer about what you consider sex."

"You don't consider that sex?"

I fix my eyes on him. "Semantics. I thought Wolf was screwing me. He wasn't. And why is that?"

His gaze sharpens. "Now you want to know why he wasn't screwing you?"

"Yeah. If it's all the same to you."

"I never said it was the same," he says quickly, a dark look coming over his brow.

"Then why did you let me believe it? Why did you let me think it?"

He sighs tiredly, running his hand over his face. "Why the questions, moonshine?"

"Because," I say, knowing the tequila is causing a lot of trouble for me at the moment. I don't mean to fight with him. "Because I'm in love with you, Solon. I'm in love with you and sometimes I just…I just get scared. I get scared that I'm in over my head with you, because what I feel is very deep and very real and it's…it's forever, for lack of a better word. It's forever and it's supernatural and it's a big, dark love. And you, you're this…you're still this enigma, this mystery to me. I have no idea how you think. You may have watched me when I was younger, seen me grown up, but I don't have that same privilege with you. I know next to nothing about you, and that's okay, I know I have a lifetime ahead of us, but we're standing on uneven footing here. You'll always have the upper hand. We're not equals."

"Not equals?" he whispers harshly. He reaches out and grabs my face between his hands, holding me as his eyes roam my face. "Lenore, you are my equal in every single way."

"Well, it doesn't feel like it. Not when you've got so much life behind you, more than any creature ever should. It feels like it will be centuries before I know everything about you."

"Is that such a bad thing?" he asks softly. "To spend those centuries with me, getting to know who I am?"

"No. No, of course not. But it's hard when there's no mystery when it comes to me. Like you say, I wear my emotions on my sleeve. What you see is what you get. I'm twenty-one years old Solon, how the hell am I even compelling enough to be with someone like you?"

"*You* compel me, my dear," he says. "Your emotions compel me. Your softness, your heart. The fact that right now you're telling me all these things, these truths about you, things I didn't expect to hear, that compels me. I know that we may seem different, that there are differences between us, but they have no bearing on how deeply I feel about you."

I look away, my heart fluttering.

"Look," he says quietly. He clears his throat. "I didn't tell you the whole truth about what happened with Wolf, not because it wasn't a big deal, but because I…I wanted to see if you'd care."

I stare dumbly at him. "You wanted to see if I would care? What are you, twelve?"

He bristles enough to make my heart flinch. Oh, he did not like that comment.

His chin lowers as he glowers at me beneath his dark brows. "We all have our insecurities," he says after a moment.

Okay, now we're on to something interesting. "What insecurities? You knew I was meant you from the beginning, didn't you?"

"Knowing and believing are two different things."

"Are they? Because they sound the same to me. And anyway, I did care. You saw that I did."

"I wanted to see if you'd care," he goes on, "*and* I wanted to stay in control. There's a reason why I never filled in the many blanks you had. I knew you lost a lot of time, that there was a lot you didn't remember about that period. But the more you knew, the less that I had an advantage over you. You not knowing kept you on shaky ground. I didn't want to give up an ounce of the power that I had over you."

I blink. "That's fucked up, Solon."

He stares back at me steadily. "Yes, well. I suppose I'm a little fucked up then." He runs his hand back through my hair, nails scraping along my scalp, making my eyes flutter. "But that was then. This is now. Now we are equals, and if anything, you're the one with the power over me."

Heat blooms in my chest. To think I have any power over this vampire…

I bite my lip and meet his intense gaze as his words settle into me, finding their way into my depths, spurring a warmth between my legs. "Well, as the person holding all the power, I think I'd like you to get in that bedroom and serve me."

His eyes gleam. "Very well."

He grabs my hand and pulls me into the bedroom, practically throwing me across the room so I stumble backward onto the bed. He kicks the door closed and in a flash he's on top of me.

I'm in a burgundy baby-doll dress and leggings and boots, he's in a suit, but unlike the last time we got naked, where he moved at supersonic speed, this time he's taking things slowly. He unzips my boots, tossing them across the room, before reaching under my dress and curling his fingers along the waistband of my leggings, carefully easing them down over my thighs.

I prop myself up as his tongue flicks out, tasting the skin under my knee, then running up the sensitive flesh of my inner thighs until his nose brushes against my lace underwear.

He makes an appreciative noise, but he doesn't pull them off, not yet. Instead, he sucks at my clit through the delicate fabric, the barrier both making me moan loudly and preventing me from being overstimulated. Once again, even though I'm supposedly in control, he's the one controlling when I come by holding back just enough.

But as he sucks and I grow wetter and my panties are absolutely soaked and his tongue presses against me, I succumb to the sensations, lying back, letting it wash over my body until I'm sinking into the bed. Over and over the pressure builds and his mouth is relentless, and I keep chasing after the sweet relief.

Then, when I'm close to coming, bucking my hips up against his jaw so hard that I might crack a tooth, he pulls away and lets out a mirthless laugh.

"Not fair," I protest breathlessly. So, *so* close.

"Never is, is it?" he murmurs, prowling over me, pulling my dress up and over my head until I'm just in my bra and underwear. He takes a long, lazy look at my body, my skin prickling under the heat of his gaze.

"You can't let me be in control for one second, can you?" I ask.

A flash of a wicked grin. He reaches for the cups of my bra and pulls the lace down so my breasts are exposed. His fingers trail over them, lightly skimming over my nipples, the friction causing them to harden tightly. He stares at them in awe and hunger before dipping his head, his tongue swooping over the full curve of my breast before swirling around the middle, sucking in my nipple between sharp teeth.

"Oh god," I cry out softly, making fists in the sheets, and I swear Solon can make me come just from sucking on my tits and nothing else.

"I can be your god," he murmurs against my skin, pausing to flick my nipple with his tongue. "I can be anything you want."

"You are my god," I manage to say through a throaty moan. "*Fuck*, Solon."

He licks and sucks and teases and my whole body is writhing.

It's *so* good.

This is *so* good.

Then he takes off my bra, peels off my soaked underwear, until I'm naked and desperate beneath him, my body on fire, begging for him to put the flames out.

He takes his time looking at me, the fever in his gaze reaching a pitch, and I wonder what he sees when he sees me like this, the way he looks at me in both worship and awe. I know he makes me feel revered, like a goddess, like I have innate power all my own.

"For all time, Lenore," he says, voice dropping to a rough whisper as he runs his thumb over my lip and I bring it into my mouth, sucking, biting, tasting him. "You're mine for all time."

The back of my head tingles, my stomach flips, and I'm giddy. Giddy and alive and in love, so hopelessly, dangerously in love.

Then he pulls out his thumb and covers my mouth with his, bringing me into a deep kiss and I'm reaching up and undoing his tie, hastily opening his shirt. He shrugs off his jacket, his belt, pants, everything, until he's completely naked, his body cool and taut and huge above mine, the immense weight of him against my chest.

His kiss deepens, my legs part, I feel the head of his cock, hot and slick, press against me and then he's pushing inside me, filling me whole.

I gasp, arching my back to make room for him as he pushes inside to the hilt, his cock stretching past every throbbing, aching nerve inside me, the air leaving my lungs. My head sinks back into the pillow, my mouth open, letting him possess every single inch of me.

"Lenore," he rasps in my ear as he brings his mouth to my neck. "Lenore."

All he says is my name, but it says more than enough. I

hear the desire in his voice, the lust, the hunger, the desperation, and beneath all of that, the love.

He starts moving faster, our bodies working in tandem, fitting like magnets as skin slides across skin. I am lost to him, lost to the movement of our fucking, of how deeply he penetrates me in every way, like he's sinking into my veins, my soul. Soon all I feel is him and I let my body go, let it become something feral and wild and beautiful.

Nails scratching down his back.

Teeth nipping at his neck.

Legs wrapped around his ass, pulling him in deeper, deeper, deeper.

And then I'm coming.

It hits me like a wave, knocking me over, and my heart seizes, like the whole world stops and as I cry out, limbs quaking, every single emotion I've had to juggle lately comes washing over me. It won't stop, it can't stop. I'm coming and I'm drowning and—

"I love you," I say through a gasp, my eyes closing as tears spill. "I love you so much."

My words surprise me. I've said, I always say it, but I feel it so much that it might just tear me right in two, down the middle of me. Maybe that's what love is, being halved, until one part of you exists with you and the other part exists with him.

I close my eyes and I succumb.

When the room stops spinning, and air fills my lungs again, I open my eyes, the tears falling to the sides, running down my temples.

Solon is over top of me, his large, taut body moving smoothly like a well-oiled machine, watching me closely with a look I can't read, a look that's more than pleasure. My emotions probably took him by surprise once again.

I don't want to get sentimental on him during sex, not

when he's yet to come, so I grab his ass, trying to pull him deeper inside me as he pumps his hips against me until my skin feels bruised. The bed is groaning under the movement and he's gasping for breath. I love watching him come undone, working so hard that he's actually sweating, his skin hot and tight instead of cool.

But there's something different about him right now. The lustful, driven intensity that's usually in his eyes as he's fucking me, about to come, has been replaced by something darker.

Wilder.

Chaotic.

He stares at me, mouth open, fangs bared and there's a flash of fear across his brow, his eyes widening as he fucks me harder.

"No," he says, his voice raw but the panic unmistakable, and he's shaking his head. "No, wait, no."

"What?" I ask, alarmed, digging my nails into his skin, trying to slow him down so he can talk to me. "What's happening?"

He doesn't slow. He keeps fucking me, his cock driving in deeper and harder, like he's not even in control of his body.

"Solon, what's wrong?" I cry out, my stomach sinking.

But he doesn't speak.

Instead, there's a flash of his voice inside my head.

Run.

Run Lenore!

He's telling me to run.

And that's when I see it.

See what he's trying to hold back.

The beast.

6

LENORE

IT HAPPENS AS IF IN SLOW MOTION, EVEN THOUGH SOLON'S pace doesn't slow at all.

As he's gazing down at me in sorrow and fear, his warning going through my head—*Run! Run Lenore!*—his pupils turn bright red and then grow, wider and wider until they take over the blue of the irises and the whites of his eyes, until it's all just a glossy, hateful red.

Then the transformation spreads.

It starts in the middle of his chest, where his heart is, a blackness that appears and starts to spread like an ink stain. It permeates his skin as it moves, changing the smooth pale texture to something rough and leathery, dark as onyx as it moves out to his shoulders, while more blackness spreads up his arm from his hands, encasing his whole body.

I'm too terrified to scream, too shocked to run. This has only happened once before, this terrible transformation that Solon has been so afraid of, and also during sex. But I never saw it happen, not really. I just saw what happened to his hands, watched as his claws emerged, felt him grow larger inside me as he kept fucking me, but everything about the beast remained a mystery.

I didn't run then.

I'm not going to run this time.

This beast is mine as much as Solon is.

I'm not afraid.

"Solon," I say to him in breathless awe, staring up as the darkness comes for his face and everything changes.

Everything.

If it was slow motion before, that inky spread, that oil spill that turned him from pale to tar, now it happens so fast, I can't even focus. One moment, he's still something I recognize, still a man, still a vampire, and the next he's twice the size, in every single way.

I cry out, feeling his cock expand and lengthen inside me, the pain sharp at first, then I'm lost to the horror as the beast takes shape. Solon's face is no longer his, but another creature's entirely, something from a nightmare, something so black and dark that my eyes can't pick up on the features, except for the now snarling and snapping long white teeth, and those red, red eyes, shining like crimson holes. His shoulders jut out like leathery plated armor, his hair turned into a hyena-like mane that goes halfway down his spine, his arms are tree trunk size, his torso this wide expanse of sinewy muscle. His knife-sized claws dig into the headboard behind me, and I hear the crack and splinter of wood as it breaks.

Oh god.

Oh *god.*

I don't know what to do.

Despite it all, he's still inside me, his hips are still grinding into mine, his black leathery skin rough and scraping against my pale tender flesh. He's biting and snapping at the air, making these deep animalistic sounds that would make anyone's blood run cold, make anyone feel like prey. Right now, he's the ultimate predator and he's not slowing a bit.

And it feels good.

It feels better than good.

It shouldn't. I said I wasn't scared, but that doesn't mean I'm not in shock, and yet each pass of his giant cock inside me, and I feel like I'm on the verge of coming, filled and stretched to the brink with utter ecstasy. If Solon is in control at all—and he must be a little bit—he's not letting himself get carried away too much. So far, he hasn't hurt me, he just wants to fuck me like the wild animal he is.

And I want him to.

"Solon," I say again, hoping he can understand me. His head tilts, those fathomless red eyes staring at me, and I do everything I can not to feel that cold shiver at the back of my neck. "It's okay," I assure him. I reach up and grab his hips, my fingers pressing into his ragged, almost pebbled skin. "It's okay."

I say that, even though I can't believe this is really happening.

I'm really getting fucked by the beast.

How is this okay?

He snarls at me in response, presses his hips in deeper, to the hilt, knocking the air from my lungs.

That's when I feel it.

Something brushing against my ass with tentative movements.

Testing me.

Oh my fucking god, what the hell is that?

Don't tell me he has two cocks.

No, I think to myself, *no, cocks don't move like that, with control. Whatever it is is prehensile; he's controlling it.*

I glance down, watching as he continues to slam inside

me. I quickly run my hands down his rough hips, down his lower back, and over his ass and then...

Oh my GOD.

I feel it. The hump of where it begins.

It's a fucking *tail*.

Of course the beast has a fucking tail. What beast doesn't?

And apparently, his tail has an appetite for fucking too, because it's poking and prodding my ass like it wants inside me. This is no skinny, weak appendage, but something long and thick and hard, about the same girth as his regular dick, the end blunt, and who knows how long.

Holy. Fuck.

Then the beast starts to pound me faster, the bed creaking like it's going to break, and the tail slips up between his legs and I'm just staring at it as it swipes around where his cock disappears inside me. It's too dark to see properly, but then it slides over my clit, the skin ribbed and rough against where I'm so slick and wet and—

"Fuck!" I yelp, coming hard and fast, my body jerking off the bed, and I'm writhing against him as his tail slides back and forth over my clit, over and over, until I'm coming and coming and I can't gain control, can't get any air, I'm just obliterated and then his tail slips down to my ass.

Slick and dripping with my orgasm.

And pushes inside me.

"Solon!" I scream, my nails digging into his leathery back, and his cock and tail both plunge inside me, in and out, harder, deeper, tighter, fucking me in tandem, and oh god, oh god, I've never felt so full, so wonderfully, painfully full. Every inch of my body feels stretched and filled, the slick roughness of his tail fucking my ass as deep as his cock is, a brutal, punishing rhythm, filling all my space until all I am is Solon, this beast, and—FUCK.

I'm coming so fucking hard I think my head's been

removed. I'm just a body, a boneless, shuddering, convulsing body and the rest of me has been scattered into the universe, never to be put back together again.

"Oh god," I manage to say, when I realize I'm still being fucked by the beast. "Solon."

My head is so mixed up. I can barely feel anything anymore.

But Solon, or what used to be Solon, is still going.

Except his thrusts are getting harder, rougher.

Violent.

And then the headboard snaps behind me and the bed crashes to the ground, the mattress nearly sliding off.

"Shit," I swear, trying to move back to where it's stable, but Solon growls at me viciously and when I look at his eyes, those red glossy eyes, they're emptier than they've ever been. I no longer see him deep inside, I don't see him at all. In fact, all while he was fucking me, I had a sense of him still there, still the slightest bit in control. It's why he made sure his tail was wet before he thrust it inside me, because he still somehow knows what to do for me.

But now I don't sense him at all. I don't smell him.

I just smell this sulphurous brimstone, tannis root, a stench of something evil, and now, now I'm starting to get afraid.

"Solon," I say again, firmer now, but the name means nothing to this beast, and I'm trying to pull away from him, to roll over, and somehow I manage to slide back along the crooked bed and his cock comes out of me.

He didn't like that.

He howls loudly, this awful penetrating sound that blows my eardrums, and now I'm panicking and trying to crawl away, get away, and then he's roaring in my ears and he swipes his claws against my back, just a scrape, but enough to flip me onto my back.

I cry out from the pain and stare up at him and he opens his mouth to show a row of dagger-like teeth at the back.

Oh my god.

He might actually kill me.

"Solon!" I yell at him, my voice breaking. "Stop! Please! It's me, it's Lenore!"

He snarls against and then swipes at me with his other hand, right down the middle of my chest.

The pain stuns me for a moment.

I can't breathe, can't move.

I blink, staring at his claws, at how my flesh is actually hanging off his claws in ragged strips.

Oh my god. Oh my god.

Slowly the memory comes back into my brain, the one I saw through his eyes, when he turned into the beast and killed the love of his life. I have that memory, and I realize that I will be a new one for him.

He will remember what he's done to me.

And what has he done?

I manage to move my chin to look down at my chest and…

I can see my ribs. I can see the white bone through the layers of blood and shredded skin and oh my god he's just cut me right open, almost exposing my still beating heart.

Suddenly my lungs fill with liquid and I'm choking on my own blood and then I feel it wet and spreading over the bed.

I stare at the beast, wondering if he knows what he's done yet.

But the beast just snaps its jaws at me, ready to lunge, ready to rip my head off my neck, and I know that he doesn't care, that he'll end me now, tear me limb from limb.

His leathery muscles coil and he comes at me and I throw my hands up in the air to protect myself, choking on a scream as I close my eyes and prepare to die.

But the snarling and growling only intensifies and I feel flecks of liquid on my arms and I'm so scared to open my eyes but when I do, I see him a foot away and my hand are stretched out and it's like he can't come forward, like he's stuck in place, biting the air, his saliva flying on me.

And that's when I feel it, beneath the blood in my lungs and my exposed ribs and the endless pain: The power. I feel the power coming out from the palms of my hands, buzzing like warm static, moving forward like pulsing radio waves.

It's my power.

It's what's keeping the beast back.

It might be what's going to save my life.

I keep my palms raised, keep concentrating, trying to figure out what to do next. If my power holds up, whatever this power actually is, some kind of force field or invisible shield, maybe I can buy enough time to heal.

But when I look down at my chest, at the deep ragged grooves left behind by those knife-sharp, velociraptor-sized claws, at the white bone and torn muscle, I don't see myself healing like it should. My skin feels dead, like it's not even trying.

Oh my god. What if I don't heal? I'm going to bleed out here.

"Help," I try to scream, but I choke on the word and I'm coughing up blood freely, it's running over my lips and onto the bed.

I roll over, trying to move while keeping one hand aimed at the beast, who is being held back like a snarling wolf, but I'm so weak, and every inch hurts, that I get as far as the floor before I collapse. I hold myself up against the side of the bed and try to call for help again.

I can't.

I can't form the words and I'm going to die here with the

beast staring at me, waiting for the moment for me to let my guard down.

Help, I try again, closing my eyes, keeping my hands out, palms facing the monster. The power is flowing still but it's weaker now, just as I'm weaker. I don't have a lot of time.

Help, someone help me. Solon, if you can hear me, if you're still in there, please help me. Wolf. Amethyst. Ezra. Mom. Dad! Please, someone help, help. My mother, my father. I need you, please, I need your help!

Exhausted tears are running down my face, every wet breath a struggle. My blood will drown me in the end.

Please, please, please. Someone hear me, someone help me.

Something light brushes against my hand.

My eyes fly open and I see a moth, the same moth I saw the other morning, resting on the tips of my fingers.

Are you here to help? I ask, wondering how delirious I really am that I'm asking a moth for help.

The moth turns its head toward me and stares at me and I stare at the moth and I wonder if maybe *this* is how I'm going to die, and then the moth flies off.

I turn my head to watch it go over to the window and OH MY GOD.

There is a fucking face at the fucking window.

Five stories up.

I can't even scream.

I just stare at the white face and the dark eyes peering in at me and okay, now I know *this* is how I'm going to die, not from my chest being ripped open, not from a staring contest with a moth, but because of fright, because there's a fucking ghost or a phantom or I don't know what outside my fifth-story window.

Then the window opens, by itself.

And the person just floats into the room.

I stare at them, the exhaustion and loss of blood making

me feel woozy, making me want to close my eyes, and yet I can't keep my eyes away from the stranger who just flew inside my bedroom.

Also, I'm totally naked, as well as dying.

They land right in front of me and I notice the shoes are black boots, which seems so normal and human-like, and yet when I raise my head back to take the rest of them in, I can't seem to decide what I'm looking at.

It's certainly shaped like a human, like a man, wearing a long black cloak and black clothes underneath. But the face is bizarre. I can't quite focus on it, like their features keep changing. The eyes are the only constant thing, deep-set black eyes, and the rest of the face—the nose, the chin, the mouth, the brows, the skin tone—those keep moving around, always adjusting, a constant blur.

I open my mouth to speak but only blood comes out.

Who are you? I manage to ask inside my head, hoping they can hear me.

"You don't know?" they say, a very rich, male voice. Continental accent, like rich East Coast. "You called for me."

*I didn't...*I begin. But I did call for someone and someone could be anyone. I shouldn't be choosy.

"You called for your father," he adds.

My eyes nearly fall out of my head. *"What?"* I manage to say, and then I'm coughing again and holy shit. My father? This isn't my father.

"But I am," he says. "And if you had only asked for me earlier, you could have avoided this whole mess. You need to conserve all the energy you have if you want to survive." He waves his arm at the beast and suddenly the beast just drops to the floor with a solid *thunk* that shakes the whole room, lying there in a heap like he's dead.

"No!" I scream before I'm choking again. *Stop! Solon is in there!*

The man gives me a tepid look. "He is just sleeping for now. You should be thanking me that I'm letting it live. I wanted to destroy this vampire a long time ago."

I'm not thanking him for anything yet. *You know Solon?*

He gives me a tight smile, his lips changing from fat to thin to old to young and back again. "I know everyone. And everyone knows me. Except, apparently, you. I am Jeremias. And I am your real father, Lenore."

I stare at him in disbelief, then the image of him gets blurry. The whole room gets blurry. This is my father? The evil black magic warlock witch who just flew inside my bedroom, made the beast pass out with a wave of his hands, and whose face keeps changing every five seconds?

"There isn't any time to have a proper introduction, I'm afraid," he goes on, bending down to get a better look at me. I can only stare into his beady black eyes, everything else makes my brain feel like it's melting. He looks over my wounds. "Those won't close up. If I didn't show up, you would have died."

"But I'm a vampire," I manage to say.

His lip curls in disdain at that. "You are only half a vampire. And even if you weren't, this wound would take you out. Lovely little gift that Skarde gave his first child, isn't it? The ability to maim and kill other vampires with a swipe of his claws, leaving mortal wounds in the immortal."

God, does Solon even know that? I think.

"Maybe he does, maybe he doesn't," Jeremias says, tilting his head as he looks at me. "That's the least of your concerns right now. I can fix you, if you give me a chance."

How?

He gives me a cold smile. "You'll have to come with me."

Where?

"Nowhere in particular," he says, walking around the broken bed, past the sleeping form of the beast, and into the washroom. When he comes back out, he's got a black silk robe in his hands, Solon's, and once again I realize I'm totally naked here in front of a man that's a total stranger, even if he is my father.

He crouches down and puts the over-sized robe around my shoulders in a rather tender way, covering me up. Then he peers at me closer. "I know we've only just met, dear daughter, but I don't want to lose you. You need me, and dare I say, I need you."

I swallow down the blood.

I know I don't have much time left.

I don't have a choice.

I nod slowly, unable to keep the fear out of my heart.

"Good girl," Jeremias says to me. Then he waves his hand in front of my face. "Now, sleep."

And everything goes black.

7

LENORE

I can't breathe.

I wake up, eyes flying open, and see an endless night sky of stars above, and yet I know Yanik is with me, that he has me, I can feel the unmistakable strength of his evil, endless darkness and utter madness.

He's going to kill me, he's going to kill me.

"Calm down, Lenore," a voice says, cutting through the darkness. "You're having a panic attack."

The voice is familiar, but it's not Yanik.

It doesn't belong to a vampire.

But the evil, the darkness, it remains like it runs in black veins under the ground, permeating the world from the inside out.

"Lenore," the voice says again, and suddenly the stars in the sky seem to disappear, as if covered by a black cloak. "You're all right. You've lost a lot of blood. Just stay still and wake up slowly."

Blood?

And then it all comes rushing back into my head.

Solon.

The beast.

The empty red eyes.

The feeling of five curved, knife-sized claws shredding through my chest, from my collarbone to my sternum, scraping through muscle, fat, cartilage and bone.

I gasp again for air and sit up and look down at my chest.

I'm wearing Solon's black silk robe, naked underneath, and my chest is one big gaping wound full of carnage. Pain, terror, abject horror runs through me, making my blood turn cold and fizzy and I'm close to passing out, because how can I still be alive with my body nearly ripped in two? This wound is deep and fatal, and awful, so awful.

I'm going to throw up.

"Breathe," the black cloak says, and when I look again, I see a changing face and fathomless eyes staring at me. "Breathe through it Lenore. You're safe here with me. We will fix you."

Suddenly he stands up straight and motions with his hands and I'm rising up off the ground, like a puppet on a string, until I'm standing on my feet, my toes sinking into sand.

Sand.

I look around.

I'm on a long stretch of beach, the sand cool against the soles of my feet, ocean waves crashing to one side of me, a darkened forest on the other side. No moon to be seen.

The man stands in front of me, pulling his cloak down off his head, though it doesn't make his face settle down. It keeps on changing shape, a moving blur of features, while his eerie blackened eyes remain fixed on me.

Jeremias.

My real father.

"Where am I?" I ask weakly, my voice raw, my lungs bubbling, frothy and cold. "How did I get here?"

His lips move into a smile. "We are in one of the many worlds available to you, dear daughter. Worlds that exist, if only you know where to look."

That isn't helpful.

I start coughing again, spitting out blood onto the sand. It looks black, like tar. This isn't good. "I'm going to die, aren't I?"

I feel the impatience roll off Jeremias, but I'm too tired and, well, dying, to care.

"You might if you don't stop talking," he says after a moment. Then he sighs. "You must have trust in me."

I stare down at my chest in horror again, at the mess of flesh and bone. Is this even happening? How do I know I'm not already dead?

"I can't trust a man I just met," I tell him. Oh god, I think I can see my lungs.

"Even one who is in the process of saving your life?" he asks calmly. "Besides, we have met. I have helped you before and that should be enough to warrant your trust."

"When…" I begin, but the effort to talk is too much. *When did you help me?*

"When you were tied to a chair in front of a vampire named Yanik and you asked for help. Your inner well, the moonlit one full of darkness and power, was waiting for me."

"My mother told me about that, about the well inside me."

"And your *adoptive* mother is a witch, just as I am, just as you are. Tell me, do you remember that moment? Before you harnessed Absolon's power, took his fire, and made it something of your own, something to wreak destruction and death on the Dark Order? Because I do. I heard you call, was standing by to help, and I asked, 'Are you sure, child?' And you said—"

"Yes I'm sure," I repeat absently, remembering it so well, even though I've been trying so hard to block it out. I knew I had felt something—someone—else inside me, helping me access what I needed to in order to defeat Yanik. I just didn't know it was *this guy*. My infamous evil warlock of a father.

"No, don't block it out," Jeremias says to me, reading my mind. "By blocking out what's difficult, you're refusing to face it. By refusing to face it, you can't use it to make yourself stronger. Lenore, my child, you will need all the strength you can get going forward. Not only to survive what this *monster* did to you, but to survive everything else that is to come your way. I have foreseen the future."

Suddenly Jeremias waves his hands and I'm drawn to him like an invisible hook is placed around my back, my toes dragging through the sand. "We have much to discuss," he says gravely, his face inches away. "But it will have to wait."

He moves his hand again and I'm spun around, facing the dark forest now, seeing flickering flames at the base of the bent cypress trees, the kind of forest you would see on the wind-beaten Northern California coast. Am I still near San Francisco? Or am I truly in another world?

Jeremias begins walking through the sand, though he seems to glide just above it, and I am pulled behind him, like he's dragging me along a foot off the ground.

We go up a small bluff and then he steps to the side and I'm left hovering in the air, in front of a circle of torches, the flames dancing in a non-existent breeze. A circle is drawn on the sandy ground with dark charcoal that reminds me of Solon's transformation. For a moment I wonder how he is, if he's woken up yet into his vampire form, or if he's still a beast and wreaking havoc around the house. There are scratches on the banister on the main floor, deep gouges left by his claws, so I know it had to at least have happened once before. I hope Yvonne and Amethyst are okay.

I hope he's okay.

But then my thoughts stop because outside of the torches,

holes begin to open up in the ground and thin pale arms reach out, like something rising from the grave.

Oh, no.

I stare, scared to death, watching as four girls pull themselves out of the soil. They're all ghostly white, with long black hair, barefoot, dressed in matching white dresses.

They get to their feet, taking position beside the flaming torches, and the dancing light illuminates their faces. The girls all look to be the same age, maybe a bit younger than me, but they also all look exactly the same. Like quadruplets, they all have the same small mouths, skinny noses, and piercing dark eyes. Even their posture and the way their hair falls in their face is the same, like someone copied and pasted over and over.

Who are they? I ask Jeremias, who is standing there, staring at the girls, and the girls are staring at him, like dogs awaiting a signal from their master.

"My apprentices," he says in a deep voice. "They need to learn. You will be a great example."

An example of what? I ask, my eyes going wide, but suddenly I feel wind at my back, my robe blowing around me, and I stare down in wonder as it twists and turns around me, like it's a black snake, like it's alive, and then suddenly the color fades to gray, and then to white, and now I'm in the same white dress as the girls.

I look at Jeremias in shock, but he just flicks his finger toward the flames and suddenly my spine is arching and my feet are going forward, and I'm on my back, floating in the air, moving along the path as if pushed on an invisible stretcher.

I cry out as I fly through the air, dizzy, the pain in my lungs increasing from the pressure, and now I'm in the middle of the circle, surrounded by the creepy girls and the torches, suspended above them.

What's happening? I cry out in my head, my throat filling with blood from my lungs, making it impossible to speak.

"Hush," Jeremias says as he walks toward me. He's now holding a silver chalice filled with black liquid, though when I breathe in deep, I can smell that it's blood. Not human blood, though. It seems almost alien, and entirely repulsive.

I tilt my head to the side, my hair dangling, long enough to almost reach the ground from this angle, and I watch as Jeremias lifts the silver chalice above his head. He closes his eyes and his face continues to morph and change.

"*Unum tenebris, hac nocte voco te, filia mea, ut praeter eum,*" Jeremias says in a low voice, speaking something that might be Latin. "*Nisi ab ea a venenum, venenum dare me illam.*"

"*Venenum, venenum,*" the four girls start to chant in a raspy monotone.

Venom? *Venenum* is Latin for venom, maybe?

"*Unum tenebris,*" Jeremias repeats.

"*Unum tenebris, unum tenebris,*" the girls chant, flat and unmusical.

Suddenly there is movement and sound coming from the forest. I turn my head to look as cloaked figures move through the branches. They remind me of the Dark Order, and that's enough to scare me shitless. They wait in the darkness of the trees, watching. Maybe learning like the girls, maybe biding their time.

"*Ea cura corpus cum sanguine,*" Jeremias drones on.

Corpus? Body. *Sanguine?* Blood.

Whose blood?

Mine?

"*Ea cura corpus cum sanguine,*" the girls chant flatly.

Jeremias takes a step forward and stares down at me, and now his eyes are no longer black. They are yellow. No iris, no white, just sulfur-yellow, with a black slit down the middle.

My skin crawls with horror.

"*Ea cura corpus cum sanguine*," he whispers, as if to me, then he takes the silver chalice and tips it, so the blackened blood spills out of the cup and onto my chest.

I scream.

The blood burns and hisses, steam rising from my body, and suddenly I'm contorting in the air, back arched, limbs moving and stretched in all directions. Pain throttles me from the inside out.

"*Ea cura corpus cum sanguine*," Jeremias repeats, louder now, his voice vibrating inside my skull, and my vision starts to get blurry, red tears filling my eyes. I can't stop screaming from the pain, my body won't stop burning, my skin pulled so tight I might splinter into a million pieces.

Suddenly the chanting is louder, more ominous, and through my faltering eyes I see the cloaked figures at the edge of the forest remove their hoods with skeleton hands.

They have deer skulls for faces, empty sockets for eyes, antlers that were improbably hidden by the cloaks, and they raise their arms—human arms, bare bone—to the sky as the chanting continues to grow.

I'd be horrified if I wasn't already in so much pain, if it didn't feel like the blood was causing fissures in my soul as it seeps into my wound, my chest grinding, like my ribs are moving independently.

Then suddenly, the pain stops.

The chanting stops.

The world goes painfully silent and still.

Then whatever power was holding me up dissipates and I'm falling.

I land on the ground in a heap, raising my head enough to see Jeremias step toward me. His feet are cloven hooves.

"You are saved, my child."

* * *

"Wake up, Lenore."

My eyes flutter open.

I'm lying on my side on a patch of damp moss, staring at Jeremias, who is sitting on a fallen tree trunk that is absolutely writhing with insects.

I've been in and out of consciousness for what seems like an infinite amount of time. Sometimes I come to and I'm sitting up against a tree, the bark rough on my back. Other times I'm sitting in front of the ocean, watching the waves, hugging my knees. Or lying down on the sand.

It is always dark. Forever night. There is never a moon.

I don't even know if I am still alive.

"You are alive," Jeremias says. "And you are healed. It's time for you to accept what's happened to you."

I swallow, and for once I don't taste my own blood.

I close my eyes and breathe in deeply and my lungs aren't bubbling or leaking. Slowly I push myself up so I'm sitting, keeping my legs together because I'm back in Solon's black robe, naked underneath.

I'm scared to look, to see that wound.

"Go ahead," Jeremias says. I glance at him and his nose changes from something small and petite, to something red and bulbous, then long and aquiline. Always changing. Why?

But I don't ask him that. Instead, I take in another deep, beautifully clear breath, smelling sea salt and fresh air, and then I open the collar of my robe just enough to look at my chest.

There are ugly gashes between my breasts, dark red and scabbing over.

But they *are* scabbing over.

The wounds have closed.

"How?" I ask, looking at Jeremias. "How is this possible?"

He grins, his teeth changing shape as he bares them at me.

One moment the smile looks friendly, the next it looks predatory. "Magic," he says lightly. "Of course."

Right. Magic. No matter what has happened to me in the last few months, coming to terms with the fact that magic is real, that it's something that exists in this world, and all worlds, that some humans can possess it so casually, easily, is something I still have a hard time wrapping my head around.

The fact that I myself have magic? Forget it.

"You disappoint me, Lenore," he says, observing me carefully. "You're the only daughter who has turned her back on who she is."

I stare at him sharply. "What do you mean, only daughter? You have more than me?"

His grin is both proud and malicious. "Oh. Precious soul. How ego-centric you are in your thinking. I suppose it's all gone to your head hasn't it, that you're the daughter of Jeremias. Well, perhaps that's warranted. You are the only half-witch, half-vampire with the bloodline that you have. But you are not my only child. I have many."

"How many?" I ask, intrigued, and a little frightened, at the idea of having brothers and sisters through him.

He shrugs. "A lot."

I was raised an only child. To think that I have siblings feels like a door to a whole other world just opened. I suppose it has.

"Are any of them...normal?"

He laughs. It's raspy and metallic and makes my jaw clench. "Normal? No more normal than you. Tell me, Lenore, are you ashamed of being a witch?"

I swallow hard. "No."

"But you lie. Why?"

"Why do I lie?"

"Yes."

"I don't know..."

"You're afraid of me. Still. After all I've done for you. I've saved your life twice now, doesn't that earn me your trust? I don't expect you to love me, dear daughter, but I do expect your respect."

I rub my lips together, my eyes coasting over the wound, wondering if I'll have scars for the first time in a long time, or if one day it'll be like nothing happened. But of course, I'll never forget it. I'll never forget that the beast lives inside Solon.

Now that I know what he's capable of.

Now that I know that it wants me dead.

I push that out of my head. I'm not ready to think about that yet, about what it means for us. I don't want to face it.

"How did you heal me?" I ask again. "What ritual was that? Whose blood was that? What were the animal things in the trees, the skeleton hybrids?"

"Disciples."

"Like your apprentices?"

"No," he says mildly. "They don't belong to me."

"Who do they belong to?"

"The Dark One," Jeremias says, fixing his eyes on me in a cold stare, chin raised, as if daring me to make some sort of joke. But I don't find anything humorous in the name. Instead, the name shoots fear right to the base of my skull, awakening panic in my lizard brain.

The Dark One.

I don't even want to think it.

I remember Jeremias's eyes turning yellow, like a snake, his feet turning to hooves. The blackened blood that burned my flesh.

Oh, god.

"God can't hear you here, Lenore," Jeremias says, with a conviction that chills me to the bone. "And he can't help you, either. Your god would have let you die at the hands of that vampire. But the Dark One, he can always help, if you know how to call him. And you will. With practice, you will."

He leans in closer, and I smell the stench of decay on his breath. "Did you know that you could have saved your friend Elle? That she didn't have to die?"

I glare at him, my heart thumping unevenly in my chest. "What the fuck are you talking about? How dare you even say her name."

"I dare because you deserve to know the truth. You could have turned her into a vampire. Did you even think of that?"

My mouth drops open and I snap it shut. "I did think of that. Of course I did. But Solon stopped me. Because I would have turned her into a monster." *Just like him*, I add.

"Not you, Lenore. Your powers are intention. Intention is the basis of all witchcraft. You could turn anyone into a vampire and they won't go mad, they won't turn into a monster. You have that power, and only you, because of your duality. You're prized, you know. Your blood. Why do you think Skarde wants to destroy you?"

I stare at him, trying to piece it all together, make it make sense. All that he just said about Elle, that I could have saved her...I can't. I can't even entertain the thought because the guilt will eat me alive, the idea that she could still be alive. Be a vampire. Living in the house with me.

My heart is shattering.

I push it aside.

"He wants to destroy me because I have power to destroy him," I eventually say.

He gives me a cold smile. "So much confidence for someone who has turned her back on the craft. No, Lenore. You alone can't destroy him, but you are definitely needed in the process. That is not why he wants to destroy you, however. It's because you can undo all he has done. He's creating an army, one that's both mad and monstrous, but controlled. Vampires have been forbidden from creating new ones by the bite, because it is too dangerous. Too dangerous for anyone but him. But you, you Lenore, you can do it. You can build an army of your own, of rational, sane vampires. No more monsters. Isn't that nice?"

His words fall on me like snow, taking a moment to sink in.

I can do what?

Create my own non-mad army?

I can create vampires that won't turn into a beast?

"Does…" I lick my lips, trying to swallow the enormity of it all, "does Solon know this about me?"

Because if he does, that means he's been using me all this time, and…

Jeremias stares at me, thinking it over. As if the answer is more than a yes or a no.

"No," he eventually says, and my heart flutters with relief. "He doesn't. But if you told him, it would change things."

"What do you mean?"

"Well, he already knows you're somehow instrumental in helping defeat his father. Do you really want to be pulled into that?"

I adjust myself on the moss, my legs starting to feel cramped, and pull my robe closer around me. "I'll do anything to help him defeat Skarde, because I would do anything for him. Also, and a big also, his father tried to kill me. I won't forget that. I hold grudges."

His lips twist into something like a smile. "Good. Because that is how it is foretold."

"What are you talking about?"

"I mentioned before that I have seen the future."

I stare blankly at him. "Yeah? And?"

"You will be instrumental, Lenore. Against Absolon's wishes."

"What does that mean?"

"It means," he says with a patient sigh, "he needs you, but he will do all that he can to keep you back. When the time comes, you'll know."

I frown. "Are you purposefully being vague or…?"

"I'm not. I see the future, but it's based on feelings, not visions, and not specifics."

"Great," I mutter.

"I'm not sure you understand the magnitude of what has happened to you and what is about to happen," he says, suddenly getting to his feet. I stare at his feet for a moment—boots, not cloven hooves—before I look up at him. "A man will come for you both. You must go with him. Together you can help defeat Skarde. Make no mistake, he is not easy to kill. It will take all of you to complete the task."

"The task?" I repeat. "Defeat? Do you know how bonkers that sounds?"

His eyes narrow and a flash of yellow slides across his pupils, making me flinch and feel sick to my stomach. "I know this all feels like a joke to you, but I assure you, if you don't take it seriously, the gravity will come too late. You didn't take your lover's transformation seriously, and look where it got you."

I fucking hate that he's insinuating that I brought the beast upon myself, even though it is true in a way. I mean, I didn't run when Solon told me to. Instead, I let him keep fucking me. I *wanted* the beast.

"Heed my words, my child," he says, holding out his hand for me. "The time of reckoning is coming soon, and it will not happen without you. You are needed for Skarde's destruction."

"Why can't you do it, if you're best buds with the Dark One and oh so powerful?" I ask, snarky without even meaning to, ignoring his hand.

His look could cut glass. "I've tried," he says carefully. "As you can see, I have not been successful. Skarde is not easy to get to, even for me."

"And the Dark One?"

Careful, Jeremias' voice appears inside my head and I see the heavy warning in his obsidian gaze. *Wouldn't want to give him any ideas. This is his show, after all.*

What the hell does *that* mean?

"Now," Jeremias says, his voice loud and pleasant as he pulls me to my feet, "I think you have healed enough to be on your way."

"Wait," I say, feeling a faint twinge of panic, like I've barely learned anything, like it's all happening too fast. "I don't want...I have to be able to see you again."

"You will."

"But I mean, like, I need you to show me what I'm capable of doing," I tell him, feeling shy all of a sudden. "I'm afraid of what I can do, and also afraid to even try."

"I know," he says. "Go to your well and I will be there."

Yeah, but you'll be there with all the dark magic flowing through you.

"Dark magic is the best magic there is," he goes on, with a smirk on his ever-changing façade. "You grew up in a world of light and look at how far that got you."

"My mother," I stammer, the words coming out of me. "My mother. Alice. The one I never knew. The vampire."

He goes still. "Yes?"

"What was she like?"

Jeremias stares at me for a moment before he breathes in deeply through his nose, his chest rising. "She was...a good vampire."

"I heard she killed my aunt."

"Well, that's what vampires do, isn't it? Kill people."

"Did you love her?"

He gives me a rueful smile, eyes turning darker. "I did."

"And did she love you?"

A pause. "I'm sure she did. Deep down, perhaps, even if she never knew it."

Uh oh. That sounds like borderline incel talk.

I suddenly don't want to ask any more questions.

A scurrying sound comes from behind me, snatching my attention. I look over my shoulder to see the witchy quadruplets with their white dresses and disheveled black hair coming out of the forest and scattering in different directions, like something spooked them. They dive into the holes in the ground and disappear, their slender pale feet the last traces of them.

"What's happening?" I ask. "Where are they going?"

"It's time for you to go," Jeremias says in a clipped voice. "The slayers are worried. You need to be returned."

"The slayers?" I repeat.

Then the world is ripped away.

8

ABSOLON

I WAKE UP TO DOG BREATH. A WET TONGUE LICKING MY FACE.

I open my eyes, blink, seeing Odin in front of me, his dark eyes searching mine, asking if I'm okay, telling me that he was worried, that he managed to learn how to open doors and I should be proud of him.

I stare at him for a moment, trying to get my bearings, that I'm lying on the floor, absently noticing the open door before I get a look at the rest of the bedroom.

It's destroyed.

The bed is crooked, the frame broken, the headboard ripped in two.

The mattress has slid onto the floor.

Covered in blood.

No.

No.

I get to my knees, my feet, stagger forward, lean against the slanted bedpost, the only thing keeping me up as I stare down at the sight.

There is blood everywhere.

The room hums with it.

Fresh blood, soaked into the pillow, the sheets, the mattress, the rug. I don't even have to breathe deep to know whose blood that is.

Lenore's.

"No," I croak, falling to my knees, running my hands over it, still feeling damp. There's so much blood, too much blood.

What have I done?

What have I done to her?

I feel the circuitry of my brain start snapping, wires being cut, everything going loose. My head goes back and I scream at the top of my lungs. A long, deafening, guttural scream that rips from my gut, shreds through my throat, fills the room until all the glass cracks, a symphony of explosions, from the artwork on the walls, to the mirrors in the bathroom, to the glass jar that holds her toothbrush. It all shatters like fireworks, glass raining down.

The memory comes back, all at once. I was fucking her, she was coming…she told me she loved me. Tears in her eyes. I felt all her emotions as if they were stemming from somewhere inside me, my old and weary heart expanding until it was close to bursting, and then I knew I wasn't in control.

That I was never in control.

The moment I brought Lenore into my house, I knew I had lost it all, all those centuries of carefully guarded, meticulously parcelled control gone in an instant when she fixed her eyes on me. I had watched her grow up, intrigued, curious, wondering who she would become. But it was nothing like what I felt once she was in my life. No longer someone I watched at a distance. And so I had to keep her at a distance, in every single way that I could, because the loss of all that control that kept me sane and alive meant that I would no longer be the vampire that I was.

The beast took advantage last night.

My emotions were running too high, out of the locked

box, fueled by my love for her, the very love I knew would try to destroy her. The love I've been fighting against from the start.

I knew what was happening, felt the change from deep inside, that build-up of darkness and anger and hunger that I've done everything to make sure stays buried.

It was escaping.

I told Lenore to run.

But she didn't.

She's too stubborn, or maybe she loves me too much, or maybe those two things are both connected, but either way she didn't run.

She stayed with the beast.

She thought she could tame it.

She thought she could love it.

But the beast doesn't love her.

Instead, it's driven wild by her love.

Driven mad.

I slipped away into the black, into the background, but there was just enough of me to make sure I didn't hurt her. I should have had enough control to stop fucking her like I was, tail and all, but I couldn't. Part of me wondered how far she would let it go, part of me wondered how far I would let it go. I wanted her like nothing else, even in my most vile form. I wanted to fuck her like the animal I was, make her feel pleasure she never thought was possible.

I'm not sure I achieved that.

My memory starts to sputter.

Then it goes blank.

No, it turns red.

Like the blood that's everywhere.

The blood of my lover.

Everything inside me breaks.

I open my mouth and roar again, the sound shaking my

bones, shaking the room, and then I smell Amethyst and I hear her behind me.

"Solon?" And then "Oh my god, what happened?"

I shake my head, unable to focus, to speak.

The blood, so much blood.

Did I kill her?

Where is she?

"Solon," Amethyst says again, and I feel her hand on my shoulder. "Why are you naked? Where is Lenore? My god, there's so much blood…"

I can only stare at it.

If I killed her…

If I hurt her…

"Come on, get up," Amethyst says to me, reaching under my arm, trying to pull me to my feet, but I'm deadweight.

"What the fuck happened?" Wolf's voice booms, and then he's in the room and grabbing me, hauling me up with ease. But I can't stop staring at the blood, while every structure inside of me is slowly crumbling, cracks in the foundation of everything I've tried to be.

"Solon?" he says, holding me by the shoulders and peering at me. "What happened?"

"You need clothes," Amethyst says, and she disappears into the bathroom. "Don't you have a robe?"

I nod absently while Wolf digs his nails in my skin to get my attention. I slowly bring my gaze to meet his, the horror dulling my senses. "Solon. Tell me what happened. Whose blood is that? Where is Lenore?"

I swallow. It feels like a brick in my throat. "I don't know. I woke up and I saw this. I don't…" I close my eyes, trying to breathe in deeply.

"I couldn't find your robe," I hear Amethyst say, though I know it's in the bathroom. "Pants. You need pants of some kind. I'm going to find you pants."

I hear the rustling of drawers and it all sounds far away and I wonder if perhaps none of this is real. Maybe it's a nightmare. Maybe I'm hallucinating.

"You transformed," Wolf says. He lets out a long exhale and I can practically hear his disappointment. "You don't remember."

I nod. My lips feel like sandpaper. "I told Lenore to run. She didn't. Then I don't know. Wolf," I eye him, "there's too much blood."

His brows furrow as he looks over the massacre.

"She can heal, right?" Amethyst says, coming over with a pair of black silk pajama pants and shoving them into my hands. Her smile is stiff, her voice full of false hope she's putting on for show, because she doesn't want to believe the alternative.

I glance at Wolf for a moment before looking back at her. "We don't know what can kill Lenore and what can't. That's...that's a lot of blood. That's too much blood, even for a vampire to lose."

"Then where did she go?" Amethyst says. "Why not yell for help?"

"You can't yell with your throat ripped out," I tell her. "I might have shredded her to pieces."

She flinches at the bluntness of my words, but I feel the need to be blunt. I am a monster, through and through. I did this to her friend, I did this to my love.

"She's right though," Wolf says, walking around the bed, running his fingers over the blood and smelling them. "If the wound was fatal, Lenore's body would be here. It's not. She's gone. She didn't come through the house, I would have smelled her. There would be a trail. So then, how did she leave the room?"

We all look to the open window.

Wolf walks over to it, pulling back the curtains further,

examining the edge. "No signs of damage. But you don't normally sleep with your windows open, do you?"

"Not usually," I tell him. "But Lenore, she likes the air, she..." I trail off, my heart in a vice, the image of us squabbling before bed because she wants a cool breeze and I want the room as shuttered and dark and secure as possible. I swallow. "They could have been open, I don't remember."

Wolf shakes his head while Amethyst gestures to my pajamas again. "You need to stop being naked, Solon."

"Humans," I mutter, glaring at her while I slip my pants on.

She gives me a look right back.

One that says *monster*.

"I think she went out through the window," Wolf says, peering outside. "I smell her blood here, though I don't see it. And there's something else. Brimstone."

"Brimstone?" Amethyst repeats. "That's an actual smell?"

"It is," Wolf muses, eyes darting around the window.

Now I can smell it. "Sulfur," I explain to Amethyst. "It's sulfur."

"Witches," Wolf says. "Her parents?"

"Fuck, I hope so," I say. Sulfur is often associated with magic, though her parents have never smelled like sulfur. Different herbs maybe, nothing entirely unpleasant. I've also never known them to have the ability to fly, or at least scale a house of this height, but magic is often surprising.

I head over to the wardrobe and pull out a t-shirt, slipping it on, then I create flames in the middle of the bedroom.

"Where are you going?" Wolf asks.

"To see her parents," I tell him. "They might have her."

Please let them have her. Please let her be alive.

I step into the Black Sunshine, quickly sealing it up behind me, then waste no time in leaving the house, running through the empty city in this gray dead world. Occasionally

I see a shadow soul lurking in the distance, but I know they're attracted to me because of my despair, so I keep running until I'm standing outside the house on Lily Street.

I'd like to just appear inside their apartment, but ambushing two vampire slayers, who may or may not be on edge, would probably result in my death. And while I have no doubt I probably deserve such a death, I won't welcome it until I know what happened to Lenore.

I look around me and then step up on the front stoop, at least partially sheltered from the street, and after I'm confident there are no prying eyes or passing humans milling about, I create a flaming door in the gray, stepping out into the real world again.

I place my ear against the door to Lenore's apartment, listening for signs of her, but there's nothing. I don't smell her either. Suddenly my hopes are fading.

Then I do the same to her parents door right beside hers, leading to their apartment above. I can hear faint murmurs, both Elaine and Jim talking to each other. I ring their doorbell, realizing I should have brought my phone. Perhaps texting them from the house would have been smart, but it felt like this was quicker.

In moments, the door opens.

It's Elaine, staring at me in surprise.

"Absolon," she says, then her adrenaline spikes. "Where is Lenore?"

Fuck.

"She's not here?" I ask, unable to keep the panic out of my voice.

She shakes her head, looking over me in fear. "No. No, I haven't spoken to her today."

"Can I come in?" I ask.

She hesitates. It's not wise to invite a vampire inside your house, but I know she has the slayer's blade somewhere on her body, probably strapped to her leg beneath her cargo pants. If she does, it's absolutely going wild with me standing so close to her. Every passing second the blade is telling her it needs to be driven straight into my heart.

Patience, I tell the blade. *Let's see what horrors I've done first.*

"Yes, of course," Elaine says, snapping out of it, and I wonder if she heard my thoughts. She opens the door wider and I step inside. She looks me up and down, eyeing my pajama pants and t-shirt. And I'm barefoot. I hear her heartbeat accelerate. "What happened? Where did you come from?"

"Solon," Jim says, and I look up to see him at the top of the stairs. "Why don't you come up here and we can put on some coffee. You do drink coffee?"

We don't have any blood, is what the rest of his brain is saying.

I nod and I go up the stairs, though it feels like I'm stepping into a trap, one that I might deserve to be stuck in.

I've never been in their apartment before, only Lenore's. Theirs is protected by a thousand wards, just as Lenore's was, but I was able to bypass them. Here, though, I feel like I'm walking through quicksand as I push through the doorway and into their kitchen. The pressure builds around my head, my body, making my bones rattle, and then with a *pop* I'm through.

"Sorry about that," Jim says, reaching for the coffee pot. "We have to protect ourselves more than ever now. Atlas found us with ease, there could be others."

"Are there others?" I ask. "Because Lenore is missing. We have no idea where she went, if she went anywhere. But there was the smell of sulfur in the room." And they, and their house, smells of rich Ethiopian coffee, lavender, sage, dill, and other herbal arrangements. Not a trace of sulfur.

Jim's hand starts shaking as he attempts to pour the

coffee into a mug, and he has to put the pot back on the burner. "Sorry, my arm. After Yanik..."

Any other time I would ask him how he's doing. I would be cordial. These two are my enemies at heart, not my friends, but there's always been a distant formality between us in all our dealings.

But this is not that time. There is only one thing to discuss.

"What happened?" Elaine asks, folding her arms across her chest as her eyes burn into mine. "Tell me everything that happened. Did you see who took her? Do you know? Maybe it was a vampire. Were you having a party?"

Her voice is getting higher, more frantic, but I have no inclination to calm her down because I'm not calm myself. I'm barely holding it together.

And I'm bracing myself for what I have to tell her, knowing exactly how she's going to react. That blade will be in her hand in seconds.

I swallow hard. "I think she's hurt. There's so much blood. Everywhere."

Her eyes go wide. "What?"

"What do you mean, her blood?" Jim says, looking like he's about to smash the coffee pot over my head. "Did you... were you..."

I shake my head, knowing what he thinks. "No. I was not feeding on her."

"Well what the fuck happened, Absolon?" Elaine says. "Was someone else? Another vampire?"

"I don't think so," I tell them. Shame makes me avert my eyes, concentrating on the water ring stains on the kitchen island. "It was me. I'm the one who hurt her."

"But you said..." Jim begins.

"How?" Elaine interrupts. Then she reaches out and shoves me on the shoulder, hard enough that I have to look up to meet her eyes, eyes that want to kill me. That knife is singing away. "How did you hurt her?!"

"There's another part of me," I say quietly, my voice raw, barely above a whisper and brimming with shame. "A part I've lived with for a long time."

Elaine looks horrified. "No. No, those are supposed to be legends. Fairy-tales."

"Horror stories," Jim fills in grimly.

I nod slowly. "They are true. Whatever you've heard, it's probably true. That I carry a beast inside me, that this beast… I have no control over it. I can only keep it buried, but your daughter, she—"

Suddenly the blade is in Elaine's hand, carved silver and glowing with blue electricity, and she comes at me in a blur that's fast even for my vampire eyes. She takes the blade and presses it against my chest above my heart, piercing through my t-shirt, pointing into my skin, drawing the faintest bit of blood.

"If you killed her, I will drive this knife straight into your heart and out the other side!" she screams at me, spit flying in my face as she shakes, her eyes glowing with blue crescent moons.

I wrap my hand around the blade, holding it tight, letting the painful pulsing current slice my fingers, make me bleed. "If I killed her, I will be *begging* you to end my life," I growl. "I'll want you to make it hurt. I'll want to suffer just like I made her suffer."

Her nose flares with anger, blue lighting now sparking from her eyes, her hair starting to rise like she's a living wire, a current uncontrolled, and I know how she's feeling, I know every single part of it, because I feel it too. I feel this wild, uninhibited rage directed at myself, the desire to rip my own fucking head off and shove it down my throat, to kill and torture myself a thousand times over.

"Elaine," Jim warns her quietly. "This won't help."

She ignores him, keeps her fervent eyes on me. "You're a liar. You always were. She was in love with you, so in love with you, and all I could do was watch. Watch as she gave herself to you, while you possessed her, used her. I thought you loved her!"

"I do!" I roar. "I love her with all my fucking heart, every last shriveled bit of it!"

"Then your love is poison," she snaps. "Your love is tainted and corrosive and eats away at everything that made her wonderful and good. Your love will be her ruin."

And I've told Lenore as much.

"We don't know Lenore is dead," Jim says patiently. "Elaine, please. Step away."

"Why aren't you angry?" she screams at him.

"I am angry," Jim says sharply. He gestures to me. "But he wouldn't be here right now if he didn't love Lenore. And killing him isn't going to help anything. We need to figure out where she is and if she's alive. And I know you're as connected to her as I am, but there's nothing telling me that she's dead. I would feel it. Something would be severed."

I close my eyes, trying to concentrate on Lenore. I know she's not dead either, that she's out there. I just don't know where, if she's still in pain, if she's going to be okay. If she was taken against her will.

Eventually I feel the pressure and pain lift from my chest and Elaine removes the blade. I open my eyes to see her walk across the kitchen, shaking her head as she looks out the window. Perhaps also putting her feelers out for Lenore.

"So what happened?" Jim asks me.

"I woke up on the bedroom floor. Maybe twenty minutes ago. The bed was broken. There was blood all over the mattress, the rug, the floor. So much blood. Her blood. I have no memory, except for that I knew that the transformation was coming, that I was going to turn into the beast. I told her to run and…she didn't run. She stayed."

"Why would she stay?" Elaine wonders out loud, her voice tired.

"Because she doesn't fear it," I tell her. "Or at least, she didn't before."

"This has happened before?" Jim asks in shock.

"Yes. I've turned into the beast with her."

Elaine whips around to glare at me. "And you hurt her before?"

I shake my head. "No. I never did."

"Were you in control then?" Jim asks.

I shake my head again. "No. Not really. Maybe it was luck. Either way, I never hurt her until now. She…she always thought she could tame the beast."

"None of this explains where she is now," Jim says. "Do you think she went off on her own?"

"She didn't go through the house, we would know. She went through the window. Five stories up."

"What?" Elaine exclaims. "Lenore can't fly."

"I know. But maybe she could under extreme duress. You saw what happened with the earthquake," I point out. "That said, it doesn't explain the sulfur."

Elaine swallows audibly and looks to Jim. "Do you think it could be the guild? That they kidnapped her?"

"Right after he attacked her?" Jim asks. "That doesn't make sense. Why would they be there at that time?" He looks to me, puzzled. "And you would still be the beast, wouldn't you?"

I nod. "I think so. I don't have memory of transforming back into a vampire. I assume I was still the beast when she left but…" I trail off, feeling so fucking useless.

"If it were someone from the guild, Absolon would be dead then," Jim surmises. "They would have killed the beast,

I'm sure of it. And you don't think it was a vampire? Perhaps your father?"

My stomach twists violently at the thought. "I would know if it were a vampire. I—"

Suddenly there's a faint thump from downstairs in Lenore's apartment. I stand up straighter.

"What is it?" Elaine asks, their human ears unable to pick up on the sound.

I don't answer, I just run through their ward and down the stairs and they follow after me.

9

LENORE

I'm in my old apartment.

In the bedroom.

My parents have left it the same, like I never left, hoping I guess that I might one day come back. At the very least, it's a place for me to escape when I need it.

I have only been back once since I returned from Shelter Cove, to check on my father, still healing from the damage that Yanik caused him.

And now I'm here again.

One moment I was in the forest with Jeremias, the next everything moved and the world shifted and now I'm here, crouched beside the bed, feeling like I'm going to throw up.

Slowly I rise, gathering my robe around me, not wanting to look at the wound, even though it's healing, and then I stop.

I'm not alone.

Outside the door there are voices and there are smells.

My parents.

And Solon.

I bristle with fear. I picture Solon and I see the beast and my god, I hope it's just a vampire outside there.

Then the smells get stronger, floorboards creaking, my mother says, "Is it her?" in a frantic voice and then the bedroom door opens.

I'm staring right into Solon's eyes.

His shadowed, brilliantly blue eyes.

It's him.

And yet the fear remains.

"Lenore," he says, his voice low and raspy, my name breaking on his lips.

My heart feels torn in half. Part of it wants me to run to him, to wrap my arms around him, to feel the cool, softness of his skin, to be with the one I love.

But the other part keeps me where I am. The other part lives in fear. Fear that he might change at any moment. It doesn't matter that my parents are there behind him, staring at me with worry and relief, that they could probably kill the beast. I don't want him dead, but I'm scared of him just the same.

"Lenore," he says again, and I feel him, feel the weight inside his chest, the guilt, the pain, the sorrow, and yet all I can do is throw up my hands and display my palms and say:

"Stay there."

His expression crumbles like I've slapped him. "I won't hurt you."

I shake my head. "You might."

"Lenore, sweetie," my mother says, pushing around Solon. "Are you okay? What happened to you?"

I gather the robe tighter around me, knowing that all three of them would lose their fucking minds if they saw the wound.

She approaches me like I might run away, slowly, cautiously, but then she's so close and I let go of the fear.

I throw my arms around her and she grasps me firmly, even though my chest burns from how tightly she's holding me. All the tears I've managed to hold back throughout this whole thing are finally spilling over and I'm crying, bawling into her arms. Trauma upon trauma upon trauma, and the beast was my breaking point.

So, I cry, and eventually my father comes over and joins us, holds on, and I'm so very aware that Solon is still in the room, the smell of tobacco and roses lingering, though he stays in the doorway and doesn't come any closer. I want him to leave, and yet I don't know if he'll go so easily. I can't imagine the pain and guilt he must be feeling, to know that he became the beast. He must have seen the blood, he must have suspected he did something awful, even if he has no memory of it.

And yet I can't reconcile that right now. Right now I'm falling apart, and I've been falling apart since the day I met him.

I'll leave, Solon's voice comes in my head. *If you want me to.*

I don't know what I want, I answer him. It's the truth.

I want him to go.

I want him to stay.

I want reassurance that he'll never hurt me again, but I know he can't promise that, and I know it breaks him as much as it breaks me.

"Sweetie, please," my mother says, eventually pulling away and holding my face in her hands. "Tell us what happened to you. Absolon said he…"

"Hurt her," Solon finishes, his voice grim. "I hurt her. I can smell her blood, old and dried."

My mother looks at him over her shoulder then looks at me, her eyes skimming over the robe. "What happened? How did he hurt you?"

I look over at Solon, at the haunted look in his eyes.

Then I step back and open the robe, just enough to show the space between my breasts. The mark of his claws is still there, red and angry and unmistakable.

My father gasps in horror.

My mother cries out.

Solon looks like he's dying on his feet, the pain on his face breaking my heart because I know he didn't mean it, I know this wasn't really him.

I quickly pull my robe closed, "I'm okay now," I manage to say, but my mom is reaching into her pocket and pulling out the slayer's blade and she's flinging it across the room while she screams.

Solon is fast. I don't see him move but I know he's by the front door now, probably creating flames to escape, while the blade goes through the empty doorway and hits a cupboard in the kitchen.

"Elaine!" my father yells, reaching for her, wrapping his arms around her chest to hold her back while she kicks and screams. I've never seen my mother so angry before, and I can't blame her. She sees the wound, the pain that Solon caused me, the one whom I was supposed to be safe with. She wants him dead. It was always against her nature to have let him live this long.

"Mom," I plead. "It's okay. I'm okay."

"It's not okay!" she yells at me, tears streaming down her face. "You're in love with a monster. One that almost killed you."

My jaw tenses, teeth grinding as I try to keep it together. "I know I am. But it's not Solon's fault."

"Oh my god," she says, and eventually my father's grip on her relaxes just a little. "That's what you really believe? That this wasn't his fault."

She rips out of his arms and storms on over to me,

pointing at my chest, her eyes in a frenzy of hatred. "You really think *this* wasn't his fault?"

I can tell Solon is still in the apartment somewhere. I can smell him, hear his faint breath. Out of the room, and safe, but not leaving either.

"It's…complicated," I tell her feebly. Too complicated for me to even figure out at the moment.

"Honey," my father says patiently to her, coming over to us. "Don't make this worse."

Her mouth drops open. "*I'm* making this worse?"

"Stop," I tell them. "Please, just stop. A lot has happened. This isn't just about what happened with Solon. It's about Jeremias."

Suddenly Solon appears in the doorway again, eyes blazing. "Jeremias? Is he the one who took you?"

My mom whips her head around to glare at him and go after him again, but I reach out and grab her hand, trying to keep her focused. I look at Solon and nod. "I was trying to escape, and I was able to. I was able to keep you away. I put up my hands and I felt this power, like electricity, running through my palms and you couldn't come any close. Like I had a shield protecting me. A bubble."

Solon's lips curve into a small, awestruck smile as he stares at me. "That's incredible."

"Shut up," my mom seethes at him. "None of this is incredible."

"This is the second time she's been able to use her powers to save her life," Solon says testily. "I'd say it's incredible."

"I didn't know what I was doing," I quickly tell them, not feeling the same pride that Solon is. "I just…I wanted to live, and it happened. I only got so far though. I was…the wound wasn't healing. It was fatal. And then the window opened and he came inside."

"Like he crawled inside?" my father asks.

I shake my head. "No. He straight up flew inside."

"What did he look like?" Solon asks. He takes a step toward me, but I flinch, and it's enough for him to stop where he is. I'm not ready for there not to be distance between us.

"I don't know," I tell him. "He was like a human, a man, he had on these black boots and a black cloak. But his face...it was never the same. Only his eyes remained the same, for the most part," I add, remembering them turning yellow. "But his features were always changing, like he always had a different face every few seconds. I don't know why it was like that."

Solon looks grim. "I do. Black magic usually comes at the expense of someone else. Sacrifice. Someone like Jeremias doesn't live for hundreds of years, get to amass the power and magic that he does, without having to make hundreds of sacrifices."

"You're saying his face keeps changing because it belongs to someone he sacrificed?" I ask in horror.

Solon nods. "Could be their souls trapped inside him." He pauses, studying me. "Don't tell me he brainwashed you into thinking he's all good?"

"You don't even know what happened to me!" I snap at him. "You tried to kill me! If it wasn't for Jeremias, I wouldn't be here. He saved my life. He took me somewhere and he fixed me."

"How did he fix you, sweetie?" my mother asks softly.

I tear my eyes away from Solon and look at her. "I don't know. There was a circle and lights. Fire. Torches. These four girls, they all looked the same. He said they were his apprentices. They came out of the ground. He made me float in the air above the circle and the fire and he had this cup, this chalice...it was silver."

"What was in the cup?" my father asks, looking vaguely horrified.

"Blood," I say. "But it wasn't human blood. I don't know what it was. He was chanting, Latin, about venom and blood and bodies and these...things, these creatures came out of the woods. They had deer skulls and cloaks and they were chanting too."

"The old ones," Solon says under his breath. "Lapp witches."

"Whatever they were, they scared the hell out of me. Jeremias said they belonged to the Dark One."

Both my parents visibly shudder, but Solon remains straight-faced.

"How did you get back here?" my father asks.

I shrug. "I don't know. He said I was healed and that the slayers were worried. I guess he meant you. Suddenly I was back here."

My father pats me gently on the shoulder. "We have a lot to discuss, Lenore. A lot. I want to talk more about this, about everything you saw. But you need to rest. Traveling the way you did, it will take everything out of you. And with that wound..."

"We want you to stay here," my mother says, her eyes pleading.

I nod. I was planning on it. "Okay. I will." I can feel Solon's gaze burning me, but I don't want to look at him yet. "Mom, Dad, do you mind giving me and Solon a moment alone?"

My mother narrows her eyes. "He's not staying here."

"I know he's not. But I still need to talk to him."

She sighs heavily and exchanges a weary glance with my father. Then the two of them head to the door, Solon stepping out of the way, averting his eyes from the hate in their gaze.

"I don't think you should be alone with this monster," my mother says, pausing outside the door. "It isn't safe."

"I know. It's just for a moment."

"We'll be in the living room," my father says, closing the door behind us.

Suddenly my old bedroom feels so small.

I stare at Solon, unsure of what to say. How to start.

"I'm sorry," he says to me quietly, his eyes slowly searching my face, anguish creasing his forehead. "I am so sorry, Lenore."

"I know you are," I tell him.

"Why didn't you run?"

I frown. "What do you mean? Like it's my fault?"

"It's not your fault," he says quickly. "But I told you to run. I knew it was coming and I told you to run and I know you heard me. Why didn't you run?"

I shake my head. "No. I'm not going down this path. You're trying to put the blame on me."

"No one is putting the blame on you!" he says angrily. "Obviously I did this to you. Obviously I hate myself, more than you could ever imagine. Your mother had her blade pressed against my heart and part of me wanted her to drive it in. The only thing stopping me from stepping into it was that I needed to see you again, to know that you were okay."

"Well, I'm here now. I'm okay." But fuck, please don't willingly step into any witches' blades. "I just…how did it happen? How could…I looked into your eyes, Solon, and you were gone. You were gone."

"I TOLD YOU!" he says roughly, eyes on fire. "I told you what I was. You saw with your own eyes what I was capable of doing to those I love. You knew, you can't pretend you didn't know."

"I know," I cry out. "I just thought…I thought I…"

"Did you think you were so special?"

Ouch. It feels like he just slapped me across the heart.

I swallow the pain down, my stomach sinking. "Yes," I say weakly. "I did. I thought I was special. You've told me as much, Solon, I—"

"You're special to *me*," he says, lunging forward. I gasp as he grabs my arms, fingers squeezing tight, my heart thundering in my chest. "You are everything to *me*. But I am not the beast."

I shake my head, a tear running down my cheek. "But you are, Solon. You are the beast. It is part of you, and you'll never be able to escape. I'll never be able to escape. Next time, next time he'll kill me. He'll finish the job."

His nostrils flare, jaw set in a firm, tense line. "There won't be a next time."

"Yes there will," I tell him. "Of course there will. Anytime I'm with you, I'll—"

"You won't be with me," he says sharply, a line drawn between his brows. "You won't be with me at all."

I stare at him, dumbstruck with fear. "What…what do you mean?"

"I'm not going to put you at risk," he says gravely, breathing in deep. "I can't put you at risk. We can't…we can't be together like this, not when I know what can happen."

I blink.

My heart feels on the verge of shattering, like one more hit and it's exploding into a million pieces.

He's not…

We're not…

"Are you breaking up with me?" I manage to say, and god, it sounds so dumb, but I'm so fucking scared that this is what's happening.

He presses his lips together in a firm slash, swallowing audibly. "Lenore."

I shake my head. "No. Don't. Just tell me what's happening. This isn't a solution, Solon."

"It's the only solution I have," he says, his voice soft and breaking, carrying pain in his eyes, but then I'm reeling from so much pain that it's starting to cloud my vision.

"Do you love me?" I whisper. I press my fingers to his chest, on his heart. "Do you really love me?"

His face crumbles. "I love you."

"Then this isn't the solution."

"I can't risk losing you!" he yells, throwing his arms out. "Please, god damnit Lenore, listen to me. Listen to me. I love you to the ends of the earth, but our love works best when it's alive. When I'm alive, and you're alive. I won't lose you. I won't hurt you. I need to...I need to figure myself out, to stay away from you, to—"

"You're not staying away," I tell him quickly, grabbing his hand and holding tight. "Okay. Maybe right now, maybe it makes sense to be apart for a bit. Until you...figure things out. Control yourself. Put that side of you back in the cage for a while. But this isn't a long-term solution. I won't allow it."

"You are not in control here, moonshine."

"And neither are you!" I yell. "Neither are you, Solon. We're both at the mercy of what's inside you. But I'm not going to let you walk away from me and stay that way. Okay? I'm not. I don't want to die, but I don't want to lose you either. And as long as you still love me just as I love you, I'm not going to give up on us without a fight."

He stares at me deeply, breathing hard.

"Please," I go on. "Fight with me. Don't give up."

His gaze drops to where I'm holding onto his hand. "How do you suppose we're supposed to fight this?" he asks quietly.

"I don't know, but we have to try. You owe me that."

He closes his eyes and takes in a deep breath through his nose. "Okay. Just tell me what to do."

"For now, I think…I think it's best if I stay here. We need some distance. I don't want to live in fear that the beast might escape. I don't want to set him off. I need to be ready for the next time. Maybe there's some magic I can learn. I figured out how to keep you at bay before, I could probably do it again. I just have to be sure."

His Adam's apple bobs as he swallows. "Alright." He looks to me. "I'm going to have a hard time walking away from you."

"Even though you just said we shouldn't be together."

"I never said it would be easy. Leaving you feels like going against gravity."

"I know," I say. "But for now, it's our best shot. Our only shot. Go back to the house. I'll stay here. We'll see what happens after that."

I know the words that I'm saying. I know that they make sense, that I need space from him, that he needs space from me. They sound so empty and plain coming from my mouth, but it's absolutely killing me inside that this is what's happening.

I don't want to be apart from him.

I want to rewind time so we're standing back in yesterday.

I want to go back to the moment he told me to run, and I want to run this time, run to save the both of us, run to save our relationship.

But there's no going back.

There's just here and now and I'm left with scars over my heart.

Solon places his hand at my cheek and leans in to kiss me and I let the smell of him wash over me, feed my soul, but then that fear is there, the image of the red eyes and the claws and the pain and the blood and I'm pushing him back hard.

"Don't," I tell him. "It isn't wise."

His eyes go dark and then he raises his chin, squaring his shoulders. Because he knows. He knows that the beast comes out during sex. He knows that kissing could unlock that next step. That our emotions are running too high right now, and that could be a key too.

"You know where I'll be," he says.

Then he turns and leaves the room.

And my heart finally falls.

10

ABSOLON

"Isn't it time you go home?" Jim asks, stepping outside of the apartment. "Someone is going to call the cops on you."

"They won't," I reply, staring down at the cigar in my hand, the smoke wafting up.

I feel his eyes on me. I reluctantly turn my head to look at him. Jim is far less fiery and stubborn than his wife is. He's a good father to Lenore, but I do wish he wasn't so soft. I'd trust her with him more.

"Go home, Absolon," he says, firmer now. "Lenore knows you're here."

"I *want* her to know I'm here," I tell him.

"You're the reason she's afraid, remember?" he points out.

I don't need to remember.

It's been a few days since Lenore returned from her time with Jeremias, after I turned feral and nearly killed her. She's been staying in her old apartment, I've been staying at the house. It's for the best, I know it is, and yet I can't help but come here every night. I stand here from dusk to dawn outside their house, just watching, just waiting. I don't sleep. I haven't fed in ages. I'm surviving on cigars and tenacity.

I'm fully aware that I'm the reason why Lenore is staying here. I know it was my fault, I know what I did to her. But all of that aside, I can't let her be here by herself. I know what's happened to her in the past. There was Atlas Poe on the witch's guild side, there was Yanik on the vampire side. She had people wanting to kill her and there's zero doubt in my mind that there're others out there who want their own chance. Her parents mean well, and they have done well protecting her for her whole life, but not when it truly counted. Their wards didn't work against me, they didn't work against Atlas, Yanik easily overtook Jim at the first opportunity.

To put it mildly, I know I'm what Lenore fears right now, but I don't trust her with anyone but me, not even herself.

And all that talk about Jeremias rattles me to the bone.

He so easily showed up, easily came through the window, despite the fact that I have the house under a protection spell. How long has he been able to do that? Always? If so, why not come by before Lenore came into my life? I know he knows who I am, what I do. Vampires are taught that witches exist to kill them, and they're especially taught that Jeremias would destroy us all given half the chance.

And yet, he didn't destroy us. I should take that as a good sign, that perhaps he's not as malicious as people say, but I don't. I don't trust him, and I don't trust what he wants with Lenore. He has unlimited power it seems—to break through our wards, to fly, to whisk Lenore off to some other place, to heal wounds that would have been fatal. His interest in her isn't because he's a suddenly doting father, and therefore his interest, combined with his power, is a threat.

I sigh, breathing out the cigar. "I'll leave," I tell Jim. "But you have to understand why I'm here."

"You don't trust me," he says, folding his arms and leaning

against the door. He looks like he hasn't slept in days either. Being human, it shows much more easily on him.

"I don't trust anyone," I tell him. "You know that."

"You're what's a danger to her," he says.

"And there are dangers other than me. You really think she's safe here from Jeremias?"

"He saved her. We have no evidence he would mean her harm."

"He saved her with black magic. You don't call on the Lapp witches otherwise."

"You have experience with them before?" Jim asks curiously.

"Yes," I say, puffing back on the cigar. "Long time ago. My father would use them."

"Interesting that both Jeremias and Skarde do."

I shrug. "Only interesting in that they're both connected to the Devil."

Jim watches me for a moment, mulling something over. "You're connected to that same Devil too."

"As is Lenore," I answer back. "Perhaps not by blood, but the same darkness that runs in her father's veins, runs in hers."

He glowers at me. "What's your point, Stavig?"

"I don't have one," I answer with a sigh. "Other than the fact that this doesn't bode well for anyone. If it's not Jeremias I'm worried about, then it's Skarde."

He stands up straighter. "Have you heard anything?"

"That your daughter is still on his hit list? No. I haven't. But that doesn't mean we can relax either. He's still out there." I don't bother adding what I know about Kaleid. He wouldn't believe it any more than I do.

We both fall silent for a moment. The night fog is building in the street, the air cold, and it feels like summer will never arrive. Good.

"Can I ask you something?" Jim says.

"Always."

"Do you love her?"

I sigh, staring back down at my cigar again. "Yes."

The answer burns my heart. Because I'm desperately in love with her, the woman I've hurt, the woman who now has to keep her distance from me in order to save herself. I love her despite everything I did to not. I'm stuck like this now, for all time, always to love her, never to be with her.

Love is punishment.

And I have so many sins to atone for.

He watches me for a moment, then nods. "Go home. Get some rest. Do whatever you vampires do. I promise I won't let a thing happen to her."

It goes against every instinct I have to walk away, but I know I have to. I'll just come back later, when they're asleep.

I nod at her father, then I walk down the street, smoking my cigar, disappearing into the mist. I could go into the Black Sunshine as a faster way home, but I don't want to rush at the moment. If I can't be guarding her, then I don't have anywhere I need to be. I want to enjoy my cigar, enjoy the night, enjoy this city that once made so much sense to me, provided so much comfort, but now feels like an empty husk without Lenore in my life. Even the cigar is bordering on tasteless.

I decide to walk toward downtown, going down Market Street with the electric streetcars trundling past, moving through the crowds like the fog, people piling out from a concert that just ended at the Warfield. No one looks twice at me, and no one will unless I want them to. But the smell of human blood is overwhelming at times, reminding me that I will need to feed soon, reminding me that I'll have to use one of the donors, and not Lenore as usual.

The thought of that adds another crack to my heart.

I head up Grant, toward the Chinatown gate. There are more people here, the stores open late, the air smelling of grilled meats—an appetizing scent to even someone like myself. I really must be hungry to actually crave food.

People chat in Cantonese and Mandarin, languages I understand. Their conversations are so mundane that I envy them. They talk about their families, about holidays, about the weather, about work, and for once I would give anything to enjoy a life free from my special kind of complication. Occasionally I pass by an elder who stares at me a little too long before they recoil and disappear into the stores. They know what I am. They might not be able to reconcile what I am exactly, but deep down, they know. I am predator and they are prey. They run and they hide.

Eventually I turn down a quieter street.

And that's when I smell it.

An old smell.

Aniseed, sulfur, moss, pine.

I hear his footsteps, his breath, a block away.

It's a block too close.

I whip around in time to see a shadow disappear behind a building. He's depending on me not being able to move fast in public, but he doesn't have magic. I do. I have worked for every ounce of it.

I throw up a cloaking ward, rendering anyone who might be watching from an apartment momentarily distracted, confused, so that no one will really know what they see, and then I move fast through the mist until I'm down that alley, the dark providing no shelter to my eyes.

Or his eyes either.

I'm on him in a second, throwing him against the wall, prepared for the blowback, for him to do the same to me. I'm two inches taller, my shoulders broader, my muscles bigger, but he has spent his life reveling in depravity while I have spent mine doing all I can to shutter it.

I throw him into the building so hard that it leaves cracks in the cement, something that would have crushed the bones of any human.

But he just falls to the ground, on his feet, like a cat.

And, like a cat, he stays in a crouch for a second, low to the ground, and I can tell he's fighting every instinct he has to attack.

He gets up and grins at me instead.

"This how you treat family, Solon?" Kaleid asks, brushing the dirt off his leather jacket.

"Yes," I answer simply. I won't let my guard down for a second. "Last time I saw you—"

"Was in 1850. I know. I remember," he says.

"You remember you tried to kill me?"

His grin spreads. "Of course. But only because you were trying to kill me. Come on, you can't hold that against me. Self-defense holds up in a court of law."

"There are no courts of law where we come from," I remind him. "There is no law."

"True," he muses, sauntering toward me. "It's kill or be killed. So far, neither of us have succumbed to the latter. That's pretty impressive, don't you think? The sons of Skarde are still alive and kicking."

I glare at him. "There are many sons of Skarde."

"Ah," he says, running a hand through his hair. "But there are only two first ones." He pauses, eyes going up in thought. "That's an oxymoron, isn't it? Two first sons. As if we were twins. Well, anyway. I guess you really were the first, if you wanted to go about it in a timeline of history type of way."

"I don't," I say sharply. "You can take that title and keep it."

His brows raise. "Oh. But haven't you heard? I don't want it either." His jovial smile fades for a moment, the true cunning shine of his eyes coming through. "I sent Onni here. I have to say, I'm disappointed that you didn't come as he asked."

"Why the fuck would I have done that?"

"Because we want the same thing, brother."

In a flash I'm at him, hands around his neck, then I'm pressing him against the opposite wall, my elbow crushing his jugular. "Don't you fucking call me brother," I seethe at him, seeing red. "I am not your brother."

He blinks at me, nearly rolling his eyes. "Okay. Okay." I drop him and he coughs, shaking out his shoulders. "Onni said you would be a pain in the ass."

"Pardon me for not being very hospitable. It's not every day that a parasite like you pretends to have a change of heart."

"Parasite? Why, that's a compliment, didn't you know?"

I glare at him, every nerve taut, every muscle poised and ready to attack. "Why are you here, Kaleid? You're a long way from the Baltic."

"Well, a little birdie told me you were too afraid to come on my home turf. So I decided to come to yours." He adds a smirk at the end that makes me want to break his teeth.

"Lucky me."

"You're right not to trust me brother." He catches the look on my face, smirks again. "Sorry, sorry. I forgot. I've been disowned. For good reason, I suppose. But I'm here now. That has to count for something. For all I know, you have these streets teaming with vampires ready to take me out."

I don't, but I'm not about to tell him that. "You being here means nothing, other than the fact that you're a fool."

He shrugs. "Be that as it may, I am here, and I'm here because I need your help. And you need my help. We want the same things."

"Which is?"

"Our father out of the picture."

I squint at him, studying his face. Of course, he looks the same as he always has, his hair a bit shorter, though a similar length to mine. Though I was born a human and he was born to Skarde (and a human mother), we shouldn't look alike at all, but we do. Blue eyes, dark brows, black hair, high cheekbones. Nordic through and through.

"Why would you want that?" I eventually ask.

"Because he's been in power far too long."

"Might have something to do with him being immortal."

"But we don't know that, do we? If we can die, the same probably goes for him. Just because no one has been able to kill him yet, doesn't mean we can't."

I shake my head. "Why are you doing this, Kaleid? You want to take over, is that it?"

He narrows his eyes at me. "I have no interest in ruling. I don't think anyone should be ruling over us. Let us be free to make our own choices."

"We are free to make our own choices," I remind him. "I do what I please here. You do what you please there. Why the change?"

"Because we are never truly free as long as he is in power."

"Doesn't sound like he has much power if he's hiding out in deeper worlds."

"He's not hiding," he snaps impatiently. "He's growing stronger. He's building his army."

"An army that Lenore easily defeated," I point out, though from the gleam in his eyes, I regret ever saying her name.

"Ah yes. Lenore. Where is your infamous girlfriend? I thought you'd never let her out of your sight after what our father tried to do."

I press my lips together, needing to keep her out of it. "She's around."

"I see. Vague. Okay, well, you know I hope to meet her."

I bristle. "Whatever you have planned, it won't involve her."

"So it will involve you?"

"I never said that."

He leans over and smacks my arm, hard. "Come now, Solon. Now that you know I won't try and kill you, why not invite me into your house. We have a lot to discuss."

"I'm not sure that we do," I say warily.

"The minute Skarde and his armies leave the world and come into this one, you know there's nothing that humanity can do," he says. "It's game over for them. It's game over for us."

I swallow uneasily. "Since when do you care about what happens to humanity?"

"I'm half human, if you've forgotten," he snipes, then quickly adds a smile. "I've become a lot more in touch with my human side lately. I was inspired by you."

"So I've heard."

"And if you were listening, I said it's game over for *us*. We can't survive without humans. Skarde seems to think we can, but I'm not game to test his theory by wiping everyone out. Listen, I know this seems out of left field for you, and I know you don't trust a damn word that's coming out of my mouth. But I wouldn't be here, risking my life, if it wasn't important to me and if I didn't think it wasn't important to you. And yes, this involves Lenore too, whether you like it or not. If we don't defeat him, she's the first person he's coming after. He wants her to be his bride, Solon."

I blink at him, a cold, thick feeling swimming in my chest. "His *bride*?"

Kaleid nods. "That was his intention from the start, why he sent Yanik in the first place. Did you know he would have sent me, had I not already broken away? Be glad I'm conspiring against him; I wouldn't have failed the way that Yanik did. I would have never underestimated her."

In a burst of rage, I reach out and wrap one hand around his neck, lifting him off the ground. "Don't talk about her as if you know her. You don't. You don't know a thing about her." He opens his mouth to speak, but I squeeze harder. "Now, what do you mean, he wants her to be his bride?"

He reaches up with his hands, trying to pry my fingers off him. He can survive without air, but I'm making this as painful as possible.

Finally, I let him go and he drops to his feet, coughing.

"Jesus, Solon. I thought you had manners." He straightens up. "Something about how the Dark One promised him a queen, and I guess he thinks Lenore is the one he's been waiting for."

My eyes widen. All this time, I assumed that Skarde wanted to destroy Lenore because she had some kind of power to destroy him. Now I'm realizing that wasn't the case at all. No, this is much, much worse.

"The old ones say," Kaleid goes on, "that his queen would have black magic in her veins. Enough that she would move from light to dark and rule beside him. Skarde could harness that power, use it for destruction, if she didn't give it willingly. At any rate, he could use her to breed. Create his new army that way."

Yes. This is much, *much* worse.

11

LENORE

I can't sleep.

I haven't been able to sleep since the attack, since I've been back in my old bed. I toss and I turn and even if I close my eyes for a second, I see Solon's transformation, see him turn into the beast. Sometimes the dream starts off sexual, like he's inside me again, fucking me with cock and tail and I'm enjoying it just as I had. But then he changes before I'm about to come, he becomes the beast, and yet in some of my dreams, it's still Solon. It's still him and he hurts me, aims to kill me just the same. Like the beast and him are now one.

I roll over and stare at the statue of Pazuzu on my dresser, pretending for a moment that it's a few months ago and life was easy. Back when I thought I was just a normal (ish) girl, with a normal life ahead of her.

But reality won't let me pretend. I'm hungry and I'm tired and my heart has never felt heavier. I've been spending a lot of time with my parents, a good distraction, but I don't feel safe with them—I know they can't really protect me—and the only one I ever felt safe with is someone I now fear.

Yet, when I think of Solon, the man, the vampire I know

and love, I don't feel true fear. The fear is reserved for that dark part of him, the one he can't control. That's who I truly fear. I know that there is no escaping that part of him, that Solon is stuck, and that he is a package deal. If I want Solon in my life, I have to deal with the beast as well.

There just has to be a way to get around this. Cutting him out of my life won't work—he *is* my life. If I possess the power to create non-feral vampires, why can't I figure out how to get rid of the beast? Jeremias was able to make him sleep with a wave of his hand. Can't he teach me how to do that, at the very least?

I get out of bed, my blood pumping with determination.

I head out to the kitchen, wondering if I should eat something before I attempt this, and my stomach growls in response. Then I head down the hall to the front door and open it, peering out into the street, expecting to see Solon, wanting to tell him my plan.

He's been here every single night, as soon as it gets dark. He's there waiting in the shadows, smoking his cigars. He doesn't speak to me, he doesn't come in the house. Doesn't even try to reach me through his brain telepathically. He's been staying away, out of sight out of mind, as if that works so easily with us.

But I know he's been here. It's been a comfort, to be honest. To know that no matter what I said to him, that we needed space, that he gave me that space but also refused to leave my side. I don't know if he's doing it because he's possessive or protective or both, but I've been very aware of his presence at all times.

Except, he's not here. I look both ways and gently call out "Solon?" but there's no answer. I don't smell him either. It just smells like exhaust and dog piss.

Well, fuck. Where did he go? I know my parents have been squabbling about him being out there for the last few days, maybe he had enough of them or they really laid down the guilt trip or something.

I close the door, locking it multiple times, and try to think. I can't imagine something bad happening to Solon, but still. I don't have my phone on me—it's back at the house—but my parents have one and they have his number.

I almost turn around and knock on my parents door, even though it's three in the morning, then change my mind. Solon has to be fine. He's always fine. Even when he's a beast, he's fine.

I'll just have to attempt this on my own.

I close my eyes and I try to picture the dark well within me. I imagine going inward, into myself, the world as I know it, this outside world, slipping away the deeper I go in, into the darkness, into a soft, smooth, cool place inside.

I picture diving down into the black, picture my descent until I see the well, illuminated by only a crescent moon. Everything I need, everything I want, is in that dark endless space. I imagine my arms outstretched, palms to the water, bringing the water up against gravity, like a reverse waterfall flowing into me.

Jeremias, I call him, directed at the well. *Jeremias I need your help.*

My words seem to echo inside of me, like soundwaves off the wall of a cave.

Then...

Are you sure, my child? I hear his voice slither into my head, like a centipede crawling up my spine.

The venomous kind.

Yes, I'm sure, I answer.

And I wait.

I wait to be whisked off to another dimension. Or for him to knock at my door. Perhaps teleport into my living room or fly in through the bathroom window.

But that doesn't happen.

Instead, the black infinite well that I'm imagining is changing. Becoming larger somehow. So much so that, when I open my eyes, it's all I see. I don't see my apartment, I don't see anything except the well. And when I look down at myself, I'm a ghost. My skin is transparent, showcasing the black void underneath, my pale skin is rising in tiny tendrils, like mist on a field.

Where am I? I ask, looking around, trying not to panic but the feeling of wrongness is too overwhelming. Am I...inside myself?

You are here, Jeremias says as he steps out of the void. His black cloak melts seamlessly with the nothingness, so all I see is his ever-changing face. *Here is all you need to be.*

It's cold here, and I don't get cold easily these days. I attempt to wrap my arms around myself, but they just pass through me. Okay, that is *not* a good feeling.

Why did you call upon me? he asks. *I didn't expect to see you so soon. In fact, I didn't expect to see you at all.*

I...I begin. I just need a way to figure out how to control Solon. When he's the beast. The monster. I need to be able to do what you did, how you made him sleep. It's the only way I'll be able to be with him and not live in fear.

Oh, but fear is good for you, my child, Jeremias says, giving me a fleeting smile. *It strengthens you. Are you not stronger now that you are afraid?*

That's an odd way of looking at it. *I'd rather not be afraid at all,* I admit. *Solon, he told me I wasn't special.*

Ouch, he says dryly.

I almost laugh. *Yeah, ouch. Not special enough to tame the beast and I just...you're special. You were able to control it. I want to do what you did. I want to learn. Will you teach me?*

Jeremias stares at me for a moment. With his changing

face, I have to look away. *Step forward*, he says, without answering my question.

I look down and see the water of the well beginning to lap my feet. I hesitate for a moment, then I walk with my see-through legs. Suddenly the bottom gives out from under me, if there even was a bottom to begin with, and I'm sinking straight down into the darkness, like I've been submerged in black ink. It goes over my head and I open my mouth to scream, but instead the water rushes into my lungs, choking me.

Suddenly a pair of hands appear and grabs my arms, hauling me out of the water until I find myself on dry ground, a pebbled beach. Slowly I lift my head, blinking.

It's dark here too, but it's not as dark as the void. I'm no longer inside myself, at least I don't think so. I'm lying on the shore of a lake, at night, and in front of me is a circle of fire, Jeremias standing in the middle of it, a row of dark trees behind him.

"Where am I now?" I mutter to myself, spitting out water. The water is black, and the sight sends a wave of revulsion down my spine. "Wait, let me guess, one of the many worlds I have access to."

When Jeremias doesn't respond, I glance up at him. He looks extra menacing with the flames all around him, the fire dancing in his dark eyes. "Sorry, sarcasm is a coping mechanism," I tell him.

"I can see that," he says after a moment.

"So," I say, getting to my feet and walking toward him. The flames keep me back, so I stop just outside of the circle. "Is this the magical training ground?"

He doesn't look amused. "Why did you call upon me, Lenore?"

"I told you. I want...I need to be able to control the beast side of Solon. Like you did."

"Why?"

"Why?" I repeat. "You know why. You saw what happened to me. If it wasn't for you, I would have died."

"Then you need to stay away from him."

"You know I can't do that."

He raises his chin. "And why would I know that? Is it because you love him? Because you think I care about that? Love? Love only gets in the way."

I swallow hard. "You loved my mother. Alice."

"I did," he says carefully. "But it wasn't enough. She was a vampire. She had her husband. Vampires and witches are never meant to mix."

"Because you end up with something like me."

He gives me a dry smile. "Yes. Like you. You were a happy accident, but not everyone would profit as you have."

I snort. I don't know what the hell I've profited from so far.

"You see," he goes on, "love isn't enough in our world. There's just too much at stake, and most of us are creatures of the dark and the night. Love isn't meant for us."

I mull that over for a moment. "So you can't help me? Or you won't?"

"Only darkness can drive out darkness," he says. "Absolon was born of the dark. You cannot change him with your light."

"You're severely twisting MLK's words there," I tell him.

"People have gotten things wrong for centuries," Jeremias says, walking around the circle, the flames licking his skin but never doing any damage. "So much focus on God and religion and being good, and look where that's gotten this world. Just like love, the foolish obsession with being good and pure and moral has gotten in the way for so many of us. There is only one side that helps fuel who we are, who we are meant to be. You won't become anything special, or great, by chasing the light."

I wish I could read his face, but when it's always changing, it's next to impossible.

"Come forward, my child," he says, stopping in the middle of the circle and beckoning me with a bony finger. "Let the flames bless your skin."

I hesitate. My parents told me I walked through flames unharmed when I was a child, one of the reasons they took me with them instead of leaving me to perish. Because I couldn't perish. But I don't really have memory of that, and despite being able to throw flames with my hands and destroy the Dark Order like I did, purposefully walking through fire goes against every human instinct that I have.

"Don't you want control?" he asks. "Don't you want to be able to harness your abilities, to access them whenever you want? The flames will ignite what lies beneath, what you've been too afraid to see. Come forward, for this is what you asked for."

"I'll be able to help Solon?" I ask.

He nods.

And that's all I needed to hear.

I take in a deep breath and walk through the flames.

All I feel is their warmth, like I'm being licked by heat. It's almost sensual. But there is no pain and my skin doesn't burn.

But there is something happening deep inside.

A darkness building in that well.

There's a sense of immense power, but the kind that comes with a price. I don't know how I know that, but I sense it, like the power is buried at the darkest depth, hidden in a locked box, and to open it would mean I would lose something big. Myself, my dignity, my morality. Everything that makes me who I am and everything I strive to be.

"Don't push it away," Jeremias says, searching my face closely. "That's exactly what the flames are trying to unlock. It's all there for the taking, if only you invite it in."

The way he says *it* makes me think we're not talking about abstract darkness or power here, but rather a being.

The Dark One.

Yes, a raspy metallic voice whispers from inside me, a voice that makes my blood run ice cold, my limbs suddenly heavy with dread. *Yes.*

The voice didn't come from Jeremias.

I shake it away. I push all thoughts of it out of my head, make a promise to never even think about that name again. I know now what's in that box, and that I won't ever be opening it.

Jeremias sighs with disappointment but doesn't comment.

"Tell me," I say to him, curious, "since you seem to be so obsessed with the dark, were you ever good? You were born a witch, right?"

He raises his brows. "Personal questions now? Well then. Yes, I was born a witch."

"Where?"

"Northern England."

"When?"

"About fifty years after Skarde turned into a vampire. Fourteen ten."

I stare at him in awe, my jaw dropping. What the fuck? 1410? "How are you still alive? Are you immortal?"

"Let's just say I'm hard to kill. It's a gift, for all the sacrifices I've made."

I frown. "Are you talking literal sacrifices?"

"Well, that is part of it. But no. I was born a witch, the first witch who was given a specific purpose. I was the first slayer, created to keep the vampires, which were getting out of control, in line. Every slayer that has ever existed is here because of me."

"Wait, wait. Hold up. You mean like my parents? Jim and Elaine? They somehow come from you?"

"Somehow," he says slowly. "But yes, their bloodlines can be traced back to me over the centuries. I am the father of all vampire slayers."

I hate to ask this question but... "If that's your role and always has been...well, I'm technically a vampire. Why aren't you killing me?"

"I'm not interested in that anymore. I haven't killed a vampire in a very long time."

"Okay. Then if I'm your daughter, does that mean I'm a slayer?"

He lets out a dry laugh. "You would have to kill yourself then. No. You're not one because your vampire side negates it. Any other questions?"

"Yeah. When did you become like...this?" I wave my hands at him.

"Like what?"

Evil.

"Best buds with the Dark One."

A cold wind whistles through me and I regret saying the name again. And from the deadly look in Jeremias' eyes, I can tell he feels the same.

"When I decided to live forever. And I was granted that gift. Besides, it needed something to keep up with the vampires."

"*It,*" I muse. "So, it created vampires and then created you to keep the vampires in line?"

"Yes. Sometimes creations get out of control."

"Sounds a lot like pitting two warring sides against each other and watching them fight in some sick game."

"Perhaps it is all a game," he says, eyes gleaming with flames. "But it's one I'm winning."

Is he winning though? If he doesn't kill vampires these days, then what counts as winning to a slayer? What is his end goal?

I straighten up, remembering why I'm here (wherever the fuck I am) and why I called for him.

"You said I'll be able to help Solon," I say. "So, tell me what I can do."

"Back to this again?" he asks mildly.

I stare at him and wait for him to go on.

"There is only one way to get rid of the beast," he says. "You must kill the beast."

"You can kill the beast without killing Solon?"

A quick smile. "Probably not."

I blink at that. "Well, how do you kill the beast?"

"Same as you kill a vampire. A witch's blade."

I shake my head. "I can't stab the beast with a witch's blade."

"You're right. Because you're not a slayer. It wouldn't work. You would only annoy him moments before he kills you."

"So then, I'm fucked, is what you're saying," I grumble. "At least you can teach me to make him fall asleep like you did. I need to be able to do *something*."

"As I said before," he says testily, like I'm wearing his patience thin, "you have to be willing to use darkness to fight darkness. So far, you don't seem to be receptive to that. But, perhaps next time you nearly die at his hands again, you'll finally stop being stubborn and embrace the truth. Or perhaps you'll just die—and I won't be there to save you."

I press my hands into my face, trying to think.

"You're wasting both our time," Jeremias adds. "Unless

you're willing to call upon your dark side, you're not going to get very far as a witch."

"My parents do just fine," I snap, looking up at him. "And they're dealing with the light."

He lets out a snort of contempt. "Your parents, your false parents, are foolish and weak. They can't do anything that matters. They can barely kill vampires. You will learn nothing from them. But you already know that, don't you? After all, they've taught you nothing. They don't know what to make of you, how to handle you. They sense your power, but that same power terrifies them. Your darkness terrifies them, Lenore. It scares everyone but me."

"It doesn't scare Solon," I say stubbornly.

He muses that over. "Maybe not. But Absolon needs that darkness." Suddenly he looks straight up into the black sky. "Speaking of darkness, he needs you now. The man is waiting."

Before I can ask what man, the world gets sucked away into a black vortex and he disappears into thin air. Everything is dark, so dark, and I can't feel the ground beneath my feet anymore, can't tell if my eyes are open or closed.

Slowly, it feels like I'm waking up from a dream.

I open my eyes, expecting to be back in my old apartment again.

But I'm not.

I'm in Solon's bedroom. What used to be my bedroom.

There's a new bed, king-sized as before, but without the four posters, but everything else looks the same.

Why did Jeremias put me back *here*?

I look around, half-expecting the beast to come out of the washroom, or to hear footsteps from the tower room above, but there's only silence.

I open the door to the hall and look out. I'm back in my sleep clothes from earlier, a black lace camisole and a pair of plaid boxers, nothing too risqué for this house, and I head out and quietly go down the stairs. I have no clue what time it is. Hell, I don't even know what day it is. Jeremias could have had me in that void for a long time.

I can hear faint voices though, and my senses are telling me they're coming from Dark Eyes. I pass by the dead roses and this time I don't even say the word, I don't even think, but the roses automatically start to rise, bleeding crimson.

Huh. That's a new one. When Jeremias said my magic would be easier to access now, did he mean it would be even when it wasn't intentional? Guess I have to watch myself a little closer now.

The rest of the house is dead quiet, but the closer I get to Dark Eyes, the more that I recognize Solon's voice, something that makes my heart flutter instinctively. But it's not just his voice. It's Wolf, Ezra, and a voice I don't recognize. A strange cadence that reminds me of that Onni fellow, but not quite the same.

I pause outside the doors to the club, looking down at myself again to make sure I'm not totally lewd in front of company. My nipples are hard—they always are now—and the top is flimsy, but I think I'll pass for acceptable. I was drunk and out of line when it came to Onni; I don't plan on embarrassing Solon in front of any of his other friends.

I push open the doors and walk in.

Four heads look my way.

One of them belongs to my lover, the sight of his deadly handsome face making my stomach do backflips. It's only been a few days, but *fuck*, have I missed him. My heart is aching painfully.

But my attention is then stolen by the stranger, a man who immediately gets to his feet, staring at me in a mix of hope and awe, like I'm some angel floating down from heaven.

He's cute, I'll give him that much. A total vampire, no doubt, but cute nonetheless. High cheekbones, longish dark hair that's similar to Solon's, blue eyes. Actually, he looks a lot like Solon, except a bit younger, a bit shorter and without the facial hair. He's not in a suit, but a navy-blue Henley and dark jeans, a black leather jacket hanging off the back of his chair. His muscles wear the Henley well.

"Lenore," the man says to me. He says my name like he knows me.

Before he can say anything else, Solon is at my side in a blur of movement, standing in front of him and blocking me from view of the stranger.

"What happened?" Solon asks me, reaching out and grabbing my arm, then quickly letting go when he realizes he shouldn't touch me. He swallows hard, the distance hurting him as much as it's hurting me, his eyes searching mine. "Why are you here? Dressed like this? Are you okay?"

His concern warms my heart and the urge to kiss him is hard to ignore. "I'm fine. Really. I don't...I don't know why I'm here. One minute I was with Jeremias, the next...well, I thought he'd put me back in my apartment, but for some reason he put me back here."

"Jeremias?" Solon and the stranger say at the exact same time.

"Yeah," I say. "I called to him. I..." I look around his shoulder to the stranger. "Should you be introducing us?" I ask Solon.

He grinds his teeth together. Okay, so I'm guessing this isn't a friendly visit.

Finally, he says, "Yes. I suppose I should." With a heavy sigh, he waves his hand at the stranger. "Lenore, this is Kaleid." He reluctantly adds, "My brother."

12

LENORE

"Kaleid?" I repeat, staring at the man. He is not at all what I imagined Kaleid would be. And by that, I mean he looks...normal. He doesn't look like the literal son of Skarde (not that I know what Skarde looks like, but I'm picturing something like a monstrous bat, like Gary Oldman in *Dracula*). This man looks like some hot Nordic guy with a permanent twinkle in his eye. How could this possibly be Skarde's right-hand man?

And also, what the hell is he doing here?

Should I be alarmed? I ask Solon, eyeing him. *Are you in danger?*

The corner of his mouth lifts up. *Nice to know you care.*

It takes a lot of effort to stop me from rolling my eyes. *What time is it anyway?*

Six in the morning, he says, and I blink at him in surprise.

What are you all doing up still?

Another hint of a smile. *We're vampires, Lenore. And Kaleid showing up is a very recent development.*

"Well, Lenore," Kaleid says. "Why don't you sit down and

join us? We've been discussing many things that involve you. Only fair if you get to hear about them yourself."

I give Solon a sharp look. *You've been discussing me?*

Solon's gaze is sharp in return. *I've been trying to keep you out of it. For your own good.*

Well, fuck. Now I'm more curious than anything.

I walk around Solon, warily approaching Kaleid. Wolf and Ezra seem relaxed, drinking espresso and lounging in the leather chairs, but their eyes are glued on him, their muscles tight and coiled, ready to strike if he makes a wrong move. Even so, I have no doubt that Solon would beat them to it.

And yet, I don't fear Kaleid as much as I should. I can't explain why. It's not so much the easy, casual vibe that he's putting out there—which may very well be for show—but more that I've been expecting him to show up, even though that makes no sense.

Could this possibly be the man that Jeremias told me about?

"You'll have to forgive me if I seem a little apprehensive about you being here," I say, stopping behind the chair where Solon was sitting before. "From what I know of you, you work alongside your father, and your father, well, he did try to have me killed."

Kaleid nods thoughtfully, running his fingers over his chin. "Yes, I could see how you might hold a grudge against me because of that. Rest assured, I mean you no harm. In fact, I need your help." He eyes Solon. "Just as Solon needs my help."

Solon just grumbles and returns to the chair, gesturing for me to sit down. I do so absently as he pulls over a chair for himself, positioning himself between me and Kaleid, while also trying to keep his distance from me. I have to say, it's noticeable. Not that Solon has been a very touchy-feely affectionate in public kind of guy, but when he's trying to stay away from you, you *know* it.

"So," I say, clearing my throat, fixing my eyes on Kaleid, trying to get a read on him. Solon always says it's nearly impossible for a vampire to lie to another vampire, and while I don't possess those truth-seeking skills with my diluted blood, I assume Kaleid would most likely be dead if Solon thought he was lying. I mean, he had to have invited Kaleid into this house, past the wards, into his sanctuary. That tells me that Solon has a modicum of trust in his brother. "You say you need help. Why us? Why are you here?"

Kaleid laughs and looks at Wolf and Ezra. "Wow, you weren't joking when you said she gets right down to business." But neither Wolf nor Ezra smile. Actually, Ezra never smiles, but even now he's downright glowering.

I give Kaleid a pointed stare.

He gives me a quick smile in return. "I have to respect that. I can't imagine Solon being with someone who didn't put vampires in their place. I can only hope to God you're able to do that with him." He clears his throat, his face growing completely grave in a second, like a switch has been flipped. "The reason I'm here is because I needed to see Solon —and you—in person. And since Solon didn't want to go with Onni back to Helsinki to meet with me, well, the next best thing was that I came to you. I figured I needed to earn your trust."

"And you still haven't," Wolf says, before he has a calm sip of his espresso. Then he eyes me apologetically. "Sorry, Lenore, my manners have escaped me this morning. Would you like me to make you an espresso?"

Before I can tell him not to bother, Wolf is getting up and heading over to the espresso machine behind the bar.

"Interesting," Kaleid muses, watching Wolf before looking over to Solon. "I would have thought you'd be doting on

Lenore instead, given that she belongs to you." Then, while Solon grinds his teeth together in response, Kaleid eyes me. "You still belong to him, don't you? I'm sensing some kind of tension between you here. Solon, you're barely looking at her. You don't seem like the man in love that Onni described."

"I belong to him," I tell Kaleid, keeping my voice steady. "We're just going through a rough patch."

Solon's gaze could cut diamonds as he glares at me. *What are you doing? Don't tell him anything.*

"Trouble in paradise?" his brother asks lightly. "Anything to do with those scars on your chest? Those marks look awfully familiar."

Solon emits a low growling noise, but Kaleid pays it no attention.

"It's nothing," I say, staring down at them. The wound is healed, but the ugly red scars remain, a constant reminder.

"If it was nothing, nothing would be there," Kaleid says. "You know how fast we heal." He eyes Solon. "Don't tell me you still don't know how to keep your beast on a leash."

Solon's features tighten but he manages to refrain from saying anything.

"You see, Lenore, I have one too," Kaleid says simply.

I snap to attention. "What are you talking about? A beast?"

He nods. "Benefit of being a son of Skarde. Everything that made him the monster that he is was passed to us through blood. Fortunately, my beast is a little more, well, sane than Solon's. Doesn't help that Solon was a madman for a few hundred years."

Solon's eyes lock with Kaleid's for a moment, razor-sharp. The animosity rolling off of Solo fills the air, almost has its own smell. "Enough with the fucking chit chat. Tell her what you told me and then get the hell out of my house."

Kaleid's eyes widen playfully. "Touchy, touchy." He looks to me, but my face is telling the same story. *Get the fuck on with it, buddy.*

"Right," he says, clapping his hands together, loud enough that it makes Ezra jump in his chair. "I'm here because I want to destroy my father and I need your help to do it. Both you and Solon."

I had a feeling this was where this was going. "Why?"

"Many reasons. But mainly that I want him dead."

"So go kill him."

"Not that simple. I have power, but not as much power as my father. But Solon and I together, then we can take him down."

"So you don't need me..."

"Ah, but we do," Kaleid says. "The more the better. Besides, you are the whole plan."

Solon clears his throat, glances at me briefly. "He doesn't speak for both of us."

"Right," Kaleid says carefully. "I think I've convinced Solon to help me, lord knows we want the same thing, as hard as that is for him to admit, but I have yet to convince him of your involvement. See, Lenore, what you did to Yanik and the Dark Order was very, very impressive. And that was raw, unfiltered power. Imagine what you can do if you master it."

"Well, sorry to disappoint you, but I haven't mastered it," I say, crossing my arms across my chest, since his gaze keeps dropping to my nipples every now and then. "I don't even know how to use it when I want to."

"Even with all your visits with Jeremias?" he asks doubtfully.

"Jeremias can and will only help me if I embrace my dark side. And that's something I don't want to do. I don't care to end up like him...or like you, for that matter."

Kaleid presses his hands against his heart. "Oooh, that one hurt. I'm sure in time you'll see what I'm trying to do. The darkness is what I'm trying to escape from. I commend you for not even entertaining the idea." He licks his lips. "But, despite you not being ready now, I believe you will be in time. When it counts. And more than that, we need you because you're what Skarde wants."

"So, I'm bait?" I cock my brow.

"This is exactly why I won't let you do this," Solon says gruffly to me.

Oh, but he just said the wrong thing.

"You won't let me?" I repeat. "Screw that, Solon, you don't control me or tell me what I can or can't do."

"It's not for lack of trying," he grumbles.

"Well that's for sure," I say with a dry laugh. "You can be protective or possessive or any kind of alpha you want to be, but I make my own decisions. If I go with you to…where again?"

"Helsinki," Kaleid supplies, looking hopeful.

"If I go with you to Helsinki, it's because I made the choice. Not you." I look to Kaleid. "What does Skarde want with me? Just my death?"

He shakes his head grimly. "Just the opposite. He wants you alive. He wants you to be his bride."

My mouth drops open while I simultaneously shiver. "His bride?" I squeak. Ugh, hell no. No, no, no. I haven't even seen Skarde and I'm entirely disgusted. "Why me?"

"Because it is foretold," Kaleid says. "And whether I believe it or not, Skarde believes it. He wants you, period. And you're going to get us close to him."

"I really don't think Lenore should be put in this position," Wolf says, coming over and handing me my espresso.

I take it from him. "Thank you, Wolf. But again, you don't get to make these decisions for me."

Wolf's expression darkens as he stares at me. "You have to think long and hard about this one. Solon isn't being over-protective. This is a new world, in new territory. You will be tested like never before, and before you're ready. I won't even be there to keep an eye on the two of you."

"Why not?"

"Because this asshole says we're not permitted," Ezra speaks up, his glowering expression still focused on Kaleid.

"Too many cooks in the kitchen," Kaleid explains with a show of his palms. "I can get the three of us to one of the worlds where my father has retreated, maybe four, but Wolf and Ezra would be too easy to detect. They don't blend in the same way the locals do. Besides, if we do need reinforce-ments, I can always ask Valtu."

"Dracula?" Wolf repeats. "You'd ask *him*?"

"Wait, what? Dracula?" I ask, perking up. "Like the real Dracula?"

"His name is Valtu," Kaleid says patiently, ignoring Wolf. "Valtu Dracula. He inspired Bram Stoker."

"He's an ass," Wolf says to me. "I wouldn't trust him anymore than I'd trust Kaleid."

"Then it's a good thing you're not going," Kaleid fires at him.

"Lenore isn't going either," Solon says. "And that's final."

I shake my head, feeling the anger flare up inside me. Sometimes his controlling tendencies are flattering, but right now it's annoying as fuck. "Then I am going. How about that?" I look at Kaleid. "Count me in. I want to get rid of Skarde as much as anyone, and if you need me to do it, then I will go where I'm needed."

I can't even look at Solon. His anger is palpable.

Kaleid is watching him though. "See, your lover came through. But, Jesus Solon, I think you better get some blood in you soon. You'll need your strength for this."

Solon doesn't say anything to that, and I'm reminded that both of us are starving for each other. Literally.

I slam back the espresso in one gulp, the scalding liquid not hurting my throat at all, and get out of my chair. "Then it's all settled. Just tell me when we leave so I have time to pack."

"A couple of days," Kaleid says. "I want to enjoy the city first. Feels good to be in California."

So I guess there's no real rush. Hopefully it doesn't give me too much time or I may back out of the whole thing. Clearly I haven't thought this through that much.

I give him a quick smile. "It was nice to finally meet you Kaleid. I hope for all our sakes that this works out."

Then I give Wolf and Ezra a quick head nod, catching Solon's eye briefly as I turn to leave, heading toward the doors to the house.

My vampire is quickly at my side, stopping me before I step through.

"What?" I eye Solon warily, so painfully aware of how close his body is to mine, how all the blood in my veins is rushing to the surface, begging to be with him.

"You don't have to do this," Solon whispers harshly to me.

"I know," I tell him. "But I want to. I think it's the right thing to do. The only thing to do, apparently."

"The risks are too great," he says with a firm shake of his head, pressing his lips together into a white slash.

"And some of those risks aren't yours to make," I say. Against my better judgement, and the whole giving us space aspect, I reach up and press my palm against his cheek. His cold, pale skin, the rough scrape of his stubble, send shock-waves into my hand, traveling down my arm and straight to my heart. His eyes close in response, his nostrils flaring as he takes in a deep breath. Fuck. Why does this have to be so hard? Why couldn't Jeremias have taught me what to do?

Maybe, just for this one thing, to be able to tame the beast, maybe it would be worth going dark and giving up my soul for.

Suddenly Solon's eyes open, piercing me with their intensity, the blue practically glowing. "No," he rasps. "You are not giving up your soul for anything, especially not for me."

I wince. "You weren't supposed to hear that."

"And I wasn't trying to. But I did. Lenore, listen." He covers my hand with his and pulls it off his face, intertwining his fingers with mine. "I love you. I'm not going to lose you, no matter what happens. But you can't do anything for me that comes at a high price. I won't let you. I don't deserve it."

I swallow hard, heat pricking my eyes. "Why don't you let me decide what you're worth, okay? I'm not giving up on us, okay? I'm going to figure out a way." I peer at him, noticing the gaunt look to his face, the purpling under his eyes. "But Kaleid is right in that you have to feed, especially if we're going to Finland."

He shakes his head. "I'll be fine."

"Solon," I say firmly. "You're a fucking vampire. You need blood. And maybe I'm not the one who should be giving it to you right now, but you need it from someone. Take one of the donors. Do it before we leave."

"I don't want to," he says gruffly.

"Because you don't want to feed off of anyone but me?" I ask. "That's sweet, but honestly, I don't care. It's not like sex. It's food. You can feed and not screw the person you're feeding off of, right?"

His gaze sharpens. "What do you think?"

"I'm going to assume you have some control in that area." I mean, god, I hope that's a given, because I think I'd rather risk a tussle with the beast than him sticking his dick in someone in a state of bloodlust and feeding frenzy. That would break me beyond a point of no recovery.

"I'll be fine," he says again, and jeez, he calls me the stubborn one. "I know how to handle periods of drought. You, on the other hand…"

"I'm not hungry," I lie. I'm ravenous, and food isn't cutting it. I'm getting by without blood and, honestly, I shouldn't have any withdrawals for at least another week, and maybe it's the circumstances, but I've been craving it like nothing else. My senses feel dulled, the spark inside me sputtering. It's not just any blood either—I want Solon's in particular.

But if he has to wait, then I have to wait.

I just don't know what moment we're waiting for.

And how long that will take.

Solon sighs, his expression disbelieving as his eyes skim my face. No doubt he heard what I was thinking just now too. "You should probably call your parents. Let them know where you are. And that you'll be staying over here."

My brow goes up. "I'm staying over here?"

"You didn't sleep last night if you were with Jeremias, and I can guarantee once you take a moment for yourself, it's going to hit you like a ton of bricks. Go upstairs. To your old bedroom. And stay."

I rub my lips together, wondering if this is a good idea.

"Moonshine," Solon says to me gently, "you're safe here. Safer than you are with your parents. And you're safe from me. I promise you that. Wolf is here. Ezra too. I'm giving you the space you need, but if you think you're coming with us to Helsinki, well, then you better get used to being around me again."

"I don't think I'm going," I tell him. "I *am* going."

He nods. "Very well. Come on then."

He briefly touches my elbow, leading me toward the doors and opening them. We both step through the ward and into the house, but while I go up a couple of steps, he stays where he is, staring up at me.

"Solon," I say to him. "Do you trust Kaleid?"

He looks off to the side in thought, frowning. "No. I don't. I don't trust anyone but you."

"Then why are you doing this?"

His lips twitch in amusement. "Because I know I can't stop you, no matter what I say or do." Then he turns serious. "And so, my dear, why do you want to do this?"

"I told you. It's the right thing to do. And when I search deep inside, I know that this is supposed to happen. Whether we should trust Kaleid or not is irrelevant, because I'm supposed to go with him. I'm instrumental in helping defeat Skarde and you know it." I pause. "Jeremias told me as much."

His forehead creases. "And you trust him to tell you the truth?"

"He sees the future, Solon."

"He's a fucking evil warlock who hates vampires to no end," Solon growls. "I wouldn't believe a word he says."

I sigh, knowing what he's saying is true. "I know. But sometimes you have to put your trust in someone. You can tell Kaleid is telling the truth, I can tell Jeremias is. Doesn't mean I'd make any bets, but I do believe he can see the future because I *feel* the future. And I know this is supposed to happen this way, as woo woo as it sounds."

"Woo woo?" Solon repeats, a line between his brows.

I laugh. "Yeah. Woo woo. Like, mystical, magical shit."

"You know you're a witch, right? You can just call it magic."

"We'll see," I tell him, smiling despite myself, briefly feeling the slip back into old times. Then, before I can dwell on it much longer, I turn around and head up the stairs, leaving Solon behind.

13

LENORE

THREE DAYS LATER, SOLON AND I ARE UP BEFORE DAWN TO catch the flight to Helsinki. Kaleid stayed at the Ritz, a fancy ass just like his brother, which was understandable since none of the vampires wanted him in the house. Even Yvonne put her foot down, and she's not always that savvy when it comes to the different vampires in Solon's life.

I haven't seen Kaleid since. Solon has gone to meet up with him at the hotel bar a few times, I guess to discuss the plan or perhaps try to dissuade Kaleid from involving me. But neither of them has a say in my participation anymore. Even if Kaleid changed his mind or tried to scare me off, I'd find some other way there.

"You look like shit," Kaleid says, when the private SUV shows up and we shuffle into the back row behind him.

"Thanks," I tell him.

"Obviously I meant Solon," Kaleid says. Then he frowns at me. "Though you did look better the other day. Granted, you were barely dressed." He gives me a salacious grin.

Solon stiffens beside me, and I'm worried he might throw a punch or tear out his jugular or do something bloody and violent. I kick his foot to tell him to calm down, especially since we don't want an appearance from *you know who* thirty-five thousand feet up.

"Well, it's like five a.m.," I tell Kaleid. "You're lucky you don't look like a troll."

"Speaking of trolls, Solon, did you tell her about the real trolls back home?"

Solon just clenches his jaw, looking out the window as we pull away from the house and make our way through the foggy streets. Either the driver of the SUV is a vampire too, or he can't hear us.

"What trolls?" I ask.

"You'll see," Kaleid says. "And anyway, the both of you need blood right away. I'm surprised you've been able to hold off like you have."

Okay, the driver is definitely a vampire, since he hasn't flinched once at our conversation.

"It's called discipline, Kaleid," Solon says. "You should try it sometime."

"Ah yes. Always trying to make a point. Amazing how many centuries go by and yet people never really change."

"Except for you, right?" Solon asks. "Because you've had the biggest change of heart in a millennium."

Kaleid's face goes grim. For all his easy breezy charm, the moment his face darkens, I can see the dangerous side of him coming through. The one that I believe takes after his father in ways that Solon never will. The one that I could easily see leading beside a vampire king, perhaps one day taking over the throne itself.

I clear my throat, wetting my lips for a moment. "I guess I should be making sure, before we board this plane for your kingdom, for lack of a better word, that you aren't doing all of this just to take a seat on your father's throne."

Kaleid meets my eyes, looking straight into my soul with

a vibrating energy that makes my skin crawl. "I'm not cut out for the job," he says. "Frankly, I don't think the job should even exist."

"Well, he did create vampires," I point out, playing devil's advocate. As if the Dark One needs an advocate. If humans only knew what a stupid saying that was.

Kaleid smiles, dimples appearing in his cheeks, that boyish feature attempting to hide the malice in his eyes. "Who says we should ever have been created?"

Solon snorts beside me. He's looking out the window still, shaking his head. "It pains me to think we're on the same page about something."

I look between the two estranged brothers, wondering if they'll ever be close or if they're forever doomed to be distrustful of each other. Hell, I guess the best I can wish for at this point is for us to actually get through this without anyone dying. Maybe that's asking for too much.

I was prepared for a commercial airplane, like United or something, leaving SFO, but instead the SUV takes us to a private airfield where a private jet is waiting.

I would like to say that I was totally cool about it all and acted like I took private jets all the time, but alas, that isn't the case.

"Oh my god," I say as I boarded the plane. "I feel like a celebrity!"

It's a lot smaller than I thought it would be, but obviously big enough to get us halfway across the world. But unlike any of the jets I've seen on Instagram and whatnot, this one has black leather seats, black flooring, and red walls.

"Gee, I wonder if a vampire owns this," I say as I walk down the aisle to the couches at the back.

"Kaleid has never been subtle," Solon says from behind me, sniffing distastefully.

"Says the man who lives in the Addams Family house," Kaleid speaks up. "Seems it must run in our blood."

Solon ignores that. He takes my carry-on and stows it, and then we take our seats. We each get a row of three seats that look like a leather couch, and I'm a little bereft at having to be across the aisle from Solon. The ride to the airport was the closest I had been to him in days. When I'd stayed in my old room in the house, I only would see him in passing, or we'd talk in Dark Eyes, but Amethyst, Wolf, or Ezra was always around. I think he thinks other people keep the beast at bay, and that might be true. But still, I've missed his contact something fierce.

And now, as I buckle my seatbelt, I wish he'd come over and sit next to me. I'm sure if he turned beast, Kaleid would be able to put him in his place, or I might be able to activate the powers that saved me the last time.

Then again, those claws plus a metal tube in the air don't exactly scream safety to me. They say there are only three ways to kill a vampire—witch's blade, fire, and removing the head—but surely falling from the sky would do it too.

A vampire hostess with perfect teeth comes down the aisle in a black, skimpy uniform that was no doubt Kaleid's idea, and serves us all a glass of champagne. I notice that neither Solon nor Kaleid put on their seat belt.

"Well," Kaleid says, sitting across from me. He raises his glass. "Here's to a smooth ride there. Lord knows it will be a rough one after that."

* * *

I'VE NEVER BEEN able to fall asleep on a plane before, and I certainly didn't think I would, surrounded by both Solon and Kaleid, but somehow I did, waking up only when the wheels hit the tarmac.

"Welcome to Finland," Solon whispers to me.

I raise my head, blinking.

Solon is sitting right beside me, gazing down at me with a hint of a smile.

I slowly sit up, find myself smiling right back at him.

"And good morning," he adds, watching in amusement as I try to tame my bedhead. Ugh, and I was drooling too. "You were out like a light. Good thing too, because the jet lag is no joke. Even vampires have to suffer. If anything, we're more sensitive to it than anyone."

"Were you watching me sleep?" I ask wryly.

The corners of his eyes crinkle, a softness coming over his expression. "I was." He pauses. "I'd missed it."

I swallow hard as our gaze interlocks. Everything inside me feels so tender and bruised and I know that if I kiss him, press my lips to his, that it would heal me. That my heart would fill up again, that the permanent ache between my ribs would stop. He's so close that the smell of roses and tobacco is seeping into my brain, making me feel intoxicated with him, almost dizzy.

Kiss me, I whisper inside my head. *Please.*

His eyes flare and he's wrestling with the idea, perhaps even losing to it.

"Sorry to disturb your little moment," Kaleid's voice comes through, breaking the spell. Solon immediately pulls back, and I hadn't really noticed how close our faces were until now.

I glare at Kaleid, who is sitting there looking not very sorry at all.

"I'm sure there will be plenty of time for your, uh, reconciliation once we get to the hotel," he says. "I've decided to keep it respectable. I've put you both in adjoining rooms."

"We aren't staying with you?" Solon asks, frowning.

Kaleid laughs. "I didn't think you'd want to. I know your feelings about the red world."

"What's the red world?" I ask.

Kaleid looks at me in surprise. "Solon didn't tell you? My, my, so many secrets between you two. Well, I suppose the best way to describe it is like the Black Sunshine. Except it's red. Hence the name."

I try to picture this in my head. I think I prefer the gray world better. "And that's where you live?"

He grins at me. "That's where *all* the vampires live in Helsinki. It's safer that way."

"They only leave to feed," Solon says grimly.

"That's not always true," Kaleid says. "Sometimes we bring the victims back to the red world and have at them there." He clears his throat, wincing. "Sorry. *Victims*. I have to stop thinking in that term. They aren't victims anymore. See, I've tried to borrow a page from my brother and find donors. Volunteers. I have to say, it's a lot more fun keeping them around. They get off on it."

"And I suppose every vampire has followed your lead?" Solon asks dryly.

Kaleid shrugs. "I'm not in charge of them. Or anyone. They are free to do whatever they like. If they want to keep killing people and bringing them into the red world, that's their doing. But some are coming around to the idea of consent and all that. It at least keeps the police off our backs."

Soon the plane comes to a stop and we get out. It's surprisingly hot and sunny and by the time we get to the black Land Rover, complete with Kaleid's personal driver, I'm almost sweating. I know it's early June, but for some reason I didn't think it got hot here. I was wrong.

The drive into the city from the airport is fairly boring. Lots of bland, box-like apartment buildings and shopping centers, with rows of tall pines in between. But inside I'm absolutely bursting with excitement. Okay, maybe that's not the right word—more like anxiety. My head is a bit swimmy, probably because my body thinks it's god knows what time back at home, or because I'm sitting next to Solon, shoulder pressed against his, and my gut keeps twisting on itself.

I have no idea what to expect here. In a way, I wish I had stayed awake on the plane so that I would have had time to think. Suddenly, we're here and I know we're at the mercy of Kaleid. Back in San Francisco I never feared Kaleid. Not even on the plane. But here? In his country, his world, his turf, and so close to Skarde? The fears are starting to creep up.

I mean, he's using me as bait to get access to his father. That's scary enough. I guess the only reason I have a little bit of trust that he's on my side is because he was upfront about it. He could have lied (I mean, he could have *tried* to lie) to us and said that my magic was all-powerful and could destroy Skarde. He didn't have to tell me I was to be bait. No one wants to hear that. So that honesty earns Kaleid a tiny checkmark in my trust book.

That aside, things are so tense and strained between him and Solon that I'm a little worried that this isn't some elaborate ruse to lure Solon to his father and have him sacrificed or something like that. I'm one hundred percent certain that's what Solon thinks too, so I don't have to worry about it too much, knowing Solon will do all he can to keep his head. But still.

The only thing that tempers my nerves a little is the fact that Jeremias saw this. He knew I would be instrumental in Skarde's destruction; he knew that Kaleid would come for me. He saw the future, and if I want that future to play out, then I have to suck it up and take my part in it.

Luckily, as we get closer into the city, the scenery captures my attention. There are cobblestone streets, old-timey architecture, Russian-looking churches and cathedrals, trams trundling to and fro, and everyone is blonde and tanned and smiling, shopping and eating on café patios.

Holy shit. I can't believe I'm in Helsinki! Suddenly, all the fears and worries about the vampires fade into the background and I'm eager to act like a tourist, exploring the streets.

"I forget that you've never been here before," Kaleid says, watching my expression. "We will have to make time to show you around. Nothing tastes better than finding a beer garden by the water. Or even a trip on the ferry to the fortress of Suomenlinna."

"Nice way to lure her into thinking she's here on vacation," Solon grumbles. "And not as bait for Skarde."

Kaleid narrows his eyes at him. "Oh, you're just full of fucking sunshine, aren't you?"

I burst out laughing. I can't help it. Guess all these mixed emotions have to go somewhere.

Solon just lets out a deep rumbling noise of disdain and turns his attention away.

It's not long before the car is pulling up outside a majestic looking building overlooking a busy park, a hint of the water in the distance. Bellhops rush out to help us, taking up our bags as we enter the elegant hotel.

"The Rolling Stones usually stay here," Kaleid informs us as we head through the tiled lobby to the elevators. "I couldn't get you their suite, unfortunately, but I'm sure the rooms you have will do."

Both our rooms are next to each other, on the top floor, overlooking the park. From here I can see over the trees all the way to the harbor.

But there's no time to get sorted. The bellhop deposits my suitcase and carry-on in the room, and then Kaleid is taking Solon and I out of the hotel. I would have liked to have taken a shower, put on a dress, some makeup, but he seems to be in a rush.

"Where are we going?" I ask as we head down the street. As it is back home, most people don't pay us any attention. You would think that two gorgeous, tall, striking men such as Solon and Kaleid would turn heads, but vampires are pretty adept at getting people to ignore them—until they *want* to be seen.

"Sorry, am I rushing you?" Kaleid asks. "I want to catch Valtu while I have a chance. He said he wasn't in Helsinki for long."

"Dracula?" I ask, the excitement in my voice palpable.

Kaleid laughs. "Yes. Dracula. He normally lives in Romania."

"Transylvania? Really?"

"I told you he inspired Stoker. But Valtu is all over the place. His main house is in the Carpathian Mountains, but he spends a lot of time on the beaches of Croatia too. Vampires normally don't like a lot of sun and heat, but Valtu loves it. Or maybe he just likes being around women in bikinis."

"Lemme guess. He's rich."

"We're *all* rich, baby," Kaleid says, to which Solon lets out another grumble, probably for the *baby* part.

We end up in front of a giant cathedral, white with a green dome. From my history, I know that Russia controlled Finland for a long time, and this place definitely has a Russian slant to it.

"Here we are," Kaleid says.

"What do you mean?"

He gestures to the cathedral. There are rows of steps out front, tons of tourists milling about, taking pictures or sitting in the sun and drinking cans of cider. "This is the entrance to the red world," he says.

"In the church?"

"You'll see."

He walks off and I look at Solon for explanation as we follow.

"The red world is hidden to the naked eye," Solon explains. "It takes some effort to see. Like one of those paintings that were big in the nineties."

"Magic Eye paintings?"

"They were absolutely atrocious. No magic at all."

We follow Kaleid around the back of the cathedral, onto the street. There's a long wall between the cathedral and the road, and in the wall is an ornate gated door.

I point at it. "Doesn't seem so hard to see."

"That's a door for humans," Solon says.

We walk along the wall a few feet until Kaleid stops and gestures to the wall.

"There's nothing there," I say.

"Keep looking at it," Solon says to me quietly. "Try to block out any thoughts."

Easier said than done. But I do as he says.

And suddenly a door starts to appear in the rock, just the way that one would appear in the Black Sunshine. Flames create the outline until a black wooden door with a gold latch and handle appears before me.

"So you see it," Kaleid notes. He steps toward the door and pulls the latch to the side, opening it. I see nothing but red down a long corridor that disappears into darkness, and in that darkness I sense danger.

"Welcome to the Red World," Kaleid says, gesturing for me to step through.

I glance at Solon. *Are you sure about this?*

He shakes his head. *Not even a little.*

But he's not stopping me. So that says something.

I step into the red.

Solon comes in behind me, closing the door on the world outside.

I look down at myself. I'm totally crimson, like the place is done up with red lightbulbs, except there are no lightbulbs at all. It's just…red.

Kaleid eyes me. "You okay?"

I nod. "Just takes some adjusting."

"You'll get used to it," he says. "You'll soon appreciate it."

I don't know about that. I went from being a girl who gets squeamish about blood to someone who drinks blood on a semi-regular basis, but I don't like it enough to want to live in a world that looks like it.

Kaleid starts walking down the hall, and I follow, Solon staying close behind me. His presence is both comforting and intoxicating at once.

Our footsteps echo on stone floors, making sound a feature here compared to the silent world of Black Sunshine. It's also cold and smells dank, and as we turn a corner, the ground starts to slope like we're going further underground.

Finally, we come to a stop outside one giant crimson door, and Kaleid knocks rapidly on it, as if he's a guest here.

He catches what I'm thinking because he looks at me and explains, "You never know what's going on in here. Vampires don't like to be ambushed during periods of, uh, exertion."

Sounds a lot like the Dark Room back at home. I brace myself.

The door opens, and a pale woman with high cheekbones and dark, straight hair that hangs to her waist stares at us with a blank expression.

"Natalia," Kaleid says warmly. "Just the gal I wanted to see."

She ignores him, turns her stony face toward Solon. "Absolon," she says, in what sounds like a Swedish or Norwegian accent. "What a surprise." Though she doesn't seem surprised at all.

Then she fixes her eyes on me. They must be a very pale blue, because here they're so red it's unnerving. "And you must be the witch."

"Half-witch," I correct her. I hold out my hand. "I'm Lenore."

She eyes my hand but doesn't move. Looks back to Solon. "When is the last time we saw each other?"

"Long time ago," he says gravely. "You're looking well."

I frown, taking my hand back. Their relationship already seems strange, I have to wonder if they were lovers at some point. I hate the fact that I'm getting jealous over this already.

"We're family," Solon says to me in a reassuring manner, either hearing my thoughts or picking up on my vibe.

"That's the nicest thing you've ever said to me," Natalia says, a hint of sarcasm coming through.

"Don't get used to it," Kaleid says. "He's grumpy as fuck."

"And you thought he would be any different this time?" she asks him.

"How are you related?" I ask her.

"Daughter of Skarde here," she says, raising her hand briefly.

"Oh," I say, feeling dumb. "I didn't know Skarde had any daughters."

"There are a few of his direct heirs left," she says slowly. She eyes Solon, raising a brow. "You really haven't told her much, have you? Tried to erase us from your memory?"

"You do that when your family is trying to *kill* you," Solon explains.

"Okay, enough with the chitchat," Kaleid says. "We're here to see Valtu. He hasn't left, has he?"

"No," she says carefully as she steps aside and gestures for us to come inside. "Come on in. You'll find him in the back room."

I swear there's a hint of a smile on her face when she says that.

We walk through the doors into what looks to be a lounge, a little similar to Dark Eyes, except that the furniture looks much older, with a Scandinavian slant, like nothing would be out of place in an old Nordic castle, and of course everything is red. The only light is coming from candelabras and chandeliers lit with hundreds of dripping candles. This is goth on steroids.

"What is this place?" I ask. "And don't just tell me it's *the Red World*."

"It's the gateway to the Red World," Natalia says. "This is the only way in. To access the Red World, you must walk through those doors. Then, you are free to go anywhere you want in the Red. Each corridor," she says, pointing down the sides where hallways seem to lead to nowhere, "leads to a different access point in the city. You'll see, Helsinki is a different place when you look at it through the vampire's eyes. We rule the world here."

"Technically, our father rules this world," Kaleid says. "And if we don't stop him, he'll move on to the next one. The human one."

"You don't have to give me your speech again, brother," she says. "I heard you the first time."

"And have you thought about it anymore? Because if Valtu is on board…"

"We'll see. If he's on board, then I'm on board."

Kaleid presses his hand over his heart. "It's your lack of confidence in me that kills me."

She shrugs. "Just because I think the worlds would be better if Skarde was out of the picture, doesn't mean I have faith in what your plan is. It's a death wish, Kaleid." She glances at Solon over her shoulder. "And you should know better than to think you can win this, Absolon. Frankly, I'm surprised you're here."

"You and me both," Solon says gruffly.

We stop outside a door and Natalia waves her hand at it. "He's in there. I have business to attend to, but I'll be around. Good luck."

Natalia walks off the way we came, and Kaleid looks to me and Solon with a hopeful look on his face. He puts his hand on the door and opens it.

It's a fairly large room with lush shag carpeting, a bunch of circular beds and mirrors all over the place, including the ceiling, and groups of melting red candles. In the middle of the room is a naked woman on all fours, a dog collar around her neck, the chain connected to it running to the hand of a man.

The man is sitting in a huge wooden chair, gothic as fuck. He's got longish dark hair, dark eyes, and is completely naked, holding a goblet in one hand, his mouth smeared with what looks like blood.

Below him, the woman on her knees is sucking his dick.

The man stares at us, eyes glazed with pleasure, not caring, or maybe not even seeing us. The lewd, wet sounds of the blow job fill the room.

Kaleid clears his throat. "Lenore. May I introduce you to Valtu. Better known in your world as Dracula."

14

LENORE

Of all the things I thought I'd see today, I never thought it would be Count Dracula getting his dick sucked. Then again, if I gave any thought about where we were going, I should have seen it coming. Vampires are a kinky and uninhibited bunch through and through.

I should look away, I think. But I can't. Just like it happened in the Dark Room at home, I'm watching this woman suck the life out of him and it's turning me on like crazy. But unlike before, Solon isn't pressing his cock against my ass. In fact, he actually takes a step away from me. I guess he knows exactly what I'm thinking.

"You're back," Dracula says, in a low, rich voice. His breath hitches a little with pleasure and he closes his eyes, his body tensing for a moment. He's well-built, an eight-pack, all brawny shoulders and pecs and veiny arms. "Hope you don't mind me finishing up."

"I need to know what you've decided," Kaleid says to him, as if we aren't all standing around and watching this person go down on him.

I glance over at Solon, brows raised. *Is this normal?*

He smirks at me. *You have to get over your puritanical thinking, moonshine.*

I'm not puritanical, I protest. *But I'm also not used to people having business meetings while getting blow jobs.*

"Welcome to our world," Kaleid says, picking up on my thoughts yet again. He shoots me a smile. "This place, anything goes. A lot different than in San Francisco, I know."

"Ah. This must be Lenore," Dracula says, and when I dare to look at him, his eyes are open and he's gazing directly at me. "She's pretty. For a human."

I frown. "Hey," I snap at him. "No wonder Wolf said you were an ass."

Dracula laughs, his head going back. "Oh, Wolf. How is the old boy? He still mad I stole his girlfriend?"

"That was two hundred years ago," Solon says. "I'd say he's over it now."

"Good to know," Dracula says. Then he wraps the chain around his wrist and gives the woman's neck a yank. "Deeper, sweetheart. I want to feel those tonsils."

The woman responds by batting her eyelashes and deep throating him. Dracula hisses, his stronger fingers digging into the wood of the chair's arms, then he's coming with a loud groan.

And like a total fucking pervert, I'm watching this.

Then again, Kaleid and Solon are watching too, the looks in their eyes intense and smoldering. I don't know what the fuck is going on, but the smell of sex and the woman's adrenaline is starting to turn everyone on at once. Now I totally get why vampires have so many orgies, it's like sexual arousal is contagious among them.

Somehow, I manage to compose myself, ignoring the throbbing between my legs, wishing that I had Solon alone, and also wishing the beast wasn't an issue.

Finally, when he finishes, Dracula swallows the rest of

what I'm assuming is blood in the goblet and tosses it behind him. Then he gets to his feet, his cock bobbing freely, still-half hard and, well, impressive. I'm trying not to look, I swear I am, but it's also impossible not to when it's become the focal point of the room.

"Are you hungry?" Dracula asks, strolling over to us. "You must be after watching that." He stops in front of Solon and appraises him. "I could have sworn you were more hand-some before. Did you get ugly or something?"

"He hasn't had blood in a long time," Kaleid says. Then he jerks his thumb at me. "Neither has she."

"Abstinence, hmmm," Dracula muses. "That's a different kink than I'm used to. I'd let you use my human, but I don't like to share food." Then he walks back to the woman (and I swear I'm not admiring his very tight bum) and picks up the chain, leading her away from the chair and toward the door. "Let me return her to her group," he says. "Then we'll all talk."

He leaves the room and Kaleid starts after him, pausing at the door. "You wait here. I'll be right back."

Then Kaleid shuts the door behind him.

Solon and I are alone together for the first time in a long time.

"Well," I say, crossing my arms and slowly walking along the carpet, taking in the sights of the room that wouldn't be out of place in a BDSM sex club. "That was…something."

Solon doesn't say anything to that. Probably because it wasn't much to him.

"So, is this some kind of sex room or something?" I go on, feeling strangely awkward for some reason. I think the feeling of the two of us being alone in here is too great, too overpowering, that I'm afraid of it. "Do people live here?"

Solon shakes his head, his eyes trained to my every move-ment. "Not in the gateway. Vampires will stay here of course, and this is where a lot of the feeding happens. I guess because it's easiest access to the outside world, to the humans. All the other doors lead out, but this is the only one that leads in. The vampires, though, they live all over the city, just in this world instead of the normal one."

I smell the air. It smells like Dracula's cum, and the woman's arousal, and hell, probably my arousal too. But there are other smells too, human smells. Adrenaline, perfume, blood. "Do they keep humans in this place? Like as pets?"

Solon grimaces. "That would seem a little too gruesome, even to me."

Suddenly the door opens again and Kaleid steps in.

And he's not alone.

There's a man standing with him, shirtless, in a pair of swim trunks. A young man. Maybe my age. He has the face of a model—strong cheekbones, full lips, long lashes, pretty eyes, floppy thick hair. If everything wasn't tinged red, I'd wager his hair was a chestnut brown, his eyes green, his skin tanned. He's tall and there isn't an ounce of fat or hair on his body, just a primed, lean, smooth specimen.

He's also human.

"Who is this?" Solon asks sharply.

"This is Mathias," Kaleid says, putting his hand on his shoulder. "He doesn't speak English, but he understands what's happening."

I frown, bewildered. "And what's happening exactly?"

"Mathias, hold out your arm," Kaleid says.

Mathias does as he's told, staring straight ahead, a strange smile on his face.

Kaleid reaches into his jean pocket and pulls out a sharp knife.

Before I can register what's happening, Kaleid swipes the blade over Mathias's inner bicep, cutting him. A gash of blood rushes to the surface, spilling over his soft skin, the scent filling the air, filling my nose, taking over my brain.

"He's for the both of you," Kaleid says, pushing Mathias toward us. "You need to feed before we go anywhere, and you need to stop being so damn stubborn about it. Try not to kill him, okay?"

Then he closes the door behind him, leaving Solon and I with the bleeding human with the dazed look on his face.

Part of me wants to run after Kaleid, run away from what I know is going to happen.

But that part isn't as strong as the hungry part.

The one that is being driven mad by the bloodlust.

I look over at Solon for permission, even though I would do this without it. His jaw is clenched so tight, his pupils dilated into dark pools, that I think he's close to losing it too. He nods, barely.

Well, Kaleid did say he was for the both of us.

I give in.

With a throaty growl, I'm on Mathias in seconds, grabbing hold of his lean arm and wrapping my lips around the wound on his bicep.

The moment his blood hits my tongue, I'm lost to it.

I gulp the liquid down, blood so unlike Solon's, entirely human and sweet and innocent, and my nails dig into his skin and I know that I have to retain a little control or I might drain him of blood completely.

Mathias might not speak any English, but he's moaning like crazy, enjoying the feeling of me drinking from him, perhaps even getting off on it. It only heightens the experience, knowing I'm not hurting the guy, even though my teeth are sharp and tearing into his skin, even though the blood is getting all over him, all over me.

Stop, I tell myself. *He doesn't heal like you.*

Somehow, I manage to unhook my teeth and take a step

back from him, breathing hard, his blood sticking to my face. "Are you okay?" I ask him.

Mathias just smiles, his eyes glazed over. He looks as high as a kite.

Then I look over my shoulder at Solon, whose fists are clenching so hard, his own blood is dripping from his palms where his nails have cut in.

"Your turn," I tell him.

Solon's chest is heaving, he's trying so hard to compose himself. But he's being stubborn as hell. If he won't feed on me yet, then he needs to feed on Mathias, just as I have. I mean, I'm not satisfied, I still want more, but a person only has so much blood to give.

"Solon," I tell him. "Please. Do this for me."

The battle in Solon's eyes is hard to watch.

"You won't be able to protect me if you're too weak," I add.

That gets to him. His eyes blaze in response.

He slowly nods, standing up a little straighter.

He walks over to Mathias, sizing him up, though the way he's approaching him reminds me of a lion on the prowl. He walks all the way around him and stops right behind him, staring at Mathias's neck. Solon's just a bit taller, his shoulders broader, but they're both deliciously sexy and virile men and the sight of them so close together has my core aching again.

Solon starts unbuttoning his own shirt, throwing it to the side, until Solon is as shirtless as Mathias is. I know it's because Solon is thinking about later, how we have a hotel to go back to and we can't do it covered in blood (luckily, I'm wearing black), and Solon really loves his nice shirts. But it also looks extremely homoerotic and I can't help but remember what Solon said to me once, that all vampires are a little gay. I thought it funny at the time, but now I know it's because sex and feeding are so physical and intertwined. Plus, I think we would all be after so much time.

So I watch as Solon puts his hand on the side of Mathias's head and presses it down to the side, exposing his neck, showcasing a vein.

Then Solon looks me dead in the eyes, opens his mouth wide enough to bare his very sharp fangs, and clamps down on Mathias's neck. His fangs pierce the skin, the blood pouring out, until Solon's lips suck it back.

And Solon is staring at me the whole time, feeding rather tenderly given the circumstances, given how starved he must be. He's remaining in control, sucking Mathias's neck like he doesn't want to do any damage, and he's being as delicate as possible. It's almost sensual, like I'm watching two tentative lovers.

And Mathias, well, Mathias is moaning and groaning and when I tear my eyes away from Solon and look down, I see that Mathias has a fucking huge hard-on in those swim trunks.

Holy shit.

This might be the most strangely sexy thing I've ever seen. Solon sucking on a hot young guy's neck, both of them bare chested, one with a huge erection. I have to press my thighs together to quell the sharp ache that's building, the need to get off.

Before I know what's happening, I'm walking over to Mathias and dropping to my knees, very aware of his hard-on beside my head. Solon's eyes widen as he stares down at me and I know he thinks I'm about to give the guy a blow job, and while I'm glad to see Solon looking fearful and possessive, that's not the case at all.

I just want to feed from him the same time that Solon is.

I want to share this with him.

I run my hand up along Mathias's soft inner thigh, my

fingers skimming along where his femoral artery is, my fingertips tingling when they feel the pump of his blood underneath, making sure I don't hit the artery or he'd probably bleed out and die.

When I've found a safe spot, my teeth sink into his skin and I suck back, drawing out the blood. I gulp it down in small amounts, trying not to take too much, and I look up at Solon through my lashes, watching him feed as he watches me feed.

God, there's nothing hotter than this. I wonder too if Solon is hard and I'm picturing his cock large and rigid, pressed up against Mathias's ass, the way he'd press up against me. I'm watching as Solon's chest skims over Mathias's back, how tightly Solon holds him now, a hand slipping down over Mathias's waist, Solon's skin many shades lighter than his is.

All the while Solon keeps his eyes locked on mine while he drinks and drinks.

But then, the more he takes, the rougher he becomes.

His grip tightens around Mathias's waist, his teeth sink in a little deeper, and I watch as Solon's eyes go black as he starts to succumb to the bloodlust.

He's a powerful vampire with teeth that will always be sharper than mine, and a powerful, lockjaw kind of bite. I know this from personal experience. I can survive it when Solon's feeding gets out of control, but Mathias is human and he cannot.

I pull back, wiping my mouth with the back of my hand. "Solon," I manage to say. "Stop. You're going to kill him."

Solon's nostrils flare with anger and it only makes him grab Mathias harder, drink deeper, enough that Mathias's skin starts to pale before my eyes, his face looking ragged, gaunt, and he's starting to gasp for breath. I'm watching Solon drain the life out of him, and the last thing I want is for another human to die because of us. I'm supposed to be aligned with the light, not the dark.

"Stop!" I say louder, getting to my feet. "Solon, he's dying!"

I reach out and grab his arm, but he's wound so tight that I can't pull him off.

There's only one thing I can do.

I bring my wrist to my mouth and I bite it, the pain sharp, my teeth sharper. I bite and tear and create a jagged hole in my wrist, blood pouring freely.

Then I hold it out to Solon.

"Me," I plead. "Feed from me. That's how it's supposed to be."

Fear returns to his eyes, fear of losing control. He'd rather kill this innocent volunteer than risk the beast being let loose.

But I would rather he take the risk.

"Do it!" I yell at him, my voice cracking, bringing my wrist right up against his mouth and letting the blood drip on his lips.

That's all it takes.

Suddenly, Solon unhooks his fangs from Mathias's neck, who wobbles unsteadily on his feet before slumping to the ground, and then Solon is grabbing my arm tight, bringing my wrist to his mouth. He bites me with a ravenous frenzy, his eyes alternating between wild instinct and guilt.

"It's okay," I tell him softly, trying to soothe him in much the same way that I tried to soothe the beast. "Feed from me. I need you to. My blood belongs to you. I belong to you."

And that's an understatement. The feeling of him taking from me, consuming me, taking my lifeforce in order to sustain his is a feeling like no other. I've said it so many times, but the blood is love. This is love. Blood that gives, blood that saves.

Eventually, Solon's grip on my arm loosens, his drinking slows, and a clarity comes back into his eyes, though they still burn with raw intensity.

"I've missed this," I whisper to him, reaching out and brushing his hair off his forehead, marveling at how close we are, how much I've needed him like this. "I—"

In the blink of an eye, Solon pulls my wrist away from his mouth, then grabs my face, holding me in his big, strong hands, and kisses me with blood-stained lips.

I whimper into his mouth, my body responding to his like a match being struck and I'm burning all over, my skin begging to feel his skin, my blood desperate to join his. I run my hands over his chest, over his arms, relishing the feel of his cool skin, his taut muscles, and then he's groaning so deeply into my mouth that it makes my toes curl in my shoes.

We're moving backward, hands roaming desperately, clothes being torn from my body, my fingers frantic as they undo his pants, until I fall backward onto the circular bed.

We can't stand to be apart now for even a moment. I'm completely naked and so is he and he's climbing over me and I'm pulling him to me, needing to feel him against me, needing to feel him inside me.

"Lenore," he whispers harshly, "I can't promise you..."

I dig my nails into his ass, shrugging him against me, wanting his cock inside me so fucking bad that I might go mad right here. "I know," I say, pulling his face down, kissing him deeply, our tongues writhing against each other. *Fuck me, please*, I plead inside my head.

"We're not alone," he says gruffly.

I manage to raise my head to look at Mathias. He's alive, thankfully, and slumped against the wall, holding his hand to his neck. But his other hand is on his hard cock, rubbing it through his shorts. Watching us.

Let him watch.

I look back to Solon. "Does it look like I care?" My voice has gone low and throaty with lust.

He apparently doesn't either because he's kissing me again, rough and violent and deep, our mouths starved for each other for so long. The kiss is unleashing everything I've kept buried, all we've kept pent-up and kept under control.

This kiss is pure chaos.

Then Solon is spreading my legs with a rough swipe of his hand and positioning his cock and he doesn't waste a minute. He pushes inside me with one hard, powerful thrust, all the way to the hilt, knocking the air out of my lungs.

I cry out, the sound filling the room, and Solon lets loose a low rumble from deep in his chest. He's so big, so hard, and in so deep that I feel like he's literally fucked my brains out of me and I'm lying here stunned, expanding around him.

"Fuck," he growls into my ear, his lips nipping at my lobe. "I've missed this. Missed your sweet, beautiful cunt, Lenore."

I blink at his dirty talk, cheeks flaming, forgetting how he can be sometimes, when his decorum slips and he loses his control. I also know that loss of control contributes to the beast, but right now I just want him to fuck the hell out of me, I want to get off until I'm screaming from it, the beast be damned.

He lifts his head, staring deep into my eyes, and I see so much lust and love and passion in his gaze that it causes shivers to run down my spine, even though my body feels like it's burning up, getting hotter by each aching second.

Then he pulls out for a moment before thrusting back in and I'm gasping and he's diving right into a punishing rhythm, driving in deeper and deeper, like I'm being impaled into the mattress. I run my nails down his back, hard enough to draw blood, feeling the tight, powerful muscles as he moves into me. He's in me so deep that I feel like we'll be forever joined, and yet it's not enough. I need more, so much more. Body and heart and soul.

"You have them," he rasps, bringing his mouth over my breast, biting my nipple until my breath hitches. "You have all of me. Always."

He kisses me again, my blood on his lips, then he brackets me between his elbows and I marvel at the way his arms look, shoulders straining, veins visible over his ropey muscles as he starts fucking me even harder. His face contorts with the effort, mouth open, breath ragged, and the bed starts to move.

I reach down between our writhing bodies, trying to give myself a helping hand, but Solon lets out a growl of protest. Before I can move, he's pulling out of me and picking me up by the waist, flipping me over so I'm on all fours, facing Mathias, and Solon is behind me now, pulling my ass toward him.

Mathias is still on the floor, has his cock out now and he's stroking himself, watching the two of us fuck, eyes glazed over. I have a vague thought that perhaps this is wrong somehow, that this is far beyond what I'm used to with sex, even with someone like Solon, but the thought doesn't stay. The truth is, I like that he's watching us, and since we just fed from him, have his blood circulating in our systems, it feels like we already know each other on a very personal level.

"You can watch him all you want," Solon says gruffly as his grip bruises the sides of my waist, his cock pressed against me, sliding over where I'm so slick and dripping wet. "But don't forget who's fucking you."

With those growling words he thrusts inside me again and I let out a garbled cry that turns into a moan as he fills me, turning me whole, obliterating my senses.

"You like that, don't you?" he whispers, and suddenly he's reaching forward and wrapping a strong hand around my throat, pulling me back off the bed so my back is arched and I'm on my knees. "You like how deep I'm inside you. How my cock claims every inch of you."

His grip on my throat tightens and he yanks my head back even further so that his mouth is at my ear, his dick driving in even deeper from this angle, hitting all the aching nerves inside me. "You belong to me, Lenore. Every fucking inch of your tight little cunt is mine, always will be. Not his, not anyone else's." He pulls out and pushes in so hard I'm swearing, the sounds choking in my throat as he crushes my windpipe, my breasts jostling as he picks up the pace.

"Tell me I'm yours, moonshine," he rasps through a low groan, breath hot at my ear as he drives in and out of me, his hips powerful and relentless as they smack my ass. "Tell me you belong to me."

"I belong to you," I try to say, but he's choking me so hard that I can't even talk. Guess I don't need to. He knows.

He responds by letting out a deep rumbling moan and reaches down over my stomach, his fingers sliding over my clit.

"Holy fuck," I cry out, his grip loosening enough for me to scream, and then he's fucking me even harder and I have no choice but to let go. I watch as Mathias starts stroking his dick harder, mouth open, and then he's coming, his cum shooting out in a hot arc, the smell filling the room.

I come seconds later, so hard that I think I might actually have a heart attack, the orgasm ripping through me as Solon's fingers glide over my sweet spot, as his cock strokes every sensitive hollow inside me, as Mathias continues to come from watching us fuck like the wild animals we are.

"Jesus, my god!" I scream, the waves hitting me over and over, and Solon keeps up his punishing pace and I can't stop coming, I'm just a mess of cries and strangled words of release and endless moans. My body is shaking, trembling, skin hot and tight, until I feel completely boneless and brainless.

"Lenore," Solon whispers harshly at my neck. "Oh fuck. I'm coming." His voice trails off as his breath catches.

Then he bites me.

Just as I thought he would.

Just as I hoped he would.

His fangs pierce the skin on the back of my neck, sending another wave of pleasure through my already spent body, and then he's sucking back my blood while he comes. He groans loudly into my skin as he feeds from me, in such a way that I feel it vibrating in the marrow of my bones, and then I feel him coming inside me, hot and hard and filling every inch.

His hips pump hard, once, then again, the air leaving my lungs, and then he's breathing hard through his nose as he continues to drink me and I'm left in another state. One of pure bliss, pure sex, pure love. I'm beyond all the worlds right now.

Finally, he pulls his teeth out of my neck, then gently places a kiss on the wound, his lips trailing to my jaw as he lets go of my throat and grabs my chin instead, pulling my head to the side. He kisses my mouth from the side, hot and open and messy.

And mine again.

It takes a moment to realize what just happened. We had sex. Emotional, pent-up, overdue, wild, hedonistic sex in front of a stranger. In the Red World.

But more than that, we just had sex...and the beast didn't make an appearance. I know I might not be so lucky next time, but this time...we made it.

"I think we dodged a bullet there," Solon says, his voice low and rough as his hand drifts down over my breasts, over my waist, until he's pulling out of me, leaving me with an empty feeling, my body already wanting him back inside.

I nearly collapse onto the bed but Solon wraps his arms around me, lowering me gently before flipping me over so I'm on my back.

He stares down at me, his eyes sated and soft, crinkling at the corners, his mouth lifted in a small satisfied smile. "I don't regret a thing."

"You better not," I tell him. "I can't do that again. I can't go without you. I'd rather take my risks and my chances."

His smile falls, gaze turning remorseful as he looks at my chest, at the marks the beast left. "But the risks are too great, my dear. The scars remind me of what I did, what I can do, what might happen again."

I reach up and put my hand on his face, my fingertips pressing into his cheekbones, feeling the heat in his flushed cheeks, a rare feeling. "It wasn't you Solon. It was the beast who left them. And I don't let these scars remind me of what the monster did. I let them remind me of what I can survive."

"You are a survivor," he says gravely.

"And I'm yours. To the end of time. I told you we'd make it work, and we will. But I'm not going to face your father without having you with me like this. I need *you* to be the best I can be. You're my strength. And I know I'm yours too."

He seems to melt for a moment. "You are. You are, Lenore."

Then a movement catches his eye and he looks up at Mathias behind us. "Fuck. I forgot all about him."

"What happened to liking your feedings private?" I ask him playfully.

"Well," he says with a small shrug, looking back down at me. "When in Rome."

15

LENORE

I SLEEP LIKE THE DEAD.

Maybe it's the jet lag, maybe it's the fact that I fed yesterday, not just from Mathias, but from Solon as well, satisfying a hunger that had slowly been burning out of control. Or maybe it was the fact that my other hunger, the physical one for my lover, the one that burned the hottest and brightest, was finally put out.

I gave everything I had to Solon yesterday, over and over again, tempting fate, tempting that beast, each and every time we came. After we had sex in front of Mathias, we left the Red World and went back to the hotel where we fell into bed for hours on end, screwing each other silly, making up for all the lost time.

I'm sore and sated and...fuck, I'm happy. Happiest I've felt in a long time. I hang onto the feeling because I know that it will have to sustain me. The both of us are walking into a situation where we don't have the upper hand, something we might not come back from.

Don't even think about it, I tell myself. *Hang on to what's happening now.*

I feel the bed move from beside me, and I open my eyes to darkness and my eyes quickly adjust. I have no idea what time it is, because of the jet lag and the blackout curtains, but it doesn't really matter because Solon is reaching across and sliding his palm over my stomach, right between my legs. Despite having just woken up, I'm already wet as sin.

"Look at you," Solon murmurs, his eyes coasting over my face, pausing at my mouth, before sliding over my breasts, to my pussy. "Look at how fucking perfect you are." He removes his hand, admiring how shiny and slick his fingers are, before running his tongue over them, sucking them in his mouth. "I'll never get my fill of you, my dear."

"Good," I say, grinning at him like the fool in love that I am.

He grins right back, a rare but beautiful smile that knocks the wind out of me, and then he's climbing on top of me, his head sinking between my legs. He takes his time down there, licks me out, biting and feeding, until I'm coming a million times over. Then when I'm absolutely dizzy with my orgasms, he's inside me again, working me like a tireless machine until the hotel room fills with our primal cries.

We repeat this all morning, until eventually we find ourselves in the shower. He shampoos and conditions my hair, which is incredibly sensual, and then I do the same to him before ending it with a well-deserved blow job.

There's a knock at the door just as we're stepping out of the shower. Solon frowns briefly as he slips on the fluffy hotel robe, and then relaxes. "It's them."

"Who is them?" I ask, toweling off.

"Kaleid, Natalia, and Valtu," he says. He leaves the washroom, shutting the door behind him, and I slip on my robe, tying it tight. Yesterday might have been extremely voyeuristic, but I don't feel like giving everyone a peep show. I then quickly put my wet hair in a towel and step out into the room.

Kaleid, Natalia, and Valtu are standing in the middle of it, talking with Solon. It's jarring seeing Dracula in clothes, since the only impression I have of him is one where he's completely naked and coming into some chick's mouth. He's a snappy dresser though, a crisp black shirt and white linen pants, brown loafers without socks, and his hair, which was wavy and wild yesterday, is now carefully groomed.

I stand there for a moment, watching the four of them, hit with the awestruck feeling that I'm staring at a big piece of history. Kaleid, Natalia, and Solon are practically ageless and all direct children of Skarde, and I'm sure Dracula has been around for centuries as well. They're all well-oiled killing machines, powerful animals that could easily wipe humans out if they wanted to. Sure, they need them for sustenance, but who is to say vampires of their caliber, shaped and molded by hundreds of years of unique life experience as cunning and wealthy predators, couldn't kill most of the humans on the planet and enslave the rest, farming them the same way that humans farm cattle?

I shudder at the thought. It's only by the grace of god that these four wouldn't do that, and even then I can only really be sure about Solon. He's the outsider in this group, and outsider to the vampire world in general. No one likes a bounty hunter that makes a living in trading vampires to witches in exchange for magic.

And yet, Solon is here. Perhaps because he's more powerful than the rest of them, maybe because of being the first turned vampire, or maybe because of the magic he's accrued.

Or maybe he's only here because you're here, I tell myself.

At that, Solon looks my way and beckons me over. "You're a part of this, Lenore. Come over here."

I swallow, feeling nervous all of a sudden in their presence, especially when Kaleid, Natalia, and Dracula all look at me at once, their eyes piercing. To see them in the Red World was one thing, but to have them in the real world, in my hotel room—I'm aware of how dangerous this group could be to someone like me.

Fuck, I better be doing the right thing.

Kaleid smirks, as if he heard me. "We were just discussing the plan. Since you and Solon left so abruptly yesterday, you missed out on what I'd talked to Valtu and Natalia about. But, I have to say, you're both looking the picture of health now."

"Far less ugly," Dracula comments, eying Solon.

"So what's the plan?" I ask, folding my arms across my chest.

"The four of us will leave tonight," Kaleid says. "We'll take my jet. It'll take us as far as Tromso in Norway, above the Arctic Circle. Our father had been living in a village, hidden in the Red World, but he's moved on. Further north. Into deeper worlds."

"There are deeper worlds?" I ask, but just as the words leave my lips, I hear Jeremias in my head. *We are in one of the many worlds available to you, dear daughter. Worlds that exist, if only you know where to look.*

"Ones that Skarde created himself," Natalia says in her monotone voice. "Some, like the Red World, we have access to. Others we don't."

"So how do we get access, exactly?" Solon asks. "Because getting dropped off in the Arctic Circle and just sniffing out the woods like bloodhounds doesn't sound like much of a plan."

"It'll work," Kaleid says determinedly. "I can always tell where father has been. It's been a long time for you, Solon, but I have no doubt it will be the same. Perhaps even stronger. You're not, well, diluted in the same way I am. We'll pick up the trail, we'll find out where he entered the other world."

"And again, how do we get access?" Solon asks. "If his worlds aren't open to everyone, what makes you think they'll open to us?"

"Because of her," Dracula says, eyeing me intently. "Because we have his bride."

A wave of revulsion washes over me.

"He'll know we're coming," Natalia notes.

"I'm counting on it," Kaleid says.

"Uh, excuse me," I say, raising my hand. "Bait speaking. If he's going to know we're coming for him, then why wouldn't he wipe us all out?"

Natalia shakes her head. "He would, I'm sure. If he could. But we don't think his new army can leave his world. We would have seen them already."

"Okay, but the Dark Order was his army too and they got on a fucking airplane to get me," I say.

"Actually, the Dark Order travel through interdimensional space. Much like your father does," Kaleid points out.

"How do you know that?" I ask.

He blinks at me, and for a moment I can't read his expression. It's enough though that Solon is studying him closely, a line between his brows. "Everyone knows that about Jeremias," he says. "You're new, Lenore. You have a lot of catching up to do."

"Well, she better do it quick," Dracula says, playing with the shiny silver Rolex on his wrist. "Because if we leave tonight, that doesn't give us a lot of time to prepare."

"And how do you suggest we prepare?" Kaleid asks, crossing his arms. "There are no maps to study. No battles to plan out. We just have to go and see what happens."

"This is the worst type of plan," Solon says in a low voice.

"I forget you don't know how to be spontaneous," Kaleid

says. "Listen, we don't need weapons, we don't need anything."

"Well I at least need to pack," I tell them.

Natalia laughs. "You think you're going to bring a suitcase up there? Silly girl, this is not that kind of trip. We will be hiking through the woods for who knows how long. And once we're in the other world? We have no idea what will be waiting for us."

"Oh great," I say, pasting on a fake smile. But I'm still bringing my toothbrush. Vampires don't have to worry about putting on deodorant or brushing their teeth, because they never get obnoxious body odor and their teeth never get stained or decay. But I'm still part human and I refuse to be the stinky offensive one of the group.

"We still need to figure out what to do if we get into his world," Solon says. "We can't just stroll in there with Lenore."

Kaleid puts his hand on Solon's shoulder and gives it a squeeze. "And that's why you're here, big brother. You're the brains of the operation now. You can figure that out in the meantime."

Solon glances at me, and for once I don't see that cool brazen confidence that he normally carries. He looks a little lost.

This isn't going to be easy.

* * *

AT EIGHT THAT NIGHT, the five of us board Kaleid's private jet and we fly northwest to where the sun literally doesn't set. As the plane touches down on the outskirts of Tromso, a surprisingly large city surrounded by mountains that disappear into the shimmering Arctic Ocean, I can understand why the vampires have to retreat into the darker worlds during the summer months. Though the ones I know tolerate sun just fine, I'm sure that tolerance would turn into twenty-four seven annoyance in the land where the sun barely dips down between midnight and one a.m.

We get off the plane and are picked up by another mysterious driver in a large black SUV, and we're taken out of the city, along deep blue fjords and snow-capped mountain ranges, heading east.

We don't talk a lot during the drive, all of us caught in our own heads as the sun briefly sets and then pops right back up, the sky always a pale blue, the stars never making an appearance. Something about this all is so magical. My vampire side doesn't like it, but my witch side, I can feel it coming alive. It wants to be with the sun, it wants to be running across streams and fields, becoming one with mother nature. There's a wildness inside me that wants to be unleashed, and for the first time in a long time, I have this glowing feeling deep inside, coming from the well. But it isn't darkness, it's full of light.

Solon reaches for my hand and holds it tight, giving it a squeeze that makes my stomach flip.

Your energy is radiant, he says inside my head, gazing at me with adoration. *What happened?*

I don't know, I tell him, smiling. *This land. There's something about it that's making me feel awake inside. I can feel the magic brewing.*

I can feel it too, he says. *Keep it going.* He eyes the rest of the vampires who are all looking out the window at the passing forests. *We're probably going to need it.*

The car eventually comes to a stop down the end of a long logging road. We all get out of the car and Kaleid nods at a small path that disappears into a forest of pine.

"This way," he says, taking the lead.

I look at Solon. "Are you picking anything up?"

He presses his lips together, face contorting in a

grimace as he nods. "Yes," he says with disdain. "I can...feel that he's been here. It's more than just smelling him, it's...a *knowing*."

"I told you so," Kaleid says over his shoulder. "You're still connected to Skarde in ways you never dreamed. Now, let's get going so we can sever that connection for good."

Natalia follows Kaleid, and I get behind her, Solon behind me, with Dracula at the rear. We walk single file into the woods and as the midnight sun reaches the tops of the trees, filtering into the moss and woodland bushes, I feel that energy fluttering inside me again. This is definitely a land where witches prevail. There's so much sustenance here, it's flowing through me.

We walk through the woods like this for at least a couple of hours, the sweet smell of the pine filling my soul, the sunlight giving me power where it seems to drain the rest of them a little. The well inside me feels like it's growing larger in volume, and instead of the crescent moon I usually see reflected on the inky surface, now I see the sun. It's almost blinding.

Suddenly I hear Solon make a surprised sound from behind me and I look over my shoulder in time to see a giant moth flutter out of the forest, heading straight for me.

I stop dead and instinctively hold out my arm, and the moth comes right for me. It's the same death hawk moth as before, and by same, I mean the exact same one that I saw in San Francisco. I can just tell. Like Solon, I know something innately in ways I can't explain.

The moth lands on my hand, it's wings slowly flapping, the antennae pointed my way, curious.

"That bastard is huge," Dracula says, and he's coming at me, hand outstretched, ready to crush the bug against me.

Then Solon's arm shoots out and he grabs Dracula's wrist, stopping him at the last minute. "Don't you fucking dare," Solon roars at him, eyes like daggers. "That's her familiar."

"Her what?" Natalia asks, coming over to us.

"Yeah, what?" I repeat, staring at the moth as it stares back at me. "My familiar?"

"You're still a witch, moonshine," Solon says to me, reluctantly letting go of Dracula, who nurses his hurt wrist. "All witches have a familiar."

"Yeah, but a familiar is like a cat or a fox or something… not…a bug," I protest.

"Ugly fucking bug at that," Kaleid says. There's a hint of menace in his voice that puts me on edge. From the way Solon tenses briefly, I think he feels the same.

"So what does it do?" Natalia asks. "And how do you know what it is?"

"I've seen it around Lenore before," Solon says, to my surprise.

"You have?" I ask. "Because I've only seen it twice."

"You weren't looking for it before," he says. "Or you weren't ready to see it. The familiar will make itself known when the witch is ready. I've spent enough time with your kind to know how it all works. I'm sure your parents would have told you had you asked."

"Jeremias never said anything."

"He wouldn't have a familiar," Solon says darkly. "They aren't powerful enough for him. He would have apprentices."

The image of the matching black-haired girls in their white dresses comes back to me. The way they slithered out of the ground, how identical and strange they were. I'm starting to wonder if they were even human at all.

As I ponder that, the moth takes flight again, disappearing into the forest.

"Where is it going?" I ask, suddenly feeling bereft at its absence, like it was anchoring me to my old life, something safe and comforting. "Don't I need it for something? Isn't it supposed to help me?"

"Maybe it can't help you yet," Solon says, placing his hand around my waist for a moment. "Maybe it's just letting you know it's there."

Kaleid clears his throat and glowers at us. "Well, enough talk about a fucking moth. We need to get going." He turns and starts walking again.

"Bossy fucker," Dracula mumbles from behind us.

After the incident with the moth though, it feels like something has changed. The further we go into the forest, the longer we walk, the less sunny and magical it feels. Oh, there's definitely an energy here, but it's not one from the light. It's one from the dark.

And there are mosquitos, too. Tons of them, huge ones, and they all keep buzzing around me. I spend every five seconds swatting at them while Dracula laughs at my antics. Asshole. Bloodsuckers are apparently not a problem for the other bloodsuckers, but they're still a problem to me, probably because my witch side—my human side—feels stronger than ever.

Do you feel that? Solon pops into my head as we walk.

Being eaten alive by mosquitos? Yeah, I feel it. And no, I don't like it.

No, he says. *Not the mosquitos.*

The darkness?

Yes. The darkness. The change. We're getting close, he says. *Things are going to get strange.*

I almost laugh. What could possibly be considered strange with these vamps?

But, after a while, I get what Solon meant.

Because the forest gets darker, like the sun has set again, like it can never reach this place, and I'm getting the creeping feeling that we aren't alone. I keep looking at the forest, peering through the dark trees, but I don't see anything. The feeling is strangely familiar though, like I'm being looked at by something that's looked at me before, if that makes any sense.

Are there things in the trees? I ask Solon. *I feel like we're being watched.*

We are being watched, he says, so simply that I nearly stop walking.

By who?

By what, you mean, he says. *I don't want to think about them. They get stronger when you do.*

Oh my god.

Kaleid shoots us an annoyed look over his shoulder, like he can tell I'm about to stop out of fear.

Keep going, Solon says. *Don't think about anything.*

Right. Like that's ever been easy for me.

Somehow I keep going, though now the trees are opening up a little and the ground is turning marshy, sucking at the bottoms of my boots, and we make our way through tall reeds.

"Careful," Kaleid shouts at us. "We're in the land of the old ones now. Just keep to the middle of the path and keep walking."

"What are the old ones?" I ask, feeling frantic now.

But no one answers me.

Solon! I yell in my head. *What are the old ones? Are they the ones who were watching us earlier?*

No, he says after a moment, and that's all he says.

Well fuck.

And that's when I see it. I'm watching Natalia as she walks forward, sticking to the middle of the marshy path, when suddenly hands reach out from the marsh, trying to grab her legs.

I scream. I can't help it.

"What the fuck!" I yelp, just as the hands start reaching for me now, grey hands that are twisted like branches, leaves sprouting from their skin in patches, hands that are swiping at the air, so many of them just coming from the reeds, no sign of who or what they belong to. Hands that want to drag me away.

"Keep walking!" Solon says roughly, hands at my back, pushing me forward.

I look over my shoulder at him and Dracula, both of them staring dead ahead, chins high, ignoring the hands reaching for them. On closer inspection though, there is fear in their eyes. Great.

I stumble forward, wondering why the hell we're all walking. "Why aren't we running?" I ask, shrieking again at a close call.

"Because if we run, then it'll draw the Lapp Witches out," Kaleid says.

"It's too late," Solon says. "I've already seen them."

"Shit," Natalia swears, glancing at us over her shoulder. "When?"

"Last while. They've been watching us from the forest. Keep walking Lenore, you're doing good. Just ignore them."

"Ignore the disembodied hands?" I yelp.

"I told you things would get strange."

"Fucking understatement, don't you think?" I snipe, just as another hand nearly gets my leg.

Finally the reeds start to flatten out, the hands fading with them, and then Kaleid comes to a stop.

In front of us is a lake.

A lake of blood.

At least, it looks like blood. It's all red, stretching out toward the forest on the other side.

"What the hell?" I ask.

"The lake of blood," Kaleid says, as if I know what that means.

"Is it real blood?" I ask.

He nods grimly. "But don't drink from it."

"I'm not drinking from it. I'm not going anywhere near it."

His face breaks into a grin. "Oh, don't you realize it, Lenore? We're all going in it. This is the way into his world."

My eyes widen in fear and I look to Solon for explanation. "He's kidding, right?"

Solon's jaw clenches for a moment but he shakes his head. "Unfortunately, he's telling the truth. This is where Skarde went. This is how we get to him."

"We have to go into that!" I ask, pointing wildly to the lake. I look to Natalia to back me up. "You're okay with this?"

She shrugs. "I'd rather not, but if we have to then we have to."

"So, what then, it's like the lost city of Atlantis at the bottom or what?" I ask.

"You dive in, and you dive right through to the other world," Kaleid says with an edge to his voice, his patience being tested. "You'll come out the other side. But we need to hurry. If the Lapp Witches…" then he trails off, his eyes locked on the space behind us.

The skin at the back of my neck prickles and now I know whatever Kaleid is looking at is bad. Very bad.

I take in a deep breath and turn around.

In the forest behind us are several figures standing between the trees. They are tall, thin, dressed in black cloaks, and have human skeleton hands.

And they have deer skulls for heads, sharp antlers sprouting from the top, their empty black sockets staring at us. It feels like they're staring into my soul, stirring something in the well, something I don't like.

I know these creatures. I've met them before.

"Jeremias," I whisper, reaching over for Solon's hand and holding on tight. "I've seen them with Jeremias."

"These are the Lapp Witches," Kaleid says. "We're in their territory. Same as the *vanha väki*. The old ones. We've crossed across the border back into Finland."

I'm about to ask why this is the Lapp Witch territory if I've seen them in San Francisco, but I know that where Jeremias took me doesn't exist in any place in this world. Seems I'm able to do interdimensional travel too.

"What do they want with us?" Natalia asks. "They're just staring."

"They belong to Skarde," Solon says in a low voice. "I can tell."

And just like that, the deer skull creatures start walking out of the woods, coming toward us. There's about seven of them, and they seem to glide, their feet never touching the ground.

"Oh, fuck," Dracula swears, his body tensing, as if ready for a fight. Solon's grip on my hand tightens. Natalia looks ready to run. Only Kaleid seems completely calm about all of this.

"Do you need me to light them up?" I ask, not taking my eyes away from the deer people. "I can do what I did with the Dark Order. Solon and I were a team."

"No," Kaleid says firmly. "We might need them. They might be our ticket in."

We all watch as they come over, but then they split. Three of them grab Solon, wrapping their boney skeleton hands around his shoulders, while another three do the same to Dracula, pulling them to the side.

"What are they doing?!" I yell, ready to throw down. I start going for Solon, to help him, even though he's just letting it happen.

But then one of the deer skull creatures is in front of me, palm out, pushing me back with an invisible force. I stare into the empty eye sockets, dark black holes that swirl into a void, and I feel like the world is starting to spin.

You're coming with us, a metallic voice says from deep inside of me, and I know it's coming from the creature. *You're coming to see Skarde.*

"Lenore," Solon's voice breaks through. "Don't stare too deeply."

I blink and shake my head, taking a step back until I bump into Natalia. She reaches out and grabs my hand for comfort as the deer skull continues to stare at us.

"They have to stay behind," Kaleid says. "Solon and Valtu. They won't let them come with us."

"Then Lenore isn't going either," Solon says angrily. He tries to get out of the grasp of those skeleton hands, but he can't. If these are witches, dark, dark witches, then they have power over everyone here.

Except maybe me.

But yeah, probably me too. I'm not that special.

"She has to go," Kaleid says. "If we want to do this properly."

"Then we don't do it properly," he snarls. "We don't do it at all."

"Solon," I say to him. "I'll be okay."

He blinks at me. "How the hell can you say that?"

"What, don't you trust me?" Kaleid asks.

"With *her* life? No. I don't trust anyone with her life." Solon looks at me pleadingly. "Lenore, don't do this. You don't have to."

But then the deer skull creature reaches out further and places its awful hand on my shoulder and I immediately have no control of my body anymore, like a puppet on a string.

I swallow hard, fear swarming my chest. I look at Solon. "I think I do have to."

"She doesn't have a choice now," Kaleid says.

"And this was your fucking idea!" Solon booms at him.

"Hey, hey," Natalia says. "None of us knew what would happen once we got to the other world. We didn't know how we would get there. This is how we get there. Look, Solon, I don't like this any more than you do, especially with these fucking *things*, but if we're going to do what we set out to do, then this is the only way."

"Well, I for one am glad to be sitting this one out," Dracula says.

"Yeah, and I'm only here because of you," Natalia says to him, a hint of rare emotion in her voice, and if I had any brain cells to spare, I'd wonder about their relationship. I'm pretty good at picking up on unrequited love these days.

"Come on," Kaleid says, though I'm not sure he's talking to us or to the Lapp Witches. It doesn't matter though because the one holding onto me starts leading me to the lake's edge. I want to turn my head to look at Solon one more time, but I can't. I can't do anything but move forward. I can't do anything except what this creature wants me to do.

I'll come for you, Solon's voice comes into my head. *I'll come for you, just stay safe. Do what you can to stay safe and I'll find you, I will.*

There is so much horror in his voice that it unravels me, whatever strength and resolve starting to come apart at the worst possible time, as the red water laps at my toes.

I'll be okay, I tell him. *I'll destroy him for you. I promise you that.*

Moonshine, he says, my nickname breaking in pain. *I love you. I love you.*

For the ages, I say. I want to close my eyes, sink deeper into those words in my head, let his love wash over me, bolster me, strengthen me.

But I can't. I can't even control my eyes. I'm just a puppet. I'm walking into the blood, it is rising up around my ankles, my calves, past my knees, my feet sinking into something slimy and soft, and oh god, this is awful. The stench is revolting.

"Ew," Natalia says, and while I can't turn my head to look at her, I can see her and Kaleid in my peripheral, walking into the bloody lake on either side of me.

The water rises higher and higher.

The bottom disappears.

I sink into the lake of blood and leave the world—and Solon—behind.

16

ABSOLON

I DON'T THINK I'VE EVER FELT SUCH FEAR. AND THAT IS SAYING a lot, considering what I've seen since my monstrous beginnings so many centuries ago.

But to see Lenore, my love for the ages, walk into the lake of blood, led by a Lapp Witch, accompanied by my two siblings whom I don't trust, heading to see my father Skarde, to be used as bait, I…

"I should have never let her come," I say, to no one in particular, watching the lake as their heads disappear beneath the bloody surface. The ripples from their movement cease and the lake goes still.

My heart goes still as well.

"Well, I don't know your girlfriend very well," Valtu says from beside me. "But I got the impression that she would do whatever the hell she wanted to, no matter what you said about it."

I glance at him, briefly taking in the three Lapp Witches that have him in their grasp, the same way that three are holding onto me. Their magic is far too powerful for us to break through.

"Did you know about this?" I ask him.

Valtu frowns. "About what? That Lapp Witches would appear and hold us hostage for no reason at all?"

I stare at him, studying him closely. Valtu has always been a slippery one and owns his shadiness proudly, which in a way makes him harder to read than someone like Kaleid. "Did you know that we wouldn't be able to travel into that world?" I ask eventually.

He shakes his head. "No. I'm not upset about it, but I can tell you are."

"Lenore has gone on without me. To be used as *bait*," I seethe, anger starting to bubble in my veins, but I'm not sure who the anger is directed to. Most likely myself.

Valtu eyes me. "You knew that was the plan, even before you got here."

"Not without me," I say gruffly.

"You think you can protect her from Skarde?" he asks with a snort of disbelief. "I know you're the first made, Solon, but give me a break."

"And so you think Kaleid and Natalia can do it?"

"With them alone..." he says. There's something in his voice, something I don't like.

I bristle. "What do you know, Valtu? You're not telling me the whole truth here."

He doesn't say anything and looks away.

"You fuck!" I roar, trying to get at him, to tackle him, rip his throat out, but the Lapp Witches have a tight hold on me and I'm powerless against them. "Fuck you! What do you know? Did she just walk off to her death?"

He gives me a stiff smile "Probably not. No one is lying to you, Solon. We all want Skarde out of the picture. His time has come. It's time to destroy the kingdom that created us. And Lenore is needed to do that. Skarde wants her, and she's no good to him dead." He licks his lips and attempts to give me a pitying look. "Kaleid will make sure she stays alive."

"As will I," a deep, rich voice comes from the forest behind us. The Lapp Witches tighten their grip and turn us around to face the intruder.

There is a man in black, who smells like death, who has a moving, changing face, a glowing witch's blade at his side.

"Oh, *Christ*," Dracula swears, and from the fear in his voice, I know he didn't plan on this. "This is where I die, isn't it? Right on the shores of that bloody lake, in fucking *Finland*."

"Jeremias," I say as he approaches. His face is mesmerizing, always changing, just as Lenore had described.

"The infamous Absolon Stavig," Jeremias says, stopping in front of us, giving us a predatory smile. "I've heard so much about you I feel like I actually know you. And yet, after all this time, this is the first time we've met. Can you believe that?"

"We run in different crowds," I tell him stiffly.

"Ah, you're trying to be clever but that's actually not true. You do run with the witches Absolon, just as you run with the vampires. I run with the vampires as I do with the witches. As you can see, we are very similar. Perhaps that's why Lenore is so attracted to you, like a moth to a flame." He leans in closer. "Too bad that flame has already singed her wings a little. You know it was me who glued her wings back on, Absolon. Without me, she would have died at your hands."

"I am not the beast," I say through grinding teeth.

"Yes, you are. You are the beast through and through. And my poor daughter, she was almost willing to trade her soul to save you. Did you know that I would have made it so that she could control you? That she could prevent you from ever hurting her again? But she wouldn't do it. She wouldn't succumb to the dark side."

"You sound like the fucking emperor, you know that?" Valtu comments derisively.

"I *am* an emperor," Jeremias says, not picking up on the Star Wars reference. "And I do what any good emperor does to stay in power. I expand. Tell me, Absolon, do you really think that Kaleid has any power to destroy your father? If he did, don't you think he would have done so by now?"

I stare at him. "You're working with Kaleid?"

He smirks. "Bit slow on the uptake. Yes. I am."

"Double-crosser," Valtu mutters angrily.

"Kaleid?" Jeremias asks. "I suppose he's a double-crosser if you think working with a witch is worthy of being called a traitor. To that end, I assume you would think the same of Absolon here."

"I do," Valtu says, glaring. "He is a traitor. I barely tolerate him."

Jeremias' expression turns to pity as he glances at me. "You're not very well-liked, Mr. Stavig. I can see why you prefer to stay in America. In fact, for your sake, that's where you should have stayed."

"Yes. And with Lenore."

He shakes his head. "No. Because she is still part of the plan. Did you know that I put the idea in her head to come here? I told her I foresaw the future, that a man would come for her, needing her help, that she would be instrumental in destroying Skarde. That was a lie, of course. I don't see the future. But I did want her to trust her father enough to take the chance."

There is rage building deep within me, the kind of rage that is hard to come back from. I do all that I can to keep it under control because I can't help Lenore if I don't.

"You don't deserve the privilege of calling her your daughter," I seethe.

He shrugs. "That might be so. It might be that she isn't worthy of calling me her father. She's done nothing worthwhile so far, aside from killing the Dark Order. Somehow, I doubt she'll have the power to destroy them now that they're deep in Skarde's world, close to him, the source of their energy. And she certainly won't be able to do anything if Skarde turns her dark, breeds his army through her." He steps away, the witch's blade going from one hand to the next. "Of course, we won't let that happen."

"We?" I repeat, my eyes glued to the blade, afraid to take my eyes off it in case he's about to plunge it into my heart, which I'm sure he's about to do.

"Me. And Kaleid. He's going to use Lenore to get to Skarde. Then, together, we'll kill him. Kaleid thinks he can just overtake the throne and become the new king. He hasn't said as much to me, but I'm not a fool. I know. I think you both know it too. Of course, I won't let that happen either. I'll kill your brother."

"What about Natalia?" Valtu asks, voice hard.

Jeremias shrugs with one shoulder. "Depends on how Skarde feels about her. But when I get there, if she's not dead yet, I'll kill her myself. And then I'll bring her body to you. Or maybe just her head." He gives him a quick smile.

I swallow thickly. "And Lenore?" I whisper roughly.

"Ah, Lenore," Jeremias says. He takes the blade and leans in, pressing it delicately above my heart. I can feel the blade's energy pulse deep inside me, my skin feeling like it's shrinking, the blood leaving my body. "It always comes back to Lenore, doesn't it? You must actually love her somehow in that black heart of yours."

"You know I do," I manage to say, feeling weaker by the second.

He stares at the blade, twisting it around slowly. Any more pressure and it would pierce my skin. "I don't wish my daughter any harm. But she is still a vampire. And my whole purpose in life is to keep you all in line. Well, I'm tired of doing that, and as you can see from your father, you're getting out of control. An army to take over the world? Ridiculous. No, I won't harm Lenore. She'll be the only vampire on this earth that I'll let survive." He pauses, taking the blade away. "As long as she joins me."

I shake my head, strength returning again in the form of rage. "You know she won't join you."

"Then I'm going to have to kill her, Absolon," he says. "Just as I'm going to kill the two of you. Eventually, anyway."

He puts the blade back in his pocket and starts walking off through the forest. The Lapp Witches lead Valtu and I, never letting go, and I know even if I tried to stop, they'd make my legs move with mind control. I have magic but it's not enough to fight back against them.

"Being led into the woods to die," Valtu mutters. "Nice fucking in-law you have there, Solon."

"Her actual parents are pretty nice," I say absently. My god, I don't know how they're going to take this if something happens to Lenore. She never even told them why she was going to Finland, just that she wanted to go on vacation with me. Obviously, she didn't want them to worry, because they'd try to stop her, just like I should have tried to stop her. I should have tried harder.

If she dies, her death is on my hands.

It's just that I'll probably be already dead by then.

We walk through the woods for what seems like hours, but could be days, could be minutes. All I can think about is how I have spent so long on this earth, dodging death and loss as much as I could, thinking that in time I would be hardened to everything that could try and make me soft.

And then Lenore came along.

And I lost my heart to her right away.

And I knew I would never ever be the same, that my life didn't truly begin until I saw her, until I had her in my life. Until I had her love.

I've never been one to fear death. When it's almost impossible to die, you let that fear go. In some ways, I've always welcomed it, knowing that no creature, not even a vampire, should be subjected to endless life.

But now that I have Lenore, I don't want to give an ounce of it up.

I need her by my side.

I need her as my queen.

I want to spend the ages with her, traveling through time, just the two of us, living forever, living together, until there's some grand explosion in the universe, ending it all for everyone.

And now, unless there's a miracle, that's not going to happen.

I found love and life for the first time, only to lose them both so quickly. The tighter I held on, the more they slipped away, so soft and fragile in my hardened hands.

"You done beating yourself up yet?" Jeremias asks.

I look up to see we've stopped outside a rustic cabin in the woods, a roof of mossy grass on top. "You can hear my thoughts too?" I grumble.

"No," he says. "But you definitely lean into the brooding persona very well."

Valtu has the nerve to actually laugh, which then brings a look from Jeremias. "And you," Jeremias says to him with a sniff, "Bram Stoker would be ashamed."

Then, with a wave of his hands, the door to the cabin opens—magic—and we're led inside.

I don't know why I expected some quaint and simple

216

Finnish cottage, but that's not at all what we've stepped into. Inside, it's long and cavernous and made of stone. There are no windows. It's a whole other place than what can possibly exist on the outside, and for all I know, might be another world entirely.

The only thing in the room are two sets of chains on the stone walls. Big black iron chains with five collars attached. One for the neck. Two for the wrists. Two for the ankles. All the chains are inscribed with wards, making them unbreakable.

So this is our fate.

The Lapp Witches lead us both over to the chains and they place the large one around my neck, keeping my back pressed up against the wall. If my feet ever give out, and they will, it will keep me up, make me hang by my head.

Immediately I feel the wards sink into my skin, rendering the chains strong enough to keep us in place. Vampires have super-human, preternatural strength, but we do have our limits and the magic ensures it's beyond our reach.

"Tell me, Absolon," Jeremias says smoothly, coming over to me. "What happens to a vampire when they don't feed?"

"They become grouchy," Valtu says from his set of chains beside me.

Jeremias ignores him, keeps staring at me with black fathomless eyes, the only thing on his face that doesn't change. "Well?"

"You starve," I manage to say.

"But do you die? No. You don't die, do you? You won't die until I stab you in the heart. But if you don't feed, you will live forever and ever in a state of pain and anguish so great you will be begging me to kill you and release you from this torture. In fact, in your case Absolon, your pain will double, knowing that you'll be stuck here for eternity while Lenore is out there, either dying at my hands or becoming every-thing you hate."

Then he smiles and turns around, heading to the door, the Lapp Witches following him out single file.

"I'll be seeing you one day," Jeremias says, pausing in the doorway. "Let's say, three hundred years from now? Then we'll see where you're at. Perhaps I'll feel charitable by then."

The door closes behind him, sealing us into our doom.

"Fuck," Valtu says, followed by a heavy sigh. "What the hell did we do to piss off that guy? Being stuck with you for eternity? I don't think I've ever heard of something so diabolical."

But I'm not really listening to Valtu. I'm trying to figure out what to do. I have my way with magic, I can control my own wards. Is there any way to work with these?

"Giving me the silent treatment already?" Valtu comments

I glare at him. "I'm trying to think, idiot."

"About how you're going to get us out of here?"

"Yes," I reply testily. "Now just shut up."

"I see. You think your magic will help. Don't you think Jeremias would have thought of that, since he seems to know how you operate."

He has a point there, but I refuse to think about it, refuse to give up hope this early in the game. I have to get to Lenore. That's more important than even escaping this permanent hell.

"You didn't think of that, did you?" Valtu goes on.

"Will you shut the fuck up," I snap at him, baring my fangs.

"Oh no, what's going to happen? You going to let your beast out of its cage?"

He says this as a joke, because he's a fucking smartass, but suddenly I'm struck with a terrible idea. One that might be a huge mistake, but may be the only chance we have.

"What?" Valtu says slowly, studying me.

I look at him, feeling a new spark inside me. "You're right."

"About what?"

"I should let the beast out of the cage."

Valtu blinks at me in surprise. "I was kidding, Solon."

I shake my head. "And I'm not. Jeremias may know me, but he doesn't know the beast so well. He warded these chains to keep me here, not the beast. I could break out of here."

"And kill me in the process!"

I shrug, not really caring if I do. "I might not. You're going to die here anyway. Wouldn't you rather take your chances?"

"An eternity of suffering versus being ripped to shreds and possibly eaten by you?" He shakes his head, looking haunted. "I don't know, man. I don't know."

I grin at him. "If I can give you one piece of advice, try not to piss me off after I turn. It might just save your life. In fact, just go completely still and play dead. That should do the trick."

"You're not seriously going to do this? *Can* you even do this?"

"I've never called on the beast before," I admit. "I've always done what I can to keep it away. I guess we'll just have to see, won't we?"

And I have enough anger and determination inside me to push that lever over to the other side.

I just hope to hell that the beast knows what it's doing.

I hope Lenore has the power to hold me back. Perhaps even kill me, if she has to. As long as I save her life, that's the risk I'm willing to take.

17

LENORE

I'M SUBMERGED IN A WORLD OF RED.

The blood goes into my eyes, into my nose, into my ears, a thick toxic feeling that's unlike any blood that could ever sustain life. The only thing this blood could sustain would be something dark and evil.

Someone like Skarde.

And there is no escape. The deer skull creature is pulling me under and under, making my limbs move, making me swim toward the bottom, this dark red bottom we never seem to reach.

Then, after what feels like forever, there appears a light. Something faint shining through the blood. The further we swim down, the closer we get, I have this feeling like it's a piece of glass on the lake floor, or maybe a mirror. But then it gets bigger and bigger until I realize I'm looking up at a surface of water, a big sky beyond.

The fuck?

Now I'm swimming *up*, not down, and breaking through the surface, gasping for breath.

And I realize that I'm free. That the deer skull thing is gone and it's just me, all alone, in the middle of a bloody lake.

Except this isn't the same lake I came in through.

For one, there's a dusting of white snow on the ground, for two there's a thick red river running away from the lake and disappearing over the edge of a bluff. The trees here are sparse, their leaves and needles red and littered on the ground like splattered blood, and beyond them it's like an endless space of nothing.

Suddenly I'm remembering back to when I used to have dreams about Skarde. I never saw him, not clear enough to know what he really looks like, but I saw the Dark Order in those dreams, and they were always in a snowy barren landscape, just like this one, blood splashed around in patterns of crimson.

Well, now what? Do I dive under and look for the way back out?

But before I can contemplate that in a serious way, Kaleid and Natalia burst through the surface, spitting out blood.

"There you are," Kaleid says to me, quickly swimming over at vampire speed so he's beside me in a second, grabbing hold of my arm in a manner that's way rougher than I'm used to.

"Hey," I tell him.

"Can't have you thinking about going back," he says to me, hauling me out of the blood. And by hauling, I mean he's actually dragging me on shore as I struggle to get my footing.

"Be nice, Kaleid," Natalia says, coming out of the lake after us. "Just because Solon isn't here doesn't mean I will put up with your garbage."

Kaleid laughs and lets go of me in such a way that I fall to my knees in the snow, suddenly weak and clumsy.

"Bastard," Natalia hisses at him. She marches over to me

and pulls me up to my feet. "Sorry about that," she says to me. "This world is already getting to him."

I eye Kaleid suspiciously as he starts to walk away along the river of blood. I can't tell how much of his asshole switch flipping is due to being closer to his father, or the fact that Solon isn't around anymore so he doesn't have to pretend to be nice to me.

Fuck, it's probably both. I knew he never liked me, all those smiles were just for show.

Did Solon know it? I think. Probably. Maybe not. I know he doesn't trust Kaleid, but he probably didn't think he'd turn into a jerk so fast.

"Hurry up, princess," he calls over his shoulder at me. "You have plenty of time for regret later."

Natalia gives me another sympathetic look and places her hand at my elbow, gently guiding me forward.

"So do *you* know where we are going?" I ask her, keeping my voice low, though I have no doubt that Kaleid can hear everything we're saying and probably thinking.

"No clue," she says.

"So what, we're just going to walk until we find his house or something?"

She gives me a small smile. "Or something."

"And he's going to be happy to see you?"

"Oh, fuck no." She lets out an acidic laugh. "No, we had a falling out worse than Kaleid did."

This piques my interest. "What happened? When did it happen?"

She frowns. "Maybe forty or fifty years ago? I don't know for sure, I don't really keep track of time."

I have to say, even though I'm used to being around vampires, Natalia is the first female vampire I've spent any amount of time with, and though she looks the same age as me—twenty-one—and was that age when she turned, it really throws me off to know she's been around for so much longer than that.

"But," she continues, "I just kind of snapped one day. My father, he runs a pretty tight ship. Regulated and controlled to the extreme, for everyone but him. He pretty much kept me like a fairy-tale princess in a castle. I couldn't go out, couldn't date, couldn't mate, couldn't do anything but stay with him, for hundreds of years. He even controlled who I fed on."

"My god," I say. And I thought my parents were overprotective.

"Anyway, I'd fallen in love, you know how the story goes, and my handsome prince came to rescue me and…" she trails off, sucking in her lip for a moment. "Well, Skarde killed him."

"I'm so sorry," I say, instinctively pressing my hand against my chest.

"Yeah. I'm sure his head is still on a pike outside the palace. You know how some say Vlad the Impaler was the original Dracula? Well, Skarde was doing that a century before him. It's his hobby."

"Well, Solon collects the skulls of people he's killed and keeps them in a storage locker," I say. "So I see where he gets that from."

"Mmm," she muses. "Apple doesn't fall far from the tree. But I guess that's the same for all of us."

"So then what happened after he killed him?"

"I disowned him," she says.

"And he let you leave after that?"

She nods. "He takes family seriously in a very twisted way. The minute you disown him, you're out forever. You're an enemy."

"I assume Solon went out the same way?"

"Yep."

"And Kaleid?" I whisper.

Her eyes dart up to him ahead of us and her lips thin out, giving her head a furtive shake.

As in *no*. Kaleid is still welcomed into the fold.

Suddenly Kaleid stops walking and glances at us, a cold glint in his eyes that doesn't match his dimpled grin. "You should be grateful that Skarde hasn't disowned me yet. I'm your only way in."

"And me," I point out as we catch up to him. "You need me just as much."

"So what is the plan now that Solon and Valtu aren't here?" Natalia asks, hands on her hips. "What if father decides to kill me on the spot?"

Kaleid shakes his head. "He won't. We'll just take Lenore and say that we captured her for him. Tell him that you're trying to earn your way back into his graces. Beg. Get on your knees. Cry. Make a real big show of it. He'll buy it."

"You have too much faith in him," she says. "He's changed."

"I'm the last one who saw him, not you," he points out. "It'll work. Trust me."

Natalia frowns and I realize that his own sister doesn't trust him any more than I do. I think the two of us women are going to have to stick together here.

"Anyway," Kaleid says, looking off into the distance where the river of blood runs over the edge of the snowy bluff, disappearing below. "They're here."

My heart picks up the pace, not liking the gravity in his tone. "Who is here?"

"Our escorts," he says, starting to walk again. "Come on."

I exchange a wary glance with Natalia, but we keep walking until we come to the edge of the bluff. The river of blood turns into a bloody waterfall, splashing over the rocks into a red pool below, a group of smaller streams leading out across the snow, like a heart and its arteries.

And at the foot of that red pool are two men on horseback.

Our escorts.

My scalp tingles, a feeling of uneasiness spreading through me. I know that's an understatement considering all the truly bonkers shit I've gone through today, but there's something about this sight that sends waves of fear through me. More than going into that lake, this is the real point of no return, the feeling of never going back. Once we scramble down this rocky hillside, that's it.

We'll be in Skarde's territory.

And even though the flat snowy plane seems to stretch forever, ending at the beginning of a raspberry-colored sunset, I know that Skarde lives on that horizon.

"Come on," Natalia says, touching my elbow again. "No turning back now."

I take in a deep breath and nod.

Here we go.

We quickly make our way down the cliff, the uneven and steep terrain no problem for our vampire dexterity, my footing as sure as a mountain goat, and then we're on level ground.

And I get a better look at these two horsemen.

"What the fuck," I gasp.

The men on the horses are skeletons in black cloaks, their faces hidden in darkness by their hoods. That doesn't really surprise me after having to deal with the Lapp Witches. No, what has me all 'what the fuck' are the horses.

They're skeletons made of metal and muscle, iron and copper and flesh intertwining together in a holy abomination, crimson mane and tail of blood, smoke that flows from their gaping nostrils. They don't have eyes, just sockets, and just like the deer people, you don't want to stare into them for too long.

"Oh my god, it's the *Hiisi* horses," Natalia says softly, seeming just as surprised as I am. She glances at me in awe. "It's from Finnish mythology and the *Kalevala*."

"Well, it's not mythology if they're real," I tell her. I'm glad I don't know anything about their mythology because if this is a sample of it, then I probably don't want to know what else might lie ahead of us. At school we studied the myths of Ancient Mesopotamia and if any of those myths popped up for real, we'd all be in big trouble.

"Time to get moving, *witch*," Kaleid says sharply to me, grabbing my arm so hard that his fingers bruise my inner bicep.

"Ow," I tell him, but then Natalia grabs my other arm, holding me just as tight, and I know the plan has officially come into play. I'm their prisoner, which means Kaleid gets to manhandle me all he wants.

And manhandle me he does. We walk and walk across that endless snowy landscape, the death riders on either side of us, and he's constantly tugging at me, hurting me, swearing at me. A few times Natalia shoots him daggers with her eyes to stop it, but he stays in character. I'm starting to think he's relishing it. I'm starting to think this *is* his character and that Solon's brother is a sick bastard.

Finally, a shape begins to take form on the horizon, near a blood-red sky that's ever-changing shades above a roaring crimson ocean. The Arctic Ocean? Some other ocean in another world? Either way, it's a contrast to the endless white snow, the waves powerful, the feeling of a deadly cold and fathomless deep beneath the churning red surface. Occasionally, lightning will strike, red and gold streaks that reach down from dark clouds.

And as we get closer, the shape on the shore becomes

something recognizable, like a castle of some sort. And as we get even closer, I realize what it really is—ruins. The dilapidated remains of something that I imagine was once grand and sprawling but is now just piles of rock and stone in some places.

"This is the palace you lived in?" I ask Natalia, surveying the ruins as we approach.

"God no," she whispers. "This is a world I've never been to before. I would have escaped this place a long time ago."

"Providing there is an escape," I note.

Kaleid clears his throat, glaring at me so sharply that I feel it in my blood. Right. The act. Like hell Skarde is going to believe this, I don't know why Kaleid is even bothering. We're screwed.

Fuck, I wish Solon was here. In one way I'm glad he's not, because he's safe where he is. I have no doubt he would try to kill his father, and that his father would try to kill him, and honestly I don't know how that would end. At least he's with Dracula, back in the real world where horses aren't made of metal and bone and where a depraved vampire king doesn't live in a crumbling castle, waiting for us.

Because of course he's waiting for us. He sent these death escorts our way. He knows we're coming and he's a hell of a lot more prepared than we'll ever be.

"Here we are," Kaleid says, staring at the entrance to the ruins. Once upon a time there would be a giant gate there, maybe a drawbridge, but now it's just an arch of stone and the horsemen take their place on either side, waiting for us to step through.

I feel like I'm entering a curse.

That I need to turn around and run far, far away. Every instinct, every cell and molecule in my body knows that I shouldn't step through that doorway.

But I don't have a choice. Not only because there would

be nowhere for me to run to, but the fact that Natalia and Kaleid are dragging me through.

They take me into a large courtyard, the remains of a fountain in the middle of the uneven stone ground. Above us there is only crimson sky and red lightning, the roof gone. On the other side of the fountain is another arch, a doorway that leads into darkness.

Kaleid leads me over to the doorway but then he stops, staring into the darkness.

Waiting.

I look at Natalia. Her normally placid face is faltering. She's breathing in hard through her nose, blinking fast, like she's about to have a panic attack. I know that feeling.

Then I look over at Kaleid. His posture is perfect, his chin raised as he stares into the abyss.

But even he isn't one hundred percent cool and easy like he usually is.

Beads of sweat appear on his temple and it takes a fucking *lot* to make a vampire sweat.

He's scared. So is she.

And me? Well now I'm fucking *terrified*.

"No need to be afraid, Lenore," a voice says from behind us.

My heart lurches to a stop in my chest, panic flooding my adrenals, making my whole body tense as all my internal alarm bells go off.

Run.

Run.

Don't turn around.

Don't look.

Don't look at him!

To look at him is to lose your life.

From beside me Kaleid sucks in his breath, then his nails

dig in, piercing the skin on my arm, and he whips me around, almost out of Natalia's grasp.

And I find myself face to face with Skarde.

Once again, I'm surprised at what I'm seeing. All this time I thought I would see this horrific bat-type monster thing, something my imagination or the movies have conjured up. At the very least I thought I would see someone a little fucked-up looking, like along the lines of Jeremias and his ever-rotating face.

But no.

Skarde is handsome as hell.

Looks like he's about sixty years old or so, black well-groomed hair, strong jawline, squinty blue eyes that pierce right through you, ears that stick out a little. He's wearing a navy dress shirt and black pants and looks entirely out of place amongst all the crumbling stone, like he just strolled into work as some successful CEO.

"We finally meet," he says, smiling as he presses his palms together and I swear his accent is the posh kind of British. Isn't Skarde Norwegian? Fuck it, there are more important things to ponder. Like how he's going to kill me.

He gives me another quick smile that doesn't reach his eyes and then looks at Kaleid. "You came back. I didn't think you would, son."

Kaleid nods. "I brought her, like you asked."

Skarde's dark brows raise. "Like I asked? When did I ask you for Lenore?"

Then he fixes that smile on me again and steps forward. "You must pardon this bout of awkwardness. I haven't seen my son in years, so while I have been wanting you, he hasn't known about it. And the other one there, well, that was my daughter. She disowned me, you see, and that was decades ago. I'm having a hard time believing she's here for a friendly visit."

He fixes his gaze on Natalia now. "So what is it? Why are you here? You know, I knew, deep down, I knew that you'd come into my life again, but I didn't imagine you bringing me my bride."

"Your bride?" I ask. I ask because it's what I'm supposed to ask, but also because the statement still catches me off-guard.

"Yes," Skarde says, grinning. Then he frowns at the marks that Kaleid's made in my arm. "What the fuck are you doing, hurting her like that? Release her."

At once, both Kaleid and Natalia let go of me, like they've been holding onto a hot potato. Then Skarde reaches forward, grabbing my wrist with a firm, yet gentle, grasp, and pulls me toward him. Up close, things are a little different. I smell cologne, which is strange. Vampires don't wear cologne unless they're trying to cover something up. And his face doesn't seem as...solid as it should. I blink at him, like I'm trying to see through something, thinking about those Magic Eye paintings that Solon mentioned.

"My apologies for his rough behavior," Skarde says to me with a wolfish smile. "Kaleid doesn't get around women very often."

I have to say, I appreciate that dig at him, even more so that Kaleid just stands there and takes it.

"Though I suppose," Skarde goes on, "that he's trying to prepare you for what life with me is like."

I blink up at him, caught off-guard once again. "What?"

Then his smile turns into something dark and cunning, pure evil, and for a moment I'm able to see beneath his skin, see that he has another face underneath, his real one, red eyes, and inch long fangs, no lips, no gums.

I stare in horror and then that awful underbelly fades away and he's back to his handsome self. But now I know that's not his current self, and if it *is* his real self, it's what he looked like before centuries of being the king of evil took its toll on him. Because that's what he is. He's the king of evil, I feel it permeating every pore he has, and he knows it, that's why he's doused in cologne. He's pulling out every stop in the vampire playbook in an attempt to glamor me.

He grins. He knows what I saw and he's loving it. "You're mine now, Lenore. I oughta thank my son for finding you in the first place."

I glance at Kaleid, but Skarde continues. "No, not him. Absolon. My first made. Oh, don't worry, he would never willingly give you to me, but he discovered you all the same. Sometimes I wonder what would have happened to you had he never taken you away from your parents. Would you have turned and killed them? Would they have killed you? Or would you still be in America with them, making it work, never coming across my radar? Fortunately for me, it was Absolon who found you and because I'm always watching him, always aware of what he's doing, I then found you too. My bride to be."

His hand tightens on my arm. "You don't seem to be protesting. Perhaps because none of this surprises you. Perhaps because you think you have the upper hand because of these fools that you came here with. But you don't. Not in these walls, not with any meager magic you can muster."

"I destroyed your Dark Order," I say through gritted teeth.

"You did!" he exclaims. "Oh, I forgot about that. Job well done, Lenore, and your first time too. Wow. That must have been quite the feeling to harness your father's power the way you did."

"It was my own power," I tell him, narrowing my eyes, as if I can intimidate this monster in some way. "And Solon's too."

"Ah yes, Absolon and his parlor tricks. Those can get

rather tedious, can't they? No matter, it is what it is. And you're here because you're meant to be. The *vanha väki* foretold it. Your light will be pushed away in exchange for the darkness, the very darkness your father passed down to you, the one that flows in your veins. Even if you don't see to it now, you will. I promise you that. I can be very persuasive."

Then he turns his attention to Kaleid and Natalia, all while I'm staring at his hand as it holds onto me. I swear to god his nails are growing longer and sharper by the moment until they're puncturing my skin. It's like being held in place by a giant eagle.

"Natalia," he says to her. "Why are you here? To beg forgiveness? To win me over?"

I glance up at her as she nods, her chin raised high as she stares at her father in the eyes. "Yes, sir," she says.

"Sir? Oh, I like that. I've *missed* that. God how I've missed that, Natalia. Ever since you left, things haven't been right in my life, you know? You are the last daughter I have."

Her brows knit together. "What happened to Anna?" she asks in shock. "Elena? The rest of them?"

He shrugs. "Marianna went mad and had to be destroyed. Piirko broke the rules and created a vampire, so she was dealt with accordingly. Anna was killed by a slayer. Elena got her head chopped off. It's on a pike." He jerks his thumb to the rear of the building. "Oh, I forgot, you haven't been here before. I moved the heads to the shorefront. That way when you look out the bedroom window, you just see nothing but heads for miles. Elena is there. So is your lover, what was his name? Janne? And your head will be placed right next to his."

"Father," Kaleid says, stepping between Skarde and Natalia, a rather bold move. "You can trust my sister. I wouldn't bring her here otherwise. She means you no harm."

Skarde tilts his head, appraising his son. "Is that so. You can vouch for her?"

"Yes," Kaleid says emphatically. So much so that even I believe him, and I know the truth. "Natalia wants back. This is her token. Lenore is her gift. She helped me secure her. You owe her at least the benefit of the doubt."

A smile slowly spreads across his lips. "Hmmm. Well, you certainly seem like you believe in your sister. It's funny, Kaleid, after she left, I never heard you mention her name. Like Solon, she was as dead to you as she was to me. And yet...here she is."

Skarde fixes his gaze on his daughter now and her eyes go wide, her body starting to tremble. Her fear is so visceral that I feel it inside me, how badly she wants to turn and run and never return.

But she can't. She stays in place as Skarde calmly walks toward her.

Walks behind her.

Her eyes widen further, so much shining white against the pale blue, darting from side to side, but she doesn't turn around, doesn't move as her father stands right behind her, looking every inch the killer.

"You know I'm pretty good at reading my own kind," Skarde says, his voice turning into a purr. "I can read emotions like I'm reading thoughts. Your emotions are all over the place, daughter." He closes his eyes, breathing in deep through his nose. "So much adrenaline and fear."

He opens his eyes and he's looking straight at me now as he places his hands on either side of Natalia's head. "I understand, of course. How intimidating I must be. Still, I can't help but think that your feelings are betraying why you're really here. How afraid you are that you'll be...caught."

Skarde brings his fingers over her eyes. "Perhaps if I take a closer look." He smiles at me over Natalia's shoulder and says, "Don't be alarmed if my appearance changes, Lenore. I'll always be whoever you want me to be."

Then he snarls, showing fangs, his handsome face fading away into a gray one so gaunt that it's like there's only a strip of flesh between him and his skull. His eyes are round balls in the deep sockets, his teeth without lips or gums, just a monstrous row of fangs that belong on a shark.

Kaleid screams, trying to make a move for Skarde but he can't, he's frozen in place, his arm outstretched trying desperately to reach for her.

And now I see why.

Skarde presses his long, boney fingers into Natalia's eye sockets until her eyeballs fall out like red grapes, hanging by a thread of muscle. She's screaming in horror, I'm screaming, Kaleid is screaming, and yet none of it is stopping him as he drives his fingers deeper down, down, down until he's reaching into the depths of her skull.

And being a vampire, she doesn't die easily.

She's still screaming, writhing in agony, the endless shrieks filling my brain until I know I'll never sleep again without hearing them.

And Skarde keeps going, until his fingers have busted through all the bone and he's able to grip with his hands in the middle of her face, reminding me of someone trying to eat a lobster tail, having to break apart the shell first before they get to the meat.

He smiles at me, a warning, and then he starts to pull her face apart.

Natalia screams and screams until her face is ripped down the middle, her skull coming apart, her nose, her mouth, her chin, all splitting in two.

Then the screaming stops but her father doesn't.

He keeps pulling her apart, until guts and muscle and veins and bone are being stretched like taffy, until her entire body is completely torn into two pieces and then discarded into two sickening lumps on the floor.

He looks to me, then Kaleid. "Now you know what I do when I find loved ones aren't being truthful. Are you sure you standby all the statements you've made earlier, Kaleid?"

Kaleid's face is paler than I've ever seen, his eyes brimming with tears, body shaking slightly from the onslaught of horror. "I'm sure," he manages to say, his words coming through in a whisper.

Skarde observes him for a moment, then, when finally satisfied, he looks back to me and his face morphs into the handsome one he had before, all sparkling blue eyes and a great jawline. "And you, Lenore. Well, there's no hiding your intentions. You want me dead. I don't blame you. Seeing what you saw doesn't help, does it? They say there are only three ways to kill a vampire, but did you know that I can do whatever I want to them and it still counts? Call it a benefit of being born from the Dark One. But it doesn't really matter, not in the end. No one said my bride would be a willing one. All they said is that she'd be a vampire with the power of a witch and with black magic flowing through her veins. They never said you'd love me. They never said you'd bend. But oh, my bride, I have ways of making you bend."

Then his attention goes to Kaleid. "Get her cleaned up. I don't want the stench of that other world on her. Then put her in the crown, in the holding cell. I'll come down when I'm ready."

He turns, stepping over his dead, mutilated daughter like she's a pile of dogshit, and disappears into the darkness.

18

LENORE

"SORRY LENORE," KALEID SAYS TO ME AS HE LEADS ME DOWN A narrow stone staircase that feels like it's descending into the bowels of hell.

Kaleid can say sorry all he wants, but the fact is, him leading me down here says all that it needs to. Not that I can talk much at the moment. I'm still reeling at the fact that Natalia was just literally ripped in half right in front of us. If anything, I should be apologizing to Kaleid for the gruesome and traumatizing loss of his sister.

But I'm not in the mood. I can't rely on Kaleid now and I never could. I realize that now. That if Skarde felt like morphing into the disgusting monster that he is, that if he felt like ripping his son from head to toe, he could. And he could do the exact same thing to me. So I'm going to be his bride? So what? What happens to me when he finds out I won't cooperate? He can't force me into becoming something I'm not...can he?

I wipe that thought out of my head. It won't get me anywhere. My reserve is all I have to hang on to.

Kaleid leads me down a dark corridor, the air smelling

wet and rotting, and then brings me into a bathroom with a big claw foot tub in the middle and nothing else. The water comes from a pipe suspended above.

"Strip," he says to me, pushing me into the room.

I stumble forward on the uneven rocks, catching myself from falling just in time, then whip around, hands out, ready to fight if he comes any closer.

"I'm not going to force you to do anything," Kaleid says, his eyes turning hard. "But he wants you clean, so get off your fucking bloody clothes and get into that bath."

"I'm not getting naked in front of you," I tell him.

He stares at me for a moment, dumbfounded. "Oh. Okay. Is that so? So you'll have sex in front of a total stranger, a human, but you're too good and pure to get naked in front of your brother-in-law when your life depends on it?"

My mouth drops open. "You saw us having sex?"

"You were in the red world," he hisses at me. "Every room is recorded. You and Solon fed from Mathias and then fucked in front of him. Don't act like this is shocking. Now, get your fucking clothes off or we're both dead."

I can't believe this is happening. I don't know what the fuck I expected, but it wasn't this. I expected Solon at my side, making sure I was never in a position like this.

"Yeah, well I'm not your knight in shining armor either," Kaleid says, reading my thoughts. "I look out only for myself. But sometimes, sometimes, I'll make an exception for family. And if you're with Solon, you're with family. So get in the tub and get clean. I'll be right outside the door."

Then he turns and leaves the room, shutting the door behind him. He doesn't lock it, but I have no doubt he's standing right there on guard. I can smell him, moss and pine and aniseed. Smells that are forever tainted to me.

I put my face in my hands and try to gather my nerves. Everything that just happened has left me so on edge that I

237

feel *this* close to losing it, to just crawling into a darkened corner and rocking there for a while.

But of course, this is only the start. Skarde had said Kaleid had to put me in a crown and then in the holding cell. Neither of those things sound good. They sound fucking terrifying. Of course, not as terrifying as being torn in two, but still. There are many steps between torture and death.

I sigh and turn the handle near the low ceiling, the water flowing out and splashing into the tub. Being a vampire, it doesn't matter if the water is hot or cold, it all feels fine for us, but this water is lukewarm. Then I start stripping off my clothes, my boots, socks, skinny jeans and tank top that are completely covered in blood from the lake earlier.

I step into the bathtub, naked, watching as the blood seeps off my skin and rises above me in the water in inky crimson tendrils. There's no soap, but that doesn't surprise me. Though Skarde is dressed like a well-paying guest at a hotel, I didn't think he'd have little wrapped bars of Provençal soap here.

I don't know how long I sit in the bathtub for, staring at the stone walls, wondering how long they've been here, where I am exactly, what kind of stone they have in this world. If I'll ever get back. If Solon is still okay. If there's any way I'll get out of this alive. I have a feeling that Natalia dying wasn't part of Kaleid's plan, that he needed her, no matter how callous he seems, and with her gone, how does this fare for us? It's just him and me now. Do we have the combined power to do anything to Skarde? I mean, I just saw what could be a minor display of his power, and if that's the case, neither of us stand a chance, no matter how we pool our resources together. There's just two of us. Vampire prince and a half-breed.

You could always call on Jeremias, I tell myself. *If he can travel like the Lapp Witches travel, he could be here. He could help you.*

Of course, I know that help might come with a price. Magic comes with a price. I know the first time he helped me, he was really trying to win me over. He was trying to impress me. The second time, I called on him and that didn't go as smoothly. The minute I said I didn't want to indulge the dark side was the minute he lost interest in me.

But…what if I indulged it now? Maybe not this second, but when I had to. *If* I had to. Would it be so bad to go inward, open that locked box and tap into that power I have available? Fuck, there's a chance I could easily destroy Skarde if I did that. I could destroy his whole ugly bleeding world.

And then what? Lose yourself to it? What if you never come back?

I need to ignore those thoughts for now. That's the risk, but I'm starting to realize that there's always a risk in life.

The door opens and Kaleid steps in. He doesn't avert his eyes, doesn't attempt to look bashful as he stares at me naked in the tub. But there is sorrow in his gaze that wasn't there before. Perhaps the golden child feels remorse.

Then my gaze goes to his hands. He's holding a flimsy piece of red fabric, all thin gauze, and on top of it is a head-piece. Red metal. There's a crown, then strands of red beads cascading from underneath that would crisscross across someone's face like a mask.

"Get out of the tub," he says to me in a flat voice.

I stare at him for a moment, then decide I have no choice. If he's seen me fucking Solon, then he's seen me at my most vulnerable already.

I get up, naked, head held high, and step out of the tub, walking toward him.

His nose flares as he fights to keep his eyes focused on

mine. I know that he's hard, I can smell his arousal already, but I have zero interest in appeasing him.

I stop in front of him and take the crown and fabric from his hands. "What is this?"

He swallows audibly, licking his lips. "It's what he wants you to wear."

"For what?"

His jaw tightens. "You're to be his bride, Lenore."

"Already?"

He swallows again, his Adam's apple bobbing. "I'm sorry."

"So, your plan was, what? This?"

But he doesn't say anything to that. Perhaps he can't. His father can probably hear us and he's trying to save his own ass at this point.

"Put it on," he says. "Please."

He doesn't say please the same way that his brother does. Solon rarely says please, but when he does I pay attention, because I would do anything for him, just as he would do anything for me. Kaleid doesn't have the same finesse.

"Perhaps one day," Kaleid says under his breath.

"What?" I ask, grasping the headpiece in one hand while trying to unravel the fabric with the other.

"What you were thinking," he says, without an ounce of shame. Oh, and when I look up, he's staring at my breasts too, also without shame.

"That you don't have finesse?" I ask. "Well, your father did mention your lack of luck with the ladies. In some other world, in some other time, in some other life, I would probably take you under my wing as Solon's baby brother and I would help you with that. But I think you're a lying, duplicitous asshole who would trade in whatever he could to get ahead. So, I guess what I'm saying is, fuck you, Kaleid."

Kaleid flinches, just a millimetre, enough to know that he

cares somewhere, that he's not as far gone as his father. That, or his ego is beyond manageable.

I sigh, feeling momentarily sorry for him, then try to put the fabric on. But to my surprise, it seems to take on a life of its own. The red gauze moves around and contorts on its own accord, fitting to my curves until it looks like I'm wearing an elegant designer gown of the lightest see-through fabric. At any other time I would feel both beautiful and on-display, but right now I feel like a piece of meat being wrapped up at the butcher.

Kaleid doesn't say anything, but he comes forward and takes the headpiece from my hands and places it on my head, the beads and red metal filigree draping across my face.

"How do I look?" I ask sarcastically.

"Like a blood bride," he answers. Then he reaches out, displaying his palm. "I have to take you to him either way," he says. "You might as well take my hand."

I stare at his hand then breathe in deeply, placing my palm in his.

His fingers grasp me, cold and strong, and he leans in close, lips at my ear. "I'm not going to let anything bad happen to you. I owe Solon that much."

He pulls away enough to gaze at me and I meet his eyes. "Define what *bad* means in this world."

From the way his face pales, I know he means he won't let what happened to his sister happen to me. So, great, basically everything up until being torn in half while still alive is totally game.

He doesn't say anything else after that, just takes me from the room and back down the long corridor, up the stone stairs until we're back in the courtyard. This time we go into the blackened void of a room, the one we stopped outside of before.

Are you taking me to the holding cell? I ask inside my head, directing my words at Kaleid.

I'm not surprised when he answers. *Change of plans*, he says. *You're about to get married instead.*

Well, fuck. I think I preferred the idea of a holding cell.

Just play along, he says. *Pretty sure marriages down here aren't binding.*

Pretty sure? I repeat.

He doesn't say anything else to that. Instead, he leads me into that dark cavernous room, the one he seemed afraid of earlier, and as we walk in I feel the pressure in my ears changing.

Eventually my eyes adjust to the dark and we're in a place that feels both underground—the walls are damp and smooth, like the walls of a cave—and a place that's open to the sky in places, hints of red peeking through.

In front of us is something dark, tall and large, a vague shape, then a shaft of red light comes through, illuminating Skarde. It's like he's being lit up by Hell from above.

"Here she is, the bride to be," Skarde says proudly, holding out his hands. He's dressed in a black cloak, like something an evil priest would wear, and standing at the top of a few steps, in front of the dark shape, which on closer inspection seems to be a giant throne of some sort.

I try to ground myself, pressing my bare feet into the stone, not wanting to go up the steps, but Kaleid is strong, and I know if I don't move, he'll drag me up. For some reason I don't want to be delivered kicking and screaming to Skarde. I think he'd like it too much.

I go up the steps and Kaleid brings me right over to Skarde, who immediately grasps my hands, holding tight. I try to rip mine away, but he merely tightens his hold and smirks. Yup. Definitely the type of dude that the more you struggle, the more he enjoys it. This does not bode well for me.

"I take it you've never been married before," Skarde says to me. "Don't worry, neither have I. I've been waiting for you, like a noble King." I almost snort but I manage to rein it in. "You see, I was created here." He looks behind him at the throne. "I was brought here because I wanted eternal life. The Dark One took me in and he granted me that. Made me the King of Death. But he tricked me, you see. He does that. I didn't quite know what I was getting into and then he told me that I had a bride that was willing and able. I fucked that bride, even when she was screaming at me to stop. But it was never a bride at all...I won't fill you in with the disturbing details, but that's how I became what I am."

He pauses, looking back at me, his eyes hard. "I was upset at what I'd become at first. The Dark One promised me that one day I would have my bride to rule at my side. As the years went on and the Dark One didn't interfere with my life so much, the prophecy of the bride was passed to the old folk. Oh, I had women. I bred with women, created Kaleid here, Natalia, countless others. I created vampires too, like Absolon. Did you know he used to be a clergyman? Small town in Norway, by the sea. A well-loved, light-hearted, god-fearing man. When I finally ventured out of this world, I fed on whatever human I could find. Then I found Absolon and I was so taken by his devotion, his piety, I thought...what if I could change him? What if I could drive his love for God right out of him? After all, that would impress the Dark One like nothing else. So I took Absolon and I bit him. Drank his blood. Almost killed him before making him drink my blood and bringing him back to life as a vampire."

He sighs, shaking his head in disappointment, while my heart is aching to hear of Solon's true origins. To think of him as a happy, well-loved religious man, a man of God, living his life, his calling, and then to have this monster come along and destroy every inch of his soul...it's too much.

"I didn't know that I would create such a mad creature," Skarde goes on. "I wanted Absolon to be like me, to rule with me. I had such high hopes. But he...he was filled with monstrous rage and I could barely tame him. He wasn't the son or the protégé that I had hoped for, and yet, yet I still felt I was his father. I spent centuries doing what I could to help him, hoping one day he'd gain his senses. It's a pity that when he finally did, he didn't want anything to do with me. That hurt, Lenore. It really did."

"But," he adds with another sigh, bringing my hands up to his mouth and planting cold kisses on my knuckles, disgust spreading through me, "if it weren't for Absolon, I wouldn't be here with you. So I suppose there's a reason for everything, isn't there?" He looks to Kaleid. "Are you ready to proceed over the ceremony?"

Kaleid blinks at him. "What? I'm not an officiant."

Skarde smiles. "Never mind. I suppose it wouldn't be like it is in the other world." He reaches out and places his hand behind the back of my neck, pulling me right up to him. "All I need is your blood."

I open my mouth to protest but then he's pressing his lips against mine, kissing me around the metal chains, and then FUCK.

He's biting me, gnawing on my lips, fangs sinking in, ripping my mouth apart.

I scream, trying to fight him off, but I can't. My own blood is filling my mouth, spilling down my throat, choking me.

"Father," Kaleid says sharply.

But Skarde isn't listening. He continues to bite me, his tongue snaking in my mouth, and it's piercing me, like his tongue has a row of fangs along the bottom.

What the fuck?

I scream again in horror, feeling like he's turning into a monster in front of me, but the sound gets lost and now my tongue is sliced open and bleeding and he's sucking so much of the blood back.

Finally, he pulls away, my lips and gums and tongue burning in sharp pain from all the lacerations, my blood smeared around his grin.

"I suppose it's customary to save the kiss for the end," he says, sliding his tongue out of his mouth, licking up the blood from his chin, and I see the tiny little fangs at the bottom.

I'm going to be sick.

I turn away from him and vomit, blood and who knows what flowing out of my stomach and splattering on the stones.

"You're less vampire than I thought," he says mildly. "Don't worry, you'll get the stomach for these things."

"So, you're done then," Kaleid says, taking a step closer to us. "She's now your bride. I was hoping you could show me your army."

"My army? The Dark Order?" Skarde asks. "Now?" Then he shakes his head quickly, waving Kaleid away. "It doesn't matter. We're not done here. That was only one part of the binding. I have her blood in me. Now she'll have my blood in her. And then it will be complete. Then she'll be bound to me, dark as sin, forever."

My eyes widen and I straighten up, but Skarde is so quick that I don't even see him. Suddenly he's grabbing me, slicing open his wrist with his teeth until the blood pours out, and then he's trying to bring his wrist to my mouth.

I don't dare open my mouth to scream, though I'm shrieking internally. I twist around, trying to get out of the way, but he's strong and he's pushing me back until I'm on the ground and he's on top of me, one of his knees planted between my thighs, keeping them open, one hand holding my arms above my head. He brings his wrist to my mouth, trying to get the blood inside me, all while I feel him grow harder and harder against my hip, and I know I'm going to feel a lot of pain no matter what happens.

"No!" Kaleid yells.

Skarde pauses, the blood dripping on my face, and I'm still squirming, getting my mouth as far away from him as possible, my lips pressed together until they're as tight as a vice.

"No?" Skarde repeats with a raspy growl. "What do you mean, no?"

"I need her," Kaleid says, eyes wild. He takes a step toward us. "I need her for myself. I deserve her."

Skarde is shocked. He moves off of me, and if he had eyelids I'm sure he would be blinking. I am too, I have no idea what the fuck Kaleid is saying, but at the same time I feel it in my bones that he's up to something, possibly saying anything he can to save me.

Or maybe not.

"You think you deserve her?" Skarde says. I try to roll over, to attempt to get away, but he just raises his foot and steps on my chest, pressing down until I can't breathe, until it feels like he's going to pop my lungs and heart. "You deserve nothing, Kaleid. The bride belongs to the king. Do you call yourself a king? You're just a feeble half-human who will never amount to anything."

"I'm someone," Kaleid snarls, stepping right up to his father and getting in his wretched face. "I'm the king now and forever. And Lenore belongs to me."

Skarde stares at him for a moment before he bursts out laughing, a hollow, sickening sound. "What has gotten into you?"

"This," Kaleid says.

And, in the blink of an eye, I see Kaleid pull a witch's blade out of his pocket, the silver wrapped in blue electricity.

Skarde stares down at it in shock, the sight not registering.

Then Kaleid drives the blade into Skarde's heart.

Skarde screeches, an inhuman sound that fills the space, fills my ears, echoes inside of my head, and Kaleid keeps his eyes burning on him.

"As I said, I'm the king," Kaleid seethes, staring right into his father's eyes as Skarde drops to his knees, mouth open in a now-silent scream. "Now and forever."

I watch in awe as Skarde reaches for the knife, his hand wrapping around the handle, but he can't pull it out. All he can do is hold on, staring at his son in horror and shock at the ultimate betrayal.

I scramble to my knees, then my feet, standing over Skarde as he falls back, his head smacking against the stone floor. He stares up at nothing, his body starting to change back to his handsome self, and then he goes completely still, the glowing blue knife sticking out of him.

"Is he...?" I ask, shaking my head, not trusting any of this. "Is he dead?"

Kaleid nods slowly, his eyes still locked on his father's body. "I hope so."

"That was a witch's blade," I say. "Only a slayer can use it to kill a vampire."

Kaleid finally looks at me, his mouth curving in surprise. "Unless you have magic," he says. "Black magic."

A chill runs through me. It shouldn't. I should be elated, happy that Skarde is actually, finally dead. That I'm safe and free, that the world is safe, that we accomplished what we set out to do.

But I don't feel any of those things.

I feel nothing but a growing sense of dread, like the rug is about to be pulled out from under me.

"Why do you have that blade?" I whisper. "Who gave it to you?"

"I did, my child," Jeremias' voice booms.

I whip around to see the silhouette of my estranged father in the doorway to the rest of the ruins.

Behind him, in the light, are the Dark Order. They flank Jeremias, filling the crumbling courtyard with their red cloaks and hidden faces.

"Jeremias," I say, that cold intensity inside me building.

He walks through the door, the Dark Order walking single file behind him. They keep coming in the room, filling all the dark space, hundreds of them, all staring at me. I can feel the hate and madness rolling off of them. They know what I did to their kind.

Something tells me I'm going to have a hard time doing it again.

But I can at least try.

"Don't even bother," Kaleid says to me snidely. "You won't get anywhere now." He comes over, grabbing my arm and pulling it toward him and then, before I can even move, even scream, he's sinking his teeth into my arm, tearing through my flesh and drinking my blood. I punch at him, shrieking, trying to get away, but his grip is strong and then he's holding me around the waist, biting my neck now, the pain spreading through me, the blood running down in rivers between my breasts, soaking the dress.

"I told you that you would be instrumental in helping defeat Skarde," Jeremias says, stopping at the base of the steps, not caring that Kaleid is feeding on me. "I told you a man would come for you."

"You set me up!" I scream, feeling myself growing weaker

and weaker. I try to look at Kaleid, to meet his eyes, but he's lost to the blood lust.

"I didn't set you up to fail, though," Jeremias says, folding his hands in front of him. "You can join us. Become Kaleid's princess, the daughter of the king."

If I had any strength left, I'd ask a bunch of questions. Like how on earth do either of them think this will work, a witch and a vampire ruling together? But I'm starting to fade, my knees buckling, and then I'm on the floor beside the body of Skarde, his blue unblinking eyes staring at the red sky.

Kaleid comes down with me, his fangs deep into my neck, showing no signs of stopping, his bites becoming more savage, his growls deeper.

"Kaleid," Jeremias says in a sharp tone. "We still need her to make her choice. She can't do that if she's half-dead."

Kaleid grumbles and then rips his mouth away from my neck and I'm gasping for breath. He holds the back of my head, cradling it in a way that would be tender if it were anyone else. "So, what is your choice, Lenore?" he asks, his eyes searching my face in a way that Solon's often do. "Will you accept my blood? Will you turn dark, rule a kingdom with me and your father, like you were meant to? Become the prophesized blood bride?"

I have enough strength to shake my head. "No," I manage to say. "You knew I'd say no. You fucking asshole. This is what you wanted all along."

"It's the way it was foretold," he says with a grin, those dimples showing. "My father is dead. You are here. I am king of the vampires, just as I had hoped. The choice is there if you want it."

"Why even give me a choice at all? Skarde didn't."

"I am not my father," he says with a hint of regret. "I don't have the power to turn anyone dark. I suppose I'm not evil enough."

"Yeah, but you're trying and that's what counts," I seethe.

He laughs and then looks over at Jeremias. "Your daughter is a feisty one, I'll give her that."

"Feisty, yes," he says, coming up the steps until he's looming over me. His black eyes are full of evil and hate and sickening power. "But that's where our similarities end."

I close my eyes, trying to find my way out of this. I did it once before, I lit the Dark Order on fire, I can do it again, I can set them all ablaze.

But when I search in the dark well, the only power I feel is the one buried at the bottom. The one in the box.

Open the box, Lenore, a voice says. It doesn't belong to Kaleid or Jeremias. It's the voice of the Dark One.

Yes, it hisses inside my skull, making me feel like I'm going to be sick. *Open the box and use the power. You can kill all of them. You can claim the throne for yourself. Endless power for all eternity.*

I step away from the well.

What the Dark One wants me to do is the same thing that Jeremias and Kaleid want. They want me to open that box, to get the black magic, to try and use it against them, because the moment I do is the moment I am gone.

It's the moment the prophecy becomes true.

I will turn dark and there will be no going back.

I will rule in this awful world, breeding vampires that will kill humanity in another world. I will lose myself and bring destruction to every person there is, and with Jeremias at the helm, probably every vampire too. He doesn't kill vampires anymore? Bullshit.

I open my eyes and look directly at Jeremias. "I'm not going to do it."

He sighs in disappointment, his revolving features turning hard. "As I expected." He looks to Kaleid, who is still cradling me. "And as I told you. You are not Solon, boy. Now that I had a chance to see him face to face, I know that for a fact."

My heart lurches. "What are you talking about? You saw Solon?"

Jeremias gives an awful grin. "Who do you think the Lapp Witches belong to? Me. Just as the Dark Order now belongs to me. It's a wonder what a little magic can do." He tilts his head sympathetically. "Don't worry, I didn't kill Solon or his friend. They're just chained up in a place of no escape, to starve for all eternity. His world now is an endless one of anguish and pain and torture, especially after I told him what was going to happen to you."

I blink back tears, my heart ripping open in my chest.

Solon.

No, not Solon.

"You fucking monster!" I scream.

"We're all monsters here, Lenore," he says, with a haughty raise of his chin. "You'd think you'd be used to it by now." Then he nods at Kaleid. "Do what you want with her. I won't kill her, but I won't stop you from doing so."

"Compromising already?" Kaleid comments under his breath. Then he places his cold hand at my cheek, grinning at me with bloody teeth. "Well, Lenore, I guess your no is a no. I have to respect that. Unfortunately, that means I also have no use for you anymore."

He gets up, hauling me to my feet, and I'm still so weak I can hardly stand. I don't know how he drained so much blood out of me, why I'm not recovering, but I have a feeling Jeremias has something to do with it.

Kaleid then picks me up in his arms and carries me down the stairs.

But the Dark Order stands in our way. The stench of chaos and death filling my nose as my head lolls to the side.

Kaleid's grip around me tightens and I can hear his heart rate increasing.

He's scared of the Dark Order.

He has no control over them.

"Let them pass!" Jeremias booms, and suddenly the red sea of cloaks start to part, creating a path out of the door.

Kaleid takes in a deep breath and walks forward.

Hundreds of whispering voices fill my head as we pass. I can't tell what they're saying, if it's even a language known on earth, but they hiss and they whisper and they chant and each sound is dripping with malevolency. I know Kaleid feels it too, because his pace picks up as we pass through them, until we're finally out of the palace and in the snow.

"I can't wait until they're under my control," Kaleid mumbles to himself as he walks toward the crimson ocean.

"Where are you taking me?" I ask, raising my head for a moment. We're alone out here, the Dark Order and Jeremias having stayed behind in the ruins. It's just me and Kaleid and the raging sea and the red lighting above.

"I'm easily inspired," he says, glancing down at me. "My brother inspired me in some ways, your father has inspired me too. See, I don't like the idea of killing you, Lenore. Believe it or not, that's not how I operate. I have some morals. But I do have to get rid of you, so there was always a bit of a conundrum on how to do that."

He places me down on my feet and I realize we're both standing on top of a short pier that juts out into the waves. At the end of the pier is a cage, a gold one, like it's made for a giant parrot.

"See that? That was my solution. My father liked to do this too, when he wasn't taking heads off. He had this specifically built for this sort of thing. See, I'll put you in the cage, throw you over the edge, you'll sink to the bottom. I guess no one really knows what it takes to kill you yet, so if you're really built like a vampire, then you'll be stuck in that cage, at the bottom of the sea, for all eternity. Forever alive, forever drowning. Going mad. Just as Solon will be doing the same." He laughs. "Kind of romantic, isn't it? To know you'll spend the rest of your long lives going through it together?"

"You're insane," I manage to eke out.

"Not insane," he says, grabbing me and dragging me along the dock until I'm being shoved helplessly into the cage. "Just creative."

I grasp the bars as the cage door locks me, staring at Kaleid with wide, pleading eyes as the horror takes hold of me. "Don't do this, Kaleid. This is something your father did, and you said you didn't want to be like him."

"I'm not like him," he snaps. "There's a chance I might have a change of heart and come get you out, if you're not dead. But for now, I need you out of our way. I need you out of *my* way. Once I kill Jeremias, then I'll have time to think."

He shuffles the cage back until I'm hanging off the edge of the dock, the waves licking my feet. "Send my regards to the deep," he says.

Then he kicks the cage off the pier.

And I plunge into the depths.

19

LENORE

I MANAGE TO KEEP MY MOUTH CLOSED AS I SINK, NOT WILLING to let any of the red ocean water inside me, but I'm still screaming in my head.

My fingers are pulling on the bars of the cage with all the strength that I can muster, sinking down, down, down. It feels like I'm falling forever in this icy prison, and then I'm struck with the fear that there is no bottom in this ocean because this ocean is not from my world. That I'll just fall like this forever, for all eternity, stuck in this loop of endless torture and agony until my mind scatters into a million pieces.

With any luck, I'll die. I don't know if I can live forever, I certainly don't know if I can grow gills and breathe under-water. How long do I have before my heart gives out? How long can the vampire blood inside of me keep me alive?

Please let it be swift, I find myself praying to no one in particular. Maybe the same god that Absolon worshipped before he was turned, when his life was stolen from him. Then again, that god didn't help him much either.

Actually, it's kind of amazing that Solon turned out the

way he did. He doesn't even remember his life before, that it was good and happy, that he was a man of god. All he knows is that Skarde turned him into a monster, half-vampire, half-beast, a product of tainted, evil blood. Solon spent centuries as a killing machine, as remorseless as his father, and then, eventually, he stopped. He lost the madness and fought hard against it. He buried the beast as much as he could. He stepped away from his family, he went off on his own. And while I have no doubt Solon has done countless awful and immoral things in his life, even after parting from the dark side, he's constantly striving to be better. He's trying to take back the humanity that was stolen from him so long ago.

And it's worked. Solon found his god again, even if he doesn't know it. He's nothing like the bloodlines from which he came. He is his own being with his own agency and he loves me. That he can go through all of that and love at all is nothing short of a miracle.

But now he's out there, to be tortured for eternity just like I will be. As this cage keeps sinking, I realize that if there's no bottom, there's no chance that Kaleid will have a change of heart and rescue me, and if there is a bottom, I'll be stuck in this watery prison forever. So far, I'm still alive, though I haven't taken a breath in what feels like hours.

Eventually it does stop sinking. I hit the bottom. It's so dark down here that even my night vision doesn't work. Seaweed keeps stroking my legs and the bottoms of my feet —least I hope it's seaweed, and I'm starting to realize that this is it. This is it forever.

Solon, I think out loud into the depths. *Solon, if you can hear me, I love you. I love you more than I've ever even told you because there are no words in this world or the next that can express what my heart feels for you. What my soul feels. But just know, that you are good and you are loved and I am so, so sorry for getting into this mess. I said I would be okay, and clearly I was wrong. I hope you can forgive me.*

Then I close my eyes and I go inside myself and I try to make my thoughts swim further out. I see them in the well, black and still, but this time there is that crescent moon glinting on the surface, giving me a bit of hope.

I reach out and gently touch the surface of the well with my fingertips.

I sense Solon.

He's underneath it, he's alive, he's...

He's coming for me.

I open my eyes, staring into the watery dark beyond the gold bars and I know that Solon is coming. Somehow, he's gotten out of his chains, that he's on his way here, that he's walking into a trap and a battle he can't possibly win. He's just one vampire. He is no match against Jeremias, no match against the Dark Order, and Kaleid poses a problem too.

I have to help him.

I start rattling the bars of the cage, feeling stronger now, but it's not enough. I'm locked in here, and even at the height of my vampire strength, which I am nowhere near right now, I wouldn't be able to bend metal.

Fuck! I think, panic coursing through me again, the feeling of being forever trapped down here while Solon is walking into his death. *God, someone, help me!*

Use your magic, dipshit, a voice inside my head tells me. It's my voice. *You're a witch, aren't you?*

I am, but in the past I always had help, whether it was from Jeremias or Solon or...

And that's when I see it. Out of the corner of my eye, a movement in the deep. I turn my head, and at first I think it's a fish swimming toward me but as it gets closer, the movements don't quite match up.

It's not a fish.

It's a moth.

My moth.

And it's flying underwater.

My eyes widen and I stick my fingers out of the cage and the moth lands on it like it's flying through air. It stares at me with big eyes, the antennae moving in the currents, and I feel a surge of energy leap inside me, the kind of energy that not only comes from below the well but is changing the well. The depths inside me are fading from dark to gold, like everything inside me is becoming light. The waters of the well brighten, beaming, and a rush of power starts to flow throughout my body, pulsing in my veins, making me feel gloriously alive.

I stare at the moth in awe but it just swims away, disappearing into the darkness of the cold ocean floor.

But now, I have all I need.

I close my eyes, gathering all the light that I can until it starts to shoot out of my palms and soles and fingertips, leaking from my eyes and ears and nose, and then I start to rise.

Fast.

I burst right through the top of the cage, the metal bending to my will, and then I'm shooting to the surface like a rocket, going up and up and up.

Until I'm bursting through the waves, rising above the water and I'm still going up into the sky.

Oh my god.

I'm fucking *flying*.

I let out a joyous laugh, staring at my hands as they glow with light, like I'm made of sunbeams, and I wave them around, throwing shapes at the sky, at the waves hundreds of feet below, marveling at how I can just float here suspended in air, that *I'm* the one that's doing it.

This is *my* power.

All mine.

All light and all good.

Then I hear an unmistakable chuckle, one that makes my blood run cold.

I turn to look at the crumbling ruins and see Skarde standing at the edge of the dock, staring up at me with an awestruck expression on his face, his chest marked by a blackened wound where the witch's blade went in.

He's fucking *alive*.

"It's too bad you didn't discover that earlier," Skarde shouts at me. "It would have come in handy, no?"

I gape at him, shaking my head in denial.

No. *No*.

"You're dead," I say.

"Clearly I'm not," he says. "Maybe you should come down from there Lenore."

Before I even have a chance to fly off in the opposite direction, I'm suddenly being pulled toward him, screaming as I go against my will, and then, like a cord has been severed, I drop from the sky, landing on a heap on the dock.

He picks me up by my arm, pulling me roughly to my feet, staring down at my soaked dress. "You lost your crown, but you're still dressed as a bride. Guess Kaleid didn't get his chance."

"Where is he?" I manage to ask, my bones feeling bruised from the fall, the air knocked out of me. Fear clutches my heart. A sinking, bone-deep fear.

"Oh, you care?" he asks, his gaze burning over my breasts, my neck. "He ran off. Guess he was a little embarrassed. You see, he thought a witch's blade, the blade of *mordernes*, would kill me. It did, but only for a little bit. The fool thought he was a slayer for a moment. It doesn't quite work like that, but desperate times call for desperate measures, doesn't it?"

I don't say anything about Jeremias or how he's taken

control of the Dark Order. We're all alone out here. If he knew Jeremias was here, he'd bring him up.

"Now come along," he says, yanking me along the dock and back to the shore. "Let's finish what we started. Least we can have privacy this time."

But we only just step onto the snow-crusted shore when a low rumble fills the air, shaking the ground.

Skarde stops dead, adjusting his grip on me so his hand is at the back of my neck, gripping my spine. He sucks in his breath, the first sign of uneasiness that I've ever seen from him, sending a new spike of terror through me.

The rumbling continues, the ground shaking harder.

"What's happening?" I whisper.

Skarde grunts. "Our worst nightmare," he says. He glances at me, brows raised. "This won't end well for either of us, Lenore. I'll take solace that at least we'll both die together."

Oh my god. What the fuck is he talking about?!

And then, the ruins in front of us start to shake, pieces of the building falling down, then the stones explode outward as a giant black beast bursts through the middle of the wall.

"Solon!" I scream, as the beast runs right for us, overjoyed to see him.

And then I remember what the beast did to me last time.

This *isn't* Solon.

I scream and try to wrestle out of Skarde's grasp to try and run away, but he holds me in a vice-like grip, and sticks his arm straight out in front of him.

He's using me as an offering.

"Take her!" Skarde commands as the beast gets closer. "She's what you really want."

The beast comes to a stop in front of us and snarls at me, those beady red eyes locked on mine, those knife-sized fangs bared as he snaps his jaws and my body aches in memory of the pain and horror he caused. There is no hint of Solon inside. No one in control.

"Take her!" Skarde yells again, shaking me by the neck like a ragdoll, my feet dangling off the ground.

Please no, I say to Solon inside my head, begging for my life. *I know you're in there, please don't do this. It's me, it's me. I love you, it's me.*

The beast curls its lips, showing me its gums.

Then it lunges for me, mouth open, claws out.

Guess I'm still not special.

I close my eyes, ready to be ripped to shreds.

Suddenly I feel pressure around my waist and then I'm being whipped through the air, yanked out of the way, landing on the ground in a heap, lifting up my head just in time to see the beast jump on Skarde instead.

I look up for a second, to see Jeremias standing above me, his eyes trained on the fight, and I'm momentarily thankful that he just saved me despite everything that went down earlier.

But then I too have to watch it all unfold.

It doesn't take long at all.

The beast slices Skarde right down the middle, cutting through bone, exposing his organs, his intestines falling out to the ground to a bloody lump.

Then he slices him the other way, cutting his body nearly in half.

And then, before the body completely collapses, the beast opens its jaws, wider and wider, like it's unhooking, and then it clamps its teeth around Skarde's head, fangs piercing the skull. With two rough shakes of its head, the beast rips Skarde's head right off, leaving a ragged stump behind, then spits the head out across the snow. It bounces a few times and lands facing up. Skarde's blue eyes blink at the sky a couple of times before he completely dies.

Better stick that on a pike to make sure, I think absently to myself, though I know now he's deader than dead.

I look back to the beast, which is now setting its attention on me.

"I see you've discovered how to fly now," Jeremias says to me as I quickly get to my feet. "You better make use of that."

The beast is starting to run at us now, gaining ground.

But instead of flying away, I stay where I am. I widen my stance, grounding myself, then put my palms out toward the beast, energy and light flowing outward.

It stops the beast in mid-stride. It's like it hits an invisible wall, bouncing back, then growling in anger. Giant claws rake the air in frustration, its hackles raised.

Fucking hell, why does it want to kill me so badly? I know Wolf and Ezra have tussled with it before, how come they're still alive?

"Because Absolon loves you," Jeremias says snidely. "I told you, it ruins us. The beast hates that you make Absolon better. The more he loves you, the deeper the beast gets buried. The deeper the darkness is hidden away."

Then Jeremias takes out the glowing witch's blade from his pocket. "But don't worry, my child. I'll make sure it never bothers you again."

He strides off toward the beast, moving fast, holding the blade up, ready to strike.

"No!" I scream, and start to run after him. "If you kill the beast, you'll kill Solon!"

"I don't have a problem with that," Jeremias says over his shoulder, not stopping. "All vampires will be killed soon enough."

No, no, no! I'm running at top vampire speed, about to see if flying gets me there faster to stop him, but then Jeremias waves his arm at me without looking, without slowing down, and I'm thrown backward a hundred feet, landing on the snow.

"No!" I scream again, just as the beast lunges at Jeremias.

Jeremias throws the blade.

It goes right into the beast's heart.

It stops it dead.

The beast stumbles backward, the shining handle sticking out of its chest, the blue electricity spreading outward from the wound until it's covering the beast's entire body like a network of glowing veins.

And then the beast starts to change.

It shrinks in size, getting smaller, turning pale, becoming something else.

Becoming Solon.

Solon, my beautiful, handsome Solon is now naked, the witch's blade in his chest, and he's falling to his knees, blue eyes staring right at me in love and sorrow.

A gut-wrenching cry rips out of my chest, blasting my ears, and then I'm running and running toward him and he's falling over on his side, collapsing to the ground.

"NO!" I yell, tears streaming down my face, sobs choking me, and I'm praying and praying, *please, no, be okay, please be okay. Please, please, please.*

I throw myself down on the ground beside him, my hands going to the blade and pulling it out. Blood rushes to the surface of the wound, but it's not Solon's normal blood. It's tinged with black and blue, like he's been poisoned. Dying from the inside out.

"It's no use, Lenore," Jeremias says from behind me. "I'm a slayer and that's a slayer's blade. It's how the world works."

"Fuck you!" I scream at him, and then turn my head back as Solon reaches up with his hand and places it at my cheek, my tears spilling over his fingers.

"Please, don't go," I beg him through a sob, pressing my

palm over his hand, keeping his cold skin on my cheek. "This isn't over for us. We're only just beginning. We didn't come this far through all of this to give up now."

Solon moves his lips, those beautiful lips, but only blood comes out of his mouth. He blinks up at me. *It's okay*, he says in my head, his voice faint. *I'll be okay.*

"No," I plead. "What about me? I can't do this without you. Don't let me do this life without you. You're supposed to be mine for the ages."

I am, he says, staring deep into my eyes with so much love and sorrow and my god, no, no, he's saying goodbye. *And you are mine for the ages, moonshine. I love you with all the blood in my heart. True love never dies, even if I do.*

My face crumbles and he's slowly drifting away from me. I frantically press my hands on his heart, over the wound, and I can feel him going. His heart isn't even beating anymore. His body is growing ice cold and stiff, and all the wonderful life inside him, all those centuries, all those hard-fought battles, all his memories, all the love and soul and heart that resides inside him are slipping away forever.

"Please don't leave," I whisper, the sobs throttling through me, choking on my own sobs. "Please Solon, stay with me. Love me forever."

He licks his lips slowly, swallowing hard, wheezing for breath. "I will," he manages to say, voice barely audible. "I will, my dear."

And then he stills.

His eyes stare up at nothing.

The wonderful life inside him dies.

And he is gone.

20

LENORE

I STARE DOWN AT SOLON'S BODY IN DISBELIEF, TEARS BLURRING my vision. I gently brush my fingers over his face, feeling his skin, my heart ripping in half with every square inch I touch, knowing I'll never be able to do this again.

Knowing he's no longer mine.

I love him, and somewhere in some other world he loves me, but we won't be together for the ages anymore.

I don't know how I'm supposed to survive this kind of pain, the type that scoops you out, leaving nothing behind but this aching emptiness.

And then, somewhere deep inside me, maybe in the well, maybe in my soul, that sorrow, that cutting, piercing sorrow that stabs me from the inside out, it changes.

It morphs.

Solon wasn't the only one with a beast inside of him.

I have one too.

And I'm about to let it out of its cage.

I slowly turn around, my blood running hot, my skin feeling tight, as anger erupts inside of me, using that sorrow for fuel, all that emptiness inside me turning to kindling.

I stare at Jeremias and get to my feet, feeling my palms burning.

"*You*," I say in a low, raspy voice. "You killed him."

Jeremias frowns, or at least attempts to with his changing faces. "I know I did. It's for the best, Lenore. He would have only held you back. He was too…good for you."

I swallow down the hot bile that's rising inside my throat. "You killed him. And you used me. You let Kaleid discard me like trash."

"I also saved your life," he says with a sniff. "Twice now. That counts for something."

"I loved him," I say through grinding teeth. "I loved him, and you took him from me."

"Lenore," he says with impatience.

"I'm going to take from you now," I tell him, coming toward him. My hands tingle, my fingers turning to charcoal at the tips like spent matches.

He jerks his head back and then lets out a dry laugh. "You? Take from me? You're not even a full witch Lenore. You're just half of one. You'll never amount to anything whole."

"I know I'm only half a witch," I say, my voice low and rough. "I'm also half a vampire."

He blinks, and before he can even focus on me, I'm moving.

I'm on him in a second, my fangs sinking into his neck, biting as hard and deep as I ever have before, my hands clawing at him, nails breaking skin. He tastes fucking awful, like pure primordial evil.

Jeremias yelps and tries to move out of the way, and I can feel him pulling power deep from within himself, conjuring up the black magic that will no doubt dispose of me with ease.

But I'm willing to burn us both to the ground.

Fire kills vampires.

It kills most witches too.

I bite harder, holding on, and then I close my eyes.

I draw from the well, the well of light, and I let it spread throughout my body, growing hotter and hotter and hotter. My heart feels like it's on fire, my skin is starting to smoke, my veins sparking like firecrackers.

And just when I think I'm going to explode, I erupt into flames.

I become a human fireball, every part of my skin alight.

The flames spread from me to Jeremias, and he's starting to catch on fire too.

He chuckles ruthlessly as the fire engulfs us both like torches. "Fire doesn't hurt me, my child. You know this."

"I know," I tell him as the flames lick the roof of my mouth. "It merely distracts you."

Before he can blink, I take the witch's blade that I'd hidden in the folds of my dress after I removed it from Solon's heart and I unhook my fangs from Jeremias' neck, pulling back just enough to take the blade and plunge it right into his eye.

He screams, his eyeball bursting, and I push the blade in deeper until it sinks into his brain. Then I take the blade out and do it to his other eye.

Right in. Deep.

A sickening squishy sound.

Then I stab him in the forehead, breaking through bone.

In the heart.

Then kick him over until he's on the ground, still burning, and for once I see the fire is starting to char him, singe his flesh, his magic leaving him.

I take the blade again, dripping now with his blood, then swipe it across his throat with all the vampire strength I can muster.

It slices his head clean off.

I stare at it, watching it burn, waiting for there to be nothing left of him.

Then I take the blade and stumble over to Solon, feeling drained and weak and with nothing left to live for. I fall to my knees before his lifeless body.

Then I give saving him one more shot.

Jeremias told me that I could create vampires that aren't mad.

It's time to put that to the test.

I lean over Solon, and then run my blade over my wrist, a deep cut. Blood flows out onto his mouth, splattering onto his face, into his still unblinking eyes that stare up at nothing. I reach out, saying a million silent prayers in my head, and gently open his mouth, making sure the blood drips in there.

Can you recreate a vampire? If a vampire dies, can you bring them back again? Does it count if they died by witch's blade? Will I be enough for him?

Will he still go mad, forever a beast?

Was Jeremias lying?

"Come on, Solon," I whisper to him, keeping his lips open, my wrist pressed against his mouth. "Come on, Solon, please. Please wake up, please wake up."

But nothing is happening.

"No, please," I plead. I remove my hand when his mouth fills with so much blood it starts to spill out down the sides of his face.

This isn't working.

He's dead.

You can't bring him back from the dead.

I look over at his chest, at dark open wound that looks like the marks of an electrical fire spreading across his white skin.

His heart is beneath it.

KARINA HALLE

His strong beautiful heart, the heart of a man, a vampire, a beast.

I bring my wrist to the wound, cut myself again before I start healing up, and watch as the blood flows down onto his wound, into his heart. Jeremias had fixed me by doing something similar, but he used black magic blood. I'm using my blood, full of life and light.

And love.

The blood is love.

"Solon, can you hear me?" I whisper. "Come back to me, please. I'm here. I'm waiting for you."

I let the blood run.

I let it fill the wound.

I watch it run over, spreading across his chest, running over the edges onto the snow and the pebbles of the beach below.

And still nothing.

I close my eyes, tilting my face up to the sky, letting the tears fall.

A ray of light hits my face.

I squint and realize that the clouds are parting, showing blue patches of sky underneath.

Blue.

Not a hint of red anymore.

And then beneath me he stirs.

I gasp and move back to see Solon twitch, his chest rising.

Oh my god!

"Solon," I cry out, placing my hands at his face. "Solon."

He blinks.

Staring up at the sky that matches the blue in his eyes.

Then his eyes widen and he rolls over, coughing, the blood pouring out of his mouth before he chokes on it.

"You need that," I tell him, and I'm so elated that I feel like

268

THE BLOOD IS LOVE

crying and laughing at the same time. "You need to drink from me."

He collapses back down on the ground, too weak to talk or keep himself up and I quickly slice my other wrist and hold it against his mouth, my other hand going to the back of his head and cradling it as I lift it up a few inches.

"Drink," I tell him. "You need my blood. It's the only way you'll survive."

He bites my wrist, soft at first as he drinks, then his fangs grow against my skin piercing deep out of habit. His gaze is a little lost, both ravenous and out of it, which I would expect when you've come back from the dead like this.

Then, as time goes on and I feel myself losing power and energy, a clarity comes into his eyes.

I died, he says inside my head, still feeding hungrily. *I died. You brought me back. Am I mad?*

I shake my head. *You aren't. You're you.*

Am I hurting you?

I close my eyes. *No. You can't hurt me anymore, Solon. The beast is gone, but you are here. So am I.*

What if I can't stop?

I feel like life is slipping out of me. *You'll find a way*, I whisper.

Then everything goes black.

* * *

I WAKE up to water washing up against my legs. For a moment I feel like my brain is being rewound, that I'm finding myself back in the past of not so long ago, that I'm still stuck in the depths, forever drowning, forever being kept at the bottom of the ocean in another world.

But then I slowly open my eyes, staring down at dark grey pebbles with intricate pale patterns on them, like there are maps and messages hidden within the layers. And beyond the pebbles is the crisp white of ice-crusted snow and beyond that is...blood.

So much blood. It's splattered along the pebbled beach and the white snow for as far as the eye can see. Suddenly I remember all the mayhem and death and carnage and I'm lifting up my head as panic starts to take over, stealing my breath.

"You're safe, Lenore."

Solon's voice comes from beside me and I whip my head around to see him on his back beside me, his legs half in the red ocean that keeps lapping at the shore.

"Solon," I cry out, dragging myself over the pebbles toward him, my body coming alive at the sound of him, the sight of him, the smell of him.

"Stay," he says, and he moves over, not as fast as he normally would, but then again he is a new vampire now and everything might take some getting used to. As for me, I feel like I'm moving through molasses.

He grasps my hand and lays the side of his head down on the shore, staring at me with those beautiful blues of his. "We're both a little weak," he says. "After I fed from you, you passed right out. The tide started rising. I tried to move you out of the water as much as I could but I'm...I'm learning."

"How do you feel?" I ask.

He smiles softly at me. God he's beautiful. "In some ways, like I've been hit by a truck. In other ways, like I've just been born."

I swallow thickly, my throat feeling like sandpaper. "Do you think it worked?"

He smiles. "I'm here, aren't I?" Then his smile falters. "I shouldn't be here, Lenore."

"You expected me to let you die?"

"No," he admits. "You're too stubborn for that. But...you didn't know what you were doing."

"Yes I did," I say defensively, pushing myself up on my elbows. "I was told that I wouldn't create feral vampires. I knew exactly what I was doing. You were fucking dying, Solon. No, you were *dead*. You really think I would let that happen without trying everything I could?"

"And who told you that?"

I bite my lip for a moment. "Jeremias."

"Then you didn't know for sure that it would work," he says with a pained expression. "Jeremias could have been lying."

At the mention of his name, I look over at his lifeless, charred, headless body. Fuck. He's dead. He's real dead because *I* killed him. I killed my own father, as estranged as he was.

"Moonshine," Solon says, bringing himself closer to me. "I know how badly you tend to latch onto guilt, but please don't go down this road. Not now."

"If not now, when?" I ask helplessly.

He gives me a soft smile, then lets go of my hand as he pushes himself up, getting to his feet. "There will be plenty of time of introspection later. For now, we need to get out of here. This isn't any safer than it was before."

"Even with our fathers dead?" I ask, as he reaches down and hauls me up to my feet, putting his arm around me for support as I wobble a little on the pebbles.

"Even with," he says. "Kaleid is still alive. And while I don't expect him to jump out from around the corner and get us, he did try to kill you."

"Technically he didn't know if he could kill me."

"Then he wanted to torture you," Solon says sharply. "And for that, he'll forever be a mortal enemy of mine. If I ever see his face again, I will spit in it, rip his head off, then tear the rest of him limb from limb just to make sure."

"Like you did with Skarde?" I look over at the remains of Skarde's eviscerated body. It's not lost on me that the two of us with our daddy issues just murdered the both of them, complete with two different styles of beheadings.

"Just like," he says in a low voice.

"Even though he's the king of the vampires now?" I ask, leaning into him. He's like a tree, so strong and rooted, my body instantly relaxing against his.

"We'll see how long that lasts," Solon says gruffly. "Vampires followed Skarde, but they were always looking for a way out. That's why so many end up at Dark Eyes, to disappear into that subculture, the freedom of it all. Kaleid may lead Helsinki and some other cities in Europe, but it's only because he's the son of Skarde. Or was, anyway. I'll be surprised if the majority want to follow someone under new rule."

"You willing to bet on that?"

He looks down at me and smiles. "No. Never." Then he puts his arm around my waist, supporting my weight and we start walking off across the snow, past the ruins. Every horrible thing that happened there looks differently under the light of day, because that's what's changing here. The day. The red sunset sky is growing more pale, more blue, and when I look behind us at the ocean, that too has shades of indigo mixing with the red. Whatever hold the Dark One had on this place to make it this way is losing its grip. With Skarde gone, maybe it can revert back to its natural form.

Or perhaps disappear into space altogether, I think to myself.

I glance up at Solon. "Perhaps we should pick up the pace."

"I was just thinking the same thing."

I'm drained, having given so much of my blood away, and

Solon's weary from having been born again, but somehow it doesn't take long until we're moving fast along the snow plains, heading along a red creek that's gradually turning clear, the snow melting underfoot.

"We might not have a lot of time," Solon says. "I can carry you if you want."

I shake my head. "I'm feeling stronger with every step."

"Yes. That, and more stubborn," he says.

That only spurs me on to walk faster.

Eventually we get to the bluffs where once a crimson waterfall ran over the edge, but now the water is clear and not much more than a weak stream. Of course, that stream comes from the bloody lake, which means the water in the lake is going down too.

Our way out.

"Shit," I swear, and the two of us scramble up the slope until we're up on the bluff. Up here, the snow is totally gone, leaving moss, rock, and lichen beneath our feet, and then we're running along the sluggish creek bed, following it toward the lake, hoping against all hope that it's not too late. I could be anywhere in the world as long as I had Solon by my side, but I can't attest for other worlds.

Finally we reach the lake. The water is no longer red, and it's just a small pool in the middle. As far as we know, this is the only way out of this world.

"Ready?" Solon asks, grabbing my hand and holding tight.

"Ready," I tell him.

Together we step into lake and the water is practically receding as we walk in, like it's running away from us. We're quick though and we start running through the water until we're in to our chests. Then, after a quick glance at each other, we take in a deep (though not needed) breath, and dive under.

It's much easier to swim down this time. It helps that I

don't have a Lapp Witch holding onto me as a I do, as does the fact that the water is just water now, clear and fluid and easy to move through, no longer this bloody, smelly soup.

I dive down, down, past where the natural bottom of the lake should be, and I see Solon diving beside me, keeping pace. It gets darker and darker as we go, but our night vision kicks in and then the light appears. A growing glimpse of the sky that belongs to the other world, to our beautiful world.

We kick and kick and then we're heading upward until we're breaking through the surface, gasping for breath.

I look around, treading water, blinking at the surroundings. This is where we went in. And luckily there are no Lapp Witches to be found this time.

"I think we did it," I tell Solon, brushing my soaked hair out of my face.

He grins at me, spitting out lake water. "I have my fingers crossed."

We start swimming to shore, and though I start to lose my energy by the end of it, he pulls me out of the water until I'm on solid ground beside him. The air smells fresh here, like pine needles and marsh and clean air. It smells like the real world, our world. It smells like home.

I can't help but laugh, the relief finally pouring through me. Not just that we survived Skarde (and Kaleid and Jeremias) and defeated him for good, but that we actually made it back to our world. The one that counts.

Most of all, the relief is because Solon is standing next to me, soaking wet and totally naked, and he's here and he's alive and he's mine. No longer feral, the beast inside him dead, but the rest of him living.

"I can't believe you're here," I say to him, swallowing the lump in my throat.

"I can't believe I died," he says, his gaze roaming delicately over my face. "That I died and you brought me back. You brought me back better."

"Well, that remains to be seen," I tell him, standing up on my tip toes to place a soft kiss on his kips.

He gives me a salacious grin, and the fact that he's completely naked hasn't escaped me. "I'd prove it to you," he says. "But I'm not sure exactly what I did when I was the beast. If there's a chance that Valtu is still alive, we owe it to him to find him."

I nod. I can't be the one responsible for leaving *Dracula* in the woods to die.

Solon grabs my hand and leads me through the woods. There's still a lot of magical energy in the air, but it's not dark. It's like the whole forest is sighing in relief. It's nice, it's peaceful. I think we walk for hours, but it's just enough time to slow down and take stock of everything that happened.

Unless we're lost.

"Do you smell where you've been?" I ask as we pass through blueberry bushes in a mossy clearing.

He nods. "That, and I remember the way from when Jeremias took us before."

"Did he...hurt you?" I ask.

He glances at me in surprise. "No. He didn't. But he did leave us to suffer for eternity, so suffice to say, his intentions weren't good."

"I just don't know what to make of it all," I say, gnawing on my lip. "He needed me, used me, didn't seem to care if Kaleid was going to kill me. He treated me like garbage, he was pure evil, he killed the one I love. He just...why did he save me twice? Both times from you."

He winces. "I tried to get you this time too?"

I nod. "Yeah. Unfortunately. You went for me even before you went for Skarde. You know, just to confirm the whole *I'm not special* thing."

"Fuck," he swears in a low voice. "I'm so sorry, Lenore."

"It doesn't matter," I say quickly. "Jeremias killed the beast and I was able to bring you back without it. That's all that matters. Besides, he also told me that you love me. And that love angers the beast because it reminds him of how much stronger you are."

He stops walking so abruptly I run right up against him.

"I do love you," he whispers, kissing me softly, running his hands through my hair. "Love is what brought me back. Not magic. Not anything else."

"You better be careful," I tease against his mouth. "You're getting soft on me."

"Only in the ways that count," he says, and now he's pressing his erection against me, hard as fucking steel. Man, I know we should probably wait until we get back to our luxurious hotel, but honestly I could screw him senseless right here.

Except...

Suddenly my scalp prickles, the hair rising at the back of my neck.

I stop kissing him, pulling away.

"What?" he asks, frowning at me.

"Do you sense that?" I ask. I look around. The forest of pines and birch is deep and dark, but I swear I can hear something moving. Many somethings.

Solon breathes in deeply through his nose, trying to place the scent. "I do. It's...familiar."

"Familiar good or familiar bad?" I ask warily, keeping my eyes locked on the forest.

"I don't know yet."

"Oh my god," I gasp, my hand going to my chest. Between two birch trees something moves. It looks like a person, but it also looks like a tree. Or like the forest. Like the forest personified. I immediately think of Treebeard in *Lord of the*

Rings, but he was huge and I'm pretty sure he was friendly. I don't know what the hell this is and it's highly disturbing to know that this is happening in the real world and not in one of the vampire ones.

Oh my god. What if we aren't back in our world yet? What if we only went into another one?

Easy now, moonshine, Solon's voice comes in my head. *Easy*.

Easy? I cry out, watching as more of the forest starts moving. I can see *eyes*.

"They mean you no harm," a familiar voice says, and we both whip around to see Dracula walking out of the forest. "At least, they've meant me no harm."

"You're alive," Solon says to him, relief on his face.

I'm grinning too. Dracula is a sign that we're in the right world. Besides, I didn't want him to die. He *is* an ass, but I rather like him.

"Yes," Dracula says and then stares at Solon's crotch. "And you're naked for once and happy to see me."

Solon clears his throat, not in the least bit bashful about his half-hard cock. "I'm just happy I didn't kill you."

"Well, you tried," he says with a wry grin. "You swiped at me with those dino claws of yours, but all you managed to do was break the chains before you lost interest and ran out of the door. Honestly, I didn't think I'd see you again. I've never seen your beast before, so I had no idea that the thing doesn't have one intelligent thought in its head." He pauses and eyes my dress. "So, what happened to you guys?"

"It's a long story and we have a long walk back to the road," Solon says. Then he glances behind him at the forest creatures. "Are you sure you can vouch for them?"

"That's just the old folk," he says, jerking his chin at the trees. "Least that's what they told me. They're the dead, waiting underground for Skarde to leave. Apparently waiting

KARINA HALLE

so long that they've become one with nature, or some hippie shit like that. I guess this whole land has some supernatural stuff that we have no idea about."

"Only in the mythology books," I say, remembering what poor Natalia had said.

Dracula shrugs. "You've been gone for three days. I didn't know if you'd ever come back. They kept me company in the meantime. God, they can talk your ears off. Anyway, let's get going."

Dracula waves goodbye at the tree things, who are now retreating into the background until I can't see them clearly anymore. The strange energy goes with them, but at least now I can pick up on feelings of relief, like they're finding freedom for the first time.

File that in another page of Strange Shit Lenore's Seen Today.

We start going back the way we came, walking single file, Dracula behind me, Solon in front of me. At least I can stare at Solon's perfect ass the entire walk back.

"I will say one thing," Dracula says. "Being left there for eternity has made me appreciate things."

"Like you have a new lease at life?" I ask. "Want to become a new man?"

"Something like that."

Solon eyes him over his shoulder, his eyes twinkling. "Enough to finally settle down?"

Dracula barks out a laugh. "Don't even joke about that, not after what I've been through."

I glance back at him. "What have you been through?"

He just shakes his head. "I've been screwed over twice. That's enough."

"He had a wife, ages ago," Solon explains. "She died."

"Oh no, I'm so sorry," I tell him.

He shrugs. "That's what humans do, right? They die."

278

And sometimes vampires do too.

"And then she got reincarnated," Solon adds.

"Wait, wait. *What?*" I ask. "She got reincarnated? Like…like…"

He gives me a snippy look. "Yes. Like *Dracula*. The book. The movie. Whatever you want to call it."

"So it was real?"

He shrugs again. "Some. Bram was an author. He specialized in fiction. And anyway, then she eventually died too. No happy ending for me."

"Unless she comes back again," Solon says. "Never give up hope, my friend."

"Not your fucking friend, Solon."

"Sorry, I forgot."

And it goes like this all the way back to civilization.

EPILOGUE

SOLON

Four months later

"WHAT DO YOU WANT TO DO FOR HALLOWEEN?" LENORE asks me.

I lower the copy of the San Francisco Chronicle and peer at her over it. "You're being serious?"

She grins at me, crossing her legs. She's not wearing underwear under that baby-doll dress of hers, and she's been showing off that fact all morning long.

"Oh, come on," she says, brushing her long hair back over her bare shoulder, drawing attention to her smooth skin there. Fucking hell, she knows I want to bite her too. Why is she torturing me like this when we only rolled out of bed a couple of hours ago? "You're a vampire."

"And you're also a vampire," I point out.

"Right. And this is my first Halloween as both a vampire and a witch. I need to take advantage of that."

I look back to my newspaper. "I'm sure Amethyst will go

out with you if you want to go on one of your little pub crawls."

Even though I kind of hate it when she does that. I'll admit I'm the jealous type and the idea of lots of men—humans—staring at her, hitting on her, gets me feeling all sorts of murderous. It's enough that the last two times they went out for a girl's night, I tagged along. They didn't know that of course, but I was there in the background, just in case I needed to put any classless delinquents in their place.

"We could have a Halloween party," she says, having a sip of her coffee. "For the vampires. Or the witches. Depending which way you're swinging that day."

I sigh, trying to hide my smile from her. She's adorable when she gets like this, totally obsessed and in love with her newfound identities. It makes me even more obsessed and in love with her.

"We'll see."

"Solon, you love throwing parties."

"Not theme parties, my dear. That's a very human thing."

"And you keep saying you need to embrace your humanity. Well, there you go. Let's do it. Get a band to play the Monster Mash. Dress up in capes. Hire a bunch of bats to fly around."

"Hire a bunch of bats?" I repeat, staring at her again. "Have you ever seen anyone train bats?"

"You have magic, you could do it."

"*You* have magic, Miss I Know How to Fly. Training bats is your problem."

She sticks her tongue out at me. "Whatever happened to being less grumpy?"

I lower the paper in an exasperated manner and give her a dry look. "When did I say that?"

"When you said you had a new lease on life."

"That wasn't me. That was Dracula."

That said, she's not entirely wrong. After everything that happened in the Arctic and in the Red World, I have been trying to put a better foot forward. It's not every day that you actually physically die and then come back as a vampire again.

And yet, that's what my Lenore was able to do.

She brought me back.

This time, as myself through and through. Not a hint of the beast, not a hint of madness. Just me.

And completely hers.

She owns me now. She always did, but now that she saved my life by giving me part of her life, well…I'm in it for the long run. For the ages, of course, but beyond that. Beyond life, beyond death. Beyond the universe.

And she's pretty good at reminding me of that. Has me completely wrapped around her little finger.

I just like to keep her on her toes. She doesn't need to know how damn devoted I am to her, to every inch and fiber of her being. She already has so much of the upper hand, I wouldn't want to lose all my control completely.

Especially now that she can fly. Every day she's discovering more and more of her powers. Sometimes we learn together, trading magic that innately remained within me even after dying. Other times her parents help out. Her magic is far above what they can do, but they still know the basics, and I can tell it helps bring Lenore and her parents closer together. Family is a tricky situation for the both of us, finding ways to heal rifts while also holding onto the found family in this house.

As for my family, well, Skarde is dead. He died in that other world, never to return to this one. Natalia, unfortunately, is dead too. And Kaleid, well…no one knows what happened to Kaleid. No one knows what happened to the Dark Order either. Ezra has been to Europe twice in the last four months since we left Helsinki, spying for me, since that whole lot of vampires over there are as untrustworthy as anything. He hasn't found out any information, not even any rumors. It's like all the vampires are finally free to do what they want, what I've already been doing for a long time. And without Kaleid and Natalia leading the Red World, they've moved onto the normal one. So far, they all seem to be behaving, proving that vampires don't need a ruler after all.

Then, of course, there's Dracula. He's galivanting on the beaches of Mexico or Italy or some place that sounds like hell to me. I talk to him occasionally and he's dropped a few hints that he'd like to come visit, move to San Francisco, but he hasn't bitten the bullet yet. I think he thinks that Wolf wants to kill him still, but he's so blindly obsessed with Amethyst that Wolf wouldn't pay Dracula much attention.

Unless Dracula starts going for Amethyst.

Well, that's not my problem.

"What's not your problem?" Lenore asks, putting her coffee down and getting to her feet. She walks over to me and I toss the newspaper to the side. We're in Dark Eyes, drinking coffee from the espresso machine, enjoying the cool temperatures during a hot San Francisco autumn, and the peace and quiet before the rest of the vamps wake up and things get busy.

"You're listening to my thoughts?" I ask her, teasing. "Thought we had an agreement."

"I just caught the last sentence," she says, biting her lip seductively. "Thought maybe I could give you a problem."

"Oh really?" I say, gazing up at her. She stands between my legs and reaches for my zipper. My cock is already hard as rock, having been all morning since she keeps showing me flashes of her cunt.

Plus, I can smell how aroused she's been, even though I haven't shown it. I just like to make her wait, if possible. I'm cruel like that. She once said I was the Prince of Darkness; King of Edging, and I like to lean into that as much as possible.

But as I run my hands up her inner thighs, playing with her clit, sliding my fingers inside her, I decide I don't have much patience this morning. I get her off, fucking her hard with my fingers while she stands there, head back, moans filling the nightclub, as well as the slick, X-rated sounds of her wetness.

When she's come twice already and I'm hair-trigger sensitive, my cock aching painfully for release, I bring it out of my fly, making a tight fist around the base, which elicits a deep groan from inside me. I'm not going to last long either. She quickly climbs on my lap, straddling me, then lowers her hips until I sink into her.

"Fuck," I breathe out, my arms trembling as I grab her waist, trying to control her movement, the strain making my face contort.

But she's already come. She has that look of pure lustful determination, wicked to the bone, and I know there's no point in trying to control things.

It feels good to let go sometimes.

So she starts to ride my cock, pushing down deeper and deeper, squeezing me so tight that it's hard to breathe. With each sharp thrust of her hips she rocks back and forth and I'm pulling down the neckline of her dress, biting and sucking at her soft breasts, my fingers slipping down over her slick clit again.

Heaven. Lenore feels like heaven, a place that I might have gone to when I died. It's hard to say, when I died I went to a dark place but it wasn't a bad place. It was peaceful.

It just wasn't whole because she wasn't in it.

And now that I'm deep inside her, I know that's where heaven really is. Wherever she is.

And she's with me. For now. For the ages.

Making me whole.

Making this long life one worth living.

"Fuck," I swear again as my orgasm sneaks through me and then I'm coming, grunting loudly as she rides me into oblivion, her own cries matching mine.

Eventually she collapses against me, kisses my neck, my ear, my jaw, small presses of her lips that make my skin dance.

I run my fingers through her wild hair, holding her in place while I gaze at her, feeling nothing but lucky and in love and alive.

Then, as my heart begins to bloom, making me feel dizzy with my feelings for her, feelings that are so large and powerful that I'm still having a hard time getting used to them, a hard time accepting them, she flashes me another wicked grin.

"So…" she says. "Yes to a Halloween party?"

I roll my eyes, but still I say, "Anything for you, moon-shine. Anything for you."

THE END

HOPE YOU ENJOYED the continuation of Lenore and Solon's story. If you leave a review, I would really appreciate it!

ALSO I'M ALSO DOING a spinoff with Wolf and Amethyst called NIGHTWOLF coming October 31 2021 (PREORDER here now). YAY!

. . .

AND we have Dracula's book in King of Darkness, also up for preorder.

IN THE MEANTIME you can reach out to me and keep up with what I'm working on by:

Following me on Instagram

-> joining my Facebook Group (we're a fun bunch and would love to have you)

-> Otherwise, feel free to signup for my mailing list (it comes once a month) and Bookbub alerts!

ACKNOWLEDGMENTS

I'm going to make this short but sweet (I mean it this time!). First of all, I couldn't wait to dive back into this world and I have my readers to thank for that. You let me know with all your passion and enthusiasm that you wanted more from Lenore and Solon as well. While I have no plans to continue their story going forward, I do like to leave the door open in case I get struck by inspiration. And anyway, we will see them again in both Nightwolf (Wolf and Amethyst's story) and King of Darkness (Dracula's story). And will we see Kaleid in a future book? Maybe!

Second of all, I need to thank the usual suspects, Laura for her on-the-fly editing, Chanpreet for her proofing, Hang for the gorgeously fitting cover, Nina Grinstead and all the hardworking crew at Valentine PR, plus Kathleen Tucker, Sandra Cortez, and everyone else who tried to keep me sane.

Biggest thanks to Scott who took care of me while I finished this book under incredibly stressful situations, plus a record breaking heatwave here in the normally mild PNW, that Solon would have hated haha. I'll forever associate writing this while sweating like mad (and not because I found some of these scenes sexy as hell).

Finally, I am actually a citizen of Finland (but don't ask me to speak the language) and I've been waiting for about eight years to incorporate Finnish mythology into a book. I still have my plans for a big fantasy based around this world and that's in the works for one day, but it was nice to dip my toes into it here. It goes without saying though, that this is a work of fiction and I took a lot of fictional liberties with the mythology of the Finns as well as the Sami people.

If any of you feel like bugging me to get started on that Finnish mythology dark fantasy though, feel free!

AN EXCERPT FROM NIGHTWOLF

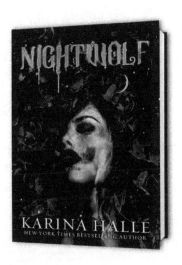

Nightwolf is Amethyst and Wolf's friends-to-lovers story, available now.

WOLF

In front of me the eucalyptus wavers in the mist, like pairs of bleeding hands. I stand in the middle of Alamo Square, taking in the night from the crest of the hill. It's my favorite time of year, my favorite time of day. Autumn in San Francisco brings with it darkness and gloom, that ever-present fog pressing down on the city like a hand from a vengeful god. I feel more at peace, more at home, during this season where the world grows a little quieter, muffled, and life slows down a little.

Humans move too fast these days. They always have, for as long as I've walked among them, but in the last half a century they've leaped forward at supersonic speed. Always rushing, too busy trying to pay for a life that they're too busy to start living.

And I get it. They only have so many years. Eighty to a hundred if they're lucky. If they're unlucky, death swoops in following a grave illness or a freak accident, cutting them off before their time. There's no escape from it either. Death lurks at every corner. I understand the urge to keep moving, keep trying to fill the days, not knowing when you'll be taken out.

Yet, they miss so much. They miss out on the fact that life isn't about getting to the next thing, the next paycheck, the next high, the next rung of the ladder. It's about the smaller moments, where there's time to breathe, when this big impossible world whittles down to one thing.

But it's that one thing that remains elusive to so many, including me.

Still, I stand in the middle of the square, letting the fog roll over me, the mist whispering things in my ears, music from the clouds and the ocean from where it all began. I feel plugged in, the sounds of the city dropping away, until it's just me and the mist and I can't tell where I begin and it ends. I am one with the dark, the way I'm supposed to be.

Laughter snags me out of my thoughts and my eyes open. Through the fog I can see a bunch of drunk teenagers, though they can't see me. They're far away, near the Painted Ladies. I can smell the booze on their breath, in their pores. Cheap beer, maybe Pabst, and one of them has been drinking a sugary vodka drink. In my gut I feel a pang of hunger, but I pay it no attention. It's been a while since I fed and when that happens, even unsavory teenagers can stoke the appetite, but I'm not who I once was. Most of us aren't. Even vampires evolve.

Still, I shove my hands in my coat pockets and turn away from them, heading up the path to the street, to the house. I don't need to be tempted, and in my experience, coming across drunk teenagers never ends well. Their growing brains are so much more open to the unknown, and often they're actively seeking it out. When a vampire appears before them, they recognize the "otherness." They feel fear. And when teenagers feel fear, especially drunk teenagers, they can lash out. And when they lash out, well...

Sometimes they die.

It's best I head back into the house anyway. Though the night is where I feel most at home, the good citizens of San Francisco aren't as desensitized to what Amethyst describes as "vibey" people as you'd think, and they're quick to call the cops. I'm tall, good-looking, dress well, am generally amiable and polite, but though the teenagers may feel fear if they see me, adults tend to find me vaguely threatening. I'm not sure why, since they don't always feel that way about all vampires, but it is what it is. Amethyst says that beneath my smile there's a snake ready to strike. She was joking at the time, but perhaps there's some truth to it.

Either way, eleven at night is too late to be standing in a foggy park by yourself without arousing suspicion, so I cross the street and go in through the back entrance of the house, the door beeping as I wave my key card at it.

"Feel better?" Solon asks from a lounge chair by the bar, Ezra sitting beside him.

The door locks behind me and the chill of the night turns to warmth as I walk across Dark Eyes.

"A bit," I say, heading right behind the bar to fix myself a drink. Solon has opened up a rare bottle of wine in my absence, drinking it with Ezra, but I need something a little stronger. I go for a classic malt, on the rocks.

"What's wrong with him?" Ezra asks Solon.

"Nothing," I answer quickly, giving him a tight smile. I don't need to get into this now, not in front of Ezra. He generally delights in other people's misery.

Knowing this, Solon remains silent. He's never one to spill someone's secrets. Not that any of this is a secret.

"Ahhh," Ezra says smugly, leaning back in his chair, the glass of wine casually dangling from his fingers. I didn't know Ezra back when he first turned in Italy, centuries ago, but I could easily see him being the wanton King of Sicily (or at the very least, the spoiled asshole son of a king who took over after his father conveniently died, and whom his new subjects had to reluctantly put up with). "Human troubles. Women, to be specific."

I sit down in the velvet chair, resting the glass on the antique table between us. "Just felt a bit off today, that's all," I explain, flashing him an easy smile. "Being in the dark always helps."

I don't even have to explain this to him. Living with Solon and Ezra for as long as I have means that we all know each other's habits like the backs of our hands. If I'm dealing with something, I'll disappear into the night. If Solon is, he'll usually be in his room of skulls, staring at their empty eye sockets until he finds some kind of absolution. If it's Ezra, well, he just gets drunk and hits things, which is a step up from when he used to get drunk and murder people. As I said before, we vampires evolve.

"A bit off because you acted like a jealous boyfriend last night," Ezra scoffs and my hackles immediately rise, along with a touch of shame. Because I wasn't at my finest. I don't think I've ever yelled at a volunteer, at least not when it came to another human. Sure, I'm the guard dog, I oversee the Dark Room, I make sure both humans and vampires are playing by the rules when it comes to feeding time, and that no one gets hurt—unless they request it. I have no problem enforcing things, no problem with giving punishment. But it wasn't like me to snap like that.

I honestly don't know what came over me. Vampires are a possessive bunch and I have always felt possessive over Amethyst. Not in that I own her, but I *want* to own her. I want her to belong to me, and I'd honestly take whatever I can get.

But I've never acted upon it, nor acted it out. It was a side of me I'm not sure I liked and made me feel like I was on shakier ground with her, something I've been feeling more of lately. I've been friends with her for nearly a decade and yet, in the last year, hell, the last few months, whatever our foundation was, the basis of who we are to each other, has been crumbling. Not necessarily in a bad way, but it's changing, the future of our relationship has been flipped like a coin, and I'm not sure which way we're going to end up.

"I wish I had seen it," Solon muses, giving me a wry smirk before he has a sip of his wine. "It's rare that our wolfhound gets worked up about anything."

I glare at him. "Temporary lapse of judgment, that's all. It happens to the best of us." *You should know that more than anyone*, I think. Solon was always cool, calm and collected, but when he wasn't, there were deadly consequences. When he had a lapse of judgment and lost his temper, his inner beast would come out and no, that wasn't a metaphor. There was a legitimate monster inside Solon that he only recently tamed, and that monster would try to kill everything in its path.

"You're right, I do know what that's like," he says with deliberation, and I loathe it when he picks up on my thoughts like that. "I also know that it made things a lot worse when I didn't deal with my problems head on."

I scoff and manage a shrug. These fucks are reaching tonight. "Who said I had problems? I didn't."

Ezra finishes his glass of wine and pounds it on the table, hard enough that it makes Solon wince. He's very particular about his furniture. "If you don't end up fucking her soon, it's going to be a problem."

"To be clear, we are talking about that cute blonde you were with last night, right?" I ask, brow raised.

"Oh, fuck you," Ezra says, getting to his feet.

"Where are you going?" I ask. "I think it's a great idea. She'd look much better on my dick than yours, don't you think?"

"Wolf, go to hell," Ezra says, glaring at me before he walks off down the length of the lounge, leaving out the back door.

"Jeez, he's a moody bitch tonight," I say, turning back in my chair to face Solon.

Solon laughs. "Turns out he has a date with the cute blonde."

"Really? Another date with the Michelle Pfieffer to his Al Pacino? Guess he didn't manage to piss her off last night. Oh well. He will."

"And if he doesn't, well...perhaps it's what he needs right now. If you haven't noticed, Ezra has been a moody bitch since 1986."

I frown, trying to think back. "What happened in 1986 again?"

"The last time he was in love."

"Oh yeah. I forgot that was a possibility for him."

"Now, I know I'm stepping on your toes here, but it's only fair since you did the same with me and Lenore," he begins, and I don't like where this is going. Solon can be secretive and minds his own business ninety-nine percent of the time but he also likes to give advice that turns into lectures. Blames it on himself being the oldest and the first-born vampire. Lenore calls it "vamp-splaining."

"Please don't tell me you're going to give me a lecture about love, because I'd just rather get drunk in peace," I tell him, taking a large burning gulp of scotch.

"No lecture," Solon says. "But I am a little concerned about you."

I throw my head back and let out a frustrated sigh. "Oh Jesus, Solon. I'm fine. So I got a little jealous last night. No harm, no foul."

"Not yet, maybe. But over time? Wolf, you know your business is your business. But, as a friend, as well as the person in charge of this house, in charge of keeping the harmony and peace which I very much need, you need to figure out just what the hell you want with her. Because I've watched the two of you for a long time now, and it's quite unbearable the way you both tiptoe around your actual feelings for each other. Now, whether you're in love with Amethyst," I open my mouth in protest but he raises his hand to shut me up, "or you just want to fuck her, as Ezra so eloquently says, you have to do something about it and make up your god damn mind. If you don't make some sort of choice, I'm afraid you're going to fuck things up royally and then I have to live in a house of angst and chaos, and frankly I had enough of that when I lived in that brothel in Bristol."

"Solon, really—"

"I'm not finished," he says firmly. "You need to figure out what you want with her and then act on it. The more you put it off, the worse it will get. Eventually she is going to have to move on from you, and then what?"

I frown, shaking my head slightly, a tightness in my chest. "What do you mean she has to move on? She's not..."

He gives me a steady look. "I don't profess to know how she feels about you, but obviously it's something, and you know it too. She's waiting for you, Wolf, whether she knows it or not. But she won't wait for long. She doesn't have long, not like we do."

I swallow thickly, the afterburn of the scotch still present. "I don't..." But there's no use in denying that I want her. And I want her to want me. "It can never be, and you know it."

He studies for a moment and then sits back in his chair. "Once upon a time I would have agreed with you," he says. "But then I met Lenore."

"Who is a vampire," I point out.

"Half-vampire," he corrects. "Who might be as immortal as us, or as mortal as her human side."

"Solon, she defeated her own powerful warlock father. She has powers unlike anyone we know. There's barely anything human about her. I have no doubt she'll be by your side for as long as you're alive. She'll be alive too."

"Be that as it may, and I pray that you're right, Lenore gave me purpose. What do you think we're supposed to do with our lives, Wolf? What do you want with yours? Are you living, or are you just existing? Just spending your many days trying to run down that elusive clock?"

I shake my head again, looking down at the scotch, the ice swirling in the glass. "Absolon Stavig, the incurable romantic." I sigh and take another sip, licking my lips. "I don't know what I'm supposed to do about her. What I do know is that as much as I feel like she's mine, as I want her to be mine, she's not supposed to be."

"Then who does she belong to?"

I shrug. "I don't fucking know. Not that douchebag she was with last night, that's for fucking sure."

"I know you are what you are. But it doesn't have to end in horror and doom."

I let out a bitter laugh. "Says the one with the monster inside him."

"You know that monster is gone now. Lenore destroyed it when I was reborn. It's not coming back."

"Solon, Amethyst is a human. I'm not. She's going to age, and while I don't have a problem with that, she will. I've seen it over and over again. The insecurities that come out, let alone the fact that you have to keep moving around the world in order to not draw suspicion."

"Then you use magic, like we do with the house. It's how we've been able to stay here for so long and no one's ever grown suspicious."

"Okay, fine. Then, say she doesn't care that she'll be seventy and look like it and I'll still look like this. She's going to *die*, Solon." My throat suddenly feels hot. "She's going to die one day and I can't...I can't go through that again. You know that's why I don't make friends with humans."

"But you have. With her, with her mother. You care about them both deeply, as do I, but can't you see the damage is already done? You already care. You can't outrun the death of other people, Wolf. You can't outrun grief."

"One day Amethyst and Yvonne will move out and move on to other things. You know they will," I tell him.

"They don't have to, not if you don't fuck things up."

"Well, then I hate to break it to you, but I'm going to fuck things up. I want her but I can't have her and at some point I'm going to do something really stupid like sleep with someone else and hurt her on purpose. Or, I'll do something worse and sleep with *her*. Lead her on. You think that's going to bring peace to this house? You think me suddenly professing my feelings to her, or fucking her, is going to make a change for the better? It's only going to make things more complicated."

And if I already felt like the foundation was weakening between us, this would crack it in two.

Solon stares at me for a long moment, his eyes unreadable. Probably probing my fucking brain. I just need my heart rate to slow down a little. It's rare that it gets this worked up.

Eventually, Solon finishes the glass of wine and pops the cork back in the empty bottle. "I know I've always given you a hard time," he says, getting to his feet. "But you deserve to be happy. You deserve to have someone in your life. I didn't know that until I met Lenore, but I do now. And even if it turns out Lenore will age and gray and die in eighty years, it's worth it, you know. It's worth it. That's all."

He walks to the bar and puts the wine in the recycling bin, dusting off his hands. "I'm going off to bed. I apologize for the saccharine late-night lecture but you were overdue for one."

And, at that, he gives me a nod and disappears through the swinging doors that lead into the house.

Alone, I exhale heavily and swallow down the rest of the scotch. Despite what Solon just told me, I'm already feeling Amethyst's absence. Normally she'd be down here with me, drinking or playing a round of pool. The fact that she's not, that she's probably in bed already, says that maybe I need to apologize for last night. I didn't think it was that big of a deal, but perhaps it was out of character enough to make her pause. Maybe she thinks I had no right.

And I don't, not really. A vampire's possession often happens without the other person even wanting it.

The thing is, I know she's attracted to me, I can feel her desire even when she's not aware of it, but that's where it stops. Whether she feels something deeper, something more, that I can't say. I don't dare let myself examine it either way. I'm used to having females—vampires and humans—wanting me. Been that way for centuries. Humans are easily compelled, even when I'm not trying, and female vampires, well, I suppose I have the right combination of charm, stature and good looks, with a bit of arrogance that they seem to love.

But my arrogance only goes so far, and I'm not cocky enough to assume that Amethyst has any deep feelings for me. Love? I'm not even sure that's her style. She's a loving person, there's no doubt there. The love she has for her mother is strong and palpable. But she has this light and breezy way about her, like she's a flower caught in the wind, never quite sure when she's going to set down and happy to just keep it easy. It's one of the reasons why I like her so much, she makes me feel like the shadows of my life, the bloody footprints I've left behind, are staying in the past and that when I'm with her, I'm practically buoyant. I escape into the darkness, but she's my light that's always there when I need it the most.

No, I don't think Amethyst is in love with me, and more than that, I wouldn't want her to be. I would only hurt her in the end, and that's the last thing I want. The only thing I do know for sure is that she might be as attracted to me as I am to her. Whether that's because I'm a vampire or because she sees the real me, that remains to be seen. It wouldn't be the first time I thought someone wanted me—Wolf Eriksen—when it turned out they just wanted the myth and the legend of what I am instead.

I'm lost in my thoughts about her when suddenly the sound of pool balls breaking fills my ears, while the temperature in the room seems to drop to freezing.

What the fuck?

I'm fast on my feet, staring at the French doors to the cigar lounge where the table is. The doors are closed, as they were before, and from my angle I can't see the table.

"Amethyst?" I call out, my voice sounding flat. A cloud of vapors forms from my breath in the chilled air. "Is that you?" Maybe she was in there the whole time.

Fuck. I sure as hell hope not. She doesn't have vampire senses, but she is awfully good at hearing things she shouldn't. The last thing I need is her having heard all that.

I walk cautiously toward the room, feeling more on edge than I should. I never get scared. It's not really a thing when you're above humans on the food chain. And yet, something has my hair standing on end, my pulse thrumming in my veins.

Maybe it's a witch, I think. *A vampire slayer that broke through the wards of the house.*

But when I look through the doors, I see the room is totally empty.

I open the doors and step into the cigar lounge, and if it's possible, this room is even colder. There's a feeling in here, one that's thick in the air with fear and dread and sadness, and even though I'm not panicking, it stirs up similar emotions from my past. There's something familiar about this, and yet I have no idea why. That's the problem with déjà vu when you're as old as I am, you can never remember where to pin it.

I walk through the room anyway, noting the balls on the pool table have all been scattered across the green felt. Except, something isn't right. There are twice the amount of balls as there should be for a game, and they've been arranged as if it's spelling something out.

I frown and walk around the table to get a better look.

Pray.

The balls spell out *pray*.

"The fuck is this?" I say out loud. We do have ghosts in the house, but none of them have ever sent a literal message before. "Pray for what?"

Suddenly, the skin on my scalp prickles and I know there's someone else here, someone behind me.

I turn around in a flash, prepared to chastise myself for actually expecting to see something.

Yet I do see something.

There's a woman standing in the middle of Dark Eyes, right where I was just sitting. Her back is to me and she's dressed in a hospital gown. Her posture seems off, like she's broken her back or her neck, her hair long and graying.

Blood flows down one side of her head, making her hair stick to her scalp, running down her arms, to the floor.

I'm dumbfounded. I know I just said I never get scared but this…this is something. This isn't right.

This is death.

I push that thought out of my head and clear my throat.

"Hello?" I ask. "Are you lost?"

Stupid fucking thing to say.

"Are you okay?" I go on.

Also stupid. Clearly she's not. She's bleeding from a massive head injury.

"Are you a ghost?" I add, as if I'll get an answer.

But in a way I do.

She starts to walk toward the doors to the house, her hair obscuring her face so I can't see it properly. There's something so familiar about it though, whether it's the person themselves, or just this overall feeling of dread and déjà vu, like I've been through this before.

And she's heading into the house.

I run out of the cigar lounge but somehow in the second it takes me to move, she's disappeared, and the doors are swinging.

For a moment I think it must all be in my head, but when I look down at the floor, her bloody footprints are in the carpet and wood, clear as day. The even weirder thing is, there's a lot of blood. I've been hungry lately. As long as it's fresh, the sight and smell of blood should be doing something to me, whether I find it appetizing or not. But this blood has no smell. Like it's real and not real all at once.

A ghost. This has to be a motherfucking ghost.

And it's going upstairs.

I run through the doors and up to the main floor. The house is quiet except for the grandfather clock ticking away in the library.

But then I hear something else.

Something new.

A flurry of wings.

I go to the staircase and look up as it leads to the levels above, each one illuminated by flickering candles throwing shadows on the walls.

But the shadows are moving. Becoming something. Flying up between the floors of the house are ravens. At least seven of them, all flapping their wings and going higher and higher until they seem to disappear into the ceiling, becoming shadows again.

The sight of them sends a literal shudder through me, stirring up something deep and dark in my gut.

And then I see a flash of blue.

The ravens disappear and the woman in the hospital walks down one of the upper hallways.

Heading toward Amethyst's room.

Fuck no.

I take the stairs two at a time, and at my speed I'm at her floor in three seconds flat.

The door to her room is open.

I hurry on over and stop in the doorway.

Amethyst is in bed, on her back, her covers down and bunched around her feet. She's wearing a pink pajama top, no bottoms, just black underwear, which makes her look both ridiculously sexy and yet also extremely vulnerable.

The urge to protect her is overpowering, and I have to hold myself back so I don't run to her side, scoop her up in my arms.

Especially since she's moving in her sleep, a whimpering sound escaping her lips.

"Amethyst?" I whisper. The light from the candles in the hall barely illuminates her, but with my eyes I can see the rest of the dark room clear as day. It's empty, no sign of the woman in the hospital gown, no ravens either, nor bloody footprints.

Amethyst turns in bed again, her black hair wrapped around her face, giving her an unsettling appearance. "No, no," she says, her words getting louder. "No, don't leave, don't leave me."

"Amethyst?" I say again. "Are you awake?"

"Don't leave me," she cries out, turning over on her side again, her hands gripping the sheets for dear life.

She's having a nightmare.

I go over to her, dropping to my knees beside her bed, reaching up with my hands to brush her hair off her face. "Shhhh," I say softly. "You're having a bad dream. It's okay."

Suddenly she gasps and her eyes fly open, staring at me in fright. All the blood in her body rises to the surface, her heart pounding hard against her chest. I can practically see it, practically smell it. Reason one hundred and five why vampires and humans shouldn't be together. It's hard to be intimate when you're aware of how much you'd like to make them bleed.

"Wolf?" she asks, her voice ragged, the whites of her eyes shining.

"It's okay," I tell her, slowly brushing a strand of hair off her forehead. The blood under her skin leaps to the surface, as if trying to make contact with my fingers, and the feel of her is so warm and full of energy, as if our skin is trying to communicate with each other. "I'm here. It was just a nightmare."

She blinks and slowly tries to sit up. My hand falls away, my fingertips vibrating without the feel of her.

"Sorry I...was I loud? Was I screaming?"

I shake my head. I rarely get to see her like this. Disheveled, unsure. Scared. That vulnerability is coming through strong, and the more it does, the more I want to step in, get closer to her. Shield her from anything that would make her feel so small and fragile.

It makes me feel like maybe she might need me after all.

"You weren't screaming and you weren't loud. But you know my hearing." I'm not about to tell her that I saw a ghost, one that was headed to her room. That's the last thing she needs to hear.

"Oh. Good." She gives me a small smile, her eyes starting to relax a little, finding strength. "What was I saying?"

I clear my throat. "Don't leave me."

"Oh," she says, then pouts, frowning. "I don't know, I don't remember it. I think I did when I woke up but..."

"It doesn't matter," I tell her. "I'm a fan of *not* remembering my dreams, bad or good. Dreams become memories. After a while it becomes hard to tell what's real and what isn't. I mean, when you've lived for as long as I have."

Another small smile. This is the one where she's feeling a little foolish, probably because of the dream, probably because she's just in a pajama top and underwear. I don't read minds, but I am an empath of sorts.

It means it's time for me to go.

I get to my feet before I do something stupid like touch her again. "I better get to sleep. Let you get back to a better dream." I pause. "Want me to leave the door open?"

She shakes her head. "No, that's okay."

I nod and head toward the door.

"Wolf," she calls out softly as I'm about to close it.

I pause in the doorway. "Yeah?"

She presses her lips together and it's like my heart might explode. "Thank you for waking me up. For being here."

And that's when I realize that whatever weird thing happened last night on account of me and my jealousy doesn't matter anymore. We've moved past it.

Perhaps Solon was wrong about everything. Maybe we're going to be okay, just as we are. Nothing has to change.

"You're welcome," I tell her, then close the door behind me as I leave.

ABOUT THE AUTHOR

Karina Halle, a former screenwriter, travel writer and music journalist, is the *New York Times*, *Wall Street Journal*, and *USA Today* bestselling author of *The Pact*, *A Nordic King*, and *Sins & Needles*, as well as over sixty other wild and romantic reads. She, her husband, and their adopted pit bull, live in a rain forest on an island off British Columbia in the summer, and in the sunny climes of Los Angeles in the winter.

www.authorkarinahalle.com

ALSO BY KARINA HALLE

Contemporary Romances

Love, in English

Love, in Spanish

Where Sea Meets Sky (from Atria Books)

Racing the Sun (from Atria Books)

The Pact

The Offer

The Play

Winter Wishes

The Lie

The Debt

Smut

Heat Wave

Before I Ever Met You

After All

Rocked Up

Wild Card (North Ridge #1)

Maverick (North Ridge #2)

Hot Shot (North Ridge #3)

Bad at Love

The Swedish Prince

The Wild Heir

A Nordic King

Nothing Personal

My Life in Shambles

Discretion

Disarm

Disavow

The Royal Rogue

The Forbidden Man

Lovewrecked

One Hot Italian Summer

The One That Got Away

All the Love in the World (Anthology)

Romantic Suspense Novels by Karina Halle

Sins and Needles (The Artists Trilogy #1)

On Every Street (An Artists Trilogy Novella #0.5)

Shooting Scars (The Artists Trilogy #2)

Bold Tricks (The Artists Trilogy #3)

Dirty Angels (Dirty Angels #1)

Dirty Deeds (Dirty Angels #2)

Dirty Promises (Dirty Angels #3)

Black Hearts (Sins Duet #1)

Dirty Souls (Sins Duet #2)

Horror & Paranormal Romance

Darkhouse (EIT #1)

Red Fox (EIT #2)

The Benson (EIT #2.5)

Dead Sky Morning (EIT #3)

Lying Season (EIT #4)

On Demon Wings (EIT #5)

Old Blood (EIT #5.5)

The Dex-Files (EIT #5.7)

Into the Hollow (EIT #6)

And With Madness Comes the Light (EIT #6.5)

Come Alive (EIT #7)

Ashes to Ashes (EIT #8)

Dust to Dust (EIT #9)

Ghosted (EIT #9.5)

Came Back Haunted (EIT #10)

In the Fade (EIT #11)

The Devil's Duology

Donners of the Dead

Veiled (Ada Palomino #1)

Song For the Dead (Ada Palomino #2)

Black Sunshine (Dark Eyes Duet #1)

The Blood is Love (Dark Eyes Duet #2)

Nightwolf

River of Shadows (Underworld Gods #1)

Crown of Crimson (Underworld Gods #2)

Printed in the USA
CPSIA information can be obtained
at www.ICGtesting.com
LVHW091928120424
777243LV00003B/359